Praise for *Texas Bound* stories

"Distinctive and majestic storehouses of Texas literature."
PAUL SCOTT MALONE, *The Dallas Morning News*

"A modern showcase of the range and vitality
of the state's rich literary heritage . . . a pleasure to read
and a privilege to recommend."
ANN W. RICHARDS

"A treasure trove . . . stories forged by humor, a preternatural
ear for conversations, and a keen sense of irony."
Texas Books in Review

"A stirring chorus of voices, no two alike.
If Louisiana's motto is 'Let the good times roll,' Texas's
should be 'Sit down and listen to this!' "
ROSELLEN BROWN

And raves for *Texas Bound*® tapes

"Tommy Lee Jones starts out the readings with Larry McMurtry. These two powerhouse talents live up to their billing."
Detroit Free Press

"Barry Corbin brought the house down, Texas style."
The New York Times

"Janet Peery's story is read by Kathy Bates—yes, *that* Kathy Bates, and she's in fine form."
JUDYTH RIGLER, *San Antonio Express-News*

"Lynna Williams' 'Personal Testimony' read by Judith Ivey will highlight your evening."
Denver Post

"Goyen's beguiling 'Texas Principessa' is glorified by Doris Roberts' reading."
LARRY SWINDELL, *Fort Worth Star-Telegram*

"Here's Star Trek's Brent Spiner throwing himself into a rich comic piece by Matt Clark and Julie White's inspired reading of Mary K. Flatten's 'Old Enough.' "
JANE SUMNER, *The Dallas Morning News*

"Listening once will not be enough!"
Review of Texas Books

A complete listing of recorded readings from the series appears on pages 259–260.

Texas Bound: Book II

SOUTHWEST LIFE AND LETTERS

A series designed to publish outstanding
new fiction and nonfiction about Texas
and the American Southwest and to
present classic works of the region in
handsome new editions.

General Editors: Kathryn Lang, Southern
Methodist University Press; Tom
Pilkington, Tarleton State University

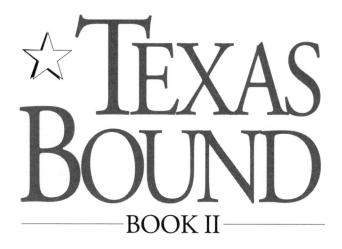

☆TEXAS BOUND

―――― BOOK II ――――

22 TEXAS STORIES

EDITED BY *Kay Cattarulla*

FOREWORD BY *John Graves*

SOUTHERN METHODIST UNIVERSITY PRESS
Dallas

Requests for permission to reproduce material from this work should be
sent to:
    Permissions
    Southern Methodist University Press
    PO Box 750415
    Dallas, Texas 75275-0415

Library of Congress Cataloging-in-Publication Data

Texas bound. Book II : 22 Texas stories / edited by Kay Cattarulla ;
    foreword by John Graves. — 1st ed.
        p.   cm. — (Southwest life and letters)
    ISBN 0-87074-426-7 (cloth). — ISBN 0-87074-427-5 (paper)
    1. Texas—Social life and customs—Fiction. 2. Short stories,
American—Texas. I. Cattarulla, Kay. II. Series.
PS558.T4T35   1998   97-48345
813'.01089764—dc21

Cover photograph *Texas* 1965 by Lee Friedlander,
courtesy of Fraenkel Gallery, San Francisco.

10 9 8 7 6 5 4 3 2 1

Copyright acknowledgments for reprinted stories appear on pages 257–258.

CONTENTS

Preface

The writers whose work appears in this book are Texans—natives or residents or, in a few cases, Texans-at-heart, who write from long familiarity with the state. Most of the twenty-two pieces were written or first published in the late 1980s and the 1990s, though there is some older work, including Katherine Anne Porter's story which dates back to 1929. Some take place in big cities; some still look to the earlier settings of farms and small towns, although usually without nostalgia. The progression of pieces winds over miles of territory, strays across state lines from time to time (as in the case of James Lee Burke's "The Convict"), and ends up on the road headed West. It's wonderful to see them all together in this book, successor to an earlier *Texas Bound* collection published in 1994, and to note that while some of the authors are well known in and outside Texas, and the majority have solid records of publications and awards, there are a few writers here whose work has not until now appeared in any book.

What unites the stories, aside from their Texas origins, is a narrative pull that makes them effective when read aloud. All were presented in readings by Texas actors at "Texas Bound," which is part of the Dallas Museum of Art's literary project "Arts & Letters Live." "Texas Bound" is modeled on "Selected Shorts," the nationally known series of short fiction readings by actors that I started with Isaiah Sheffer in 1985 at New York's Symphony Space theater. These readings are now heard via National Public Radio all over the country. Texans are as receptive as New Yorkers to what the *Wall Street Journal*, writing of "Selected Shorts," called "the power of the naked word." It has long been known here as the power of the oral tradition—"I grew up on a ranch listening to farmers and ranchers tell some of the biggest lies imaginable," said one of our audience members. Hundreds at a time are enthralled whenever "Texas Bound" performs at the Museum or goes on the road.

It takes, of course, great readers. The actors who presented the stories in this book are Kathy Bates, Esther Benson, James Black, Barry Corbin, Linda Gehringer, Peri Gilpin, Dolores Godinez, Marcia Gay Harden, John Benjamin Hickey, Norma Moore, Randy Moore, Raphael Parry, Hermine Pinson, Octavio Solis, Brent Spiner, and Julie White—all Texas born or closely connected. Other performers—Tommy Lee Jones, Judith Ivey, Tess Harper, Doris Roberts, G. W. Bailey, to name a few—contributed readings for stories in our first anthology. Some readings from both books have been published by SMU Press as *Texas Bound* audiocassettes. Titles, authors, and actors can be found on pages 259–260.

Colleagues who have helped create this project are Raphael Parry and Randy Moore, the two "Texas Bound" directors; Lisa Taylor and Paula Zeitman, the "Arts & Letters Live" associate producers, and JuLe Maxwell, Melanie Nyberg, and Barbara Roseman of our staff; George Danielson, Kay Johnson, Stone

Savage, and Wendell Sneed of the Dallas Museum of Art; and Nancy Lamb of Lambda Productions.

The Hoglund Foundation became our generous underwriter after an initial and gratefully acknowledged grant from the Lila Wallace–Reader's Digest Fund. We are lucky to be affiliated with the Dallas Museum of Art and its staff under director Jay Gates—and with the law firm of Locke Purnell Rain Harrell, where Russell Coleman, Keith Hardage, and Susan Karamanian, in particular, have watched over "Arts & Letters Live." Thanks also to our longtime copresenter, the Friends of the Dallas Public Library, currently headed by Dena Jones, and to our venturesome publishers Keith Gregory, Kathryn Lang, and Freddie Jane Goff of SMU Press.

All stories are reprinted in full, although a few were cut for reading purposes, with permission. Apologies to a few authors whose work was read at the series but, for reasons of this book's length, could not be included. We are grateful to all the writers who allowed us to use their work, and to the "Texas Bound" audience, whose wonderfully supportive members should take a bow as part of the success of the series.

Kay Cattarulla
Dallas, 1997

Foreword

Writers tend toward individualism, and I doubt that a majority of them like to view themselves as primarily part of a group, regional or thematic or ethnic or otherwise. I know I don't. But the groupings do exist, and insofar as there is a "we" comprised of authors who were born in Texas, or who live or have lived here, and have used it as a setting in their work, I believe that this anthology of short fiction called *Texas Bound: Book II* proves us to be in pretty good shape.

It builds on the achievement of the first *Texas Bound*, published in 1994, whose overall quality surprised a good many readers. Mainly, I suppose, this was because in their minds there existed a clear distinction between capitalized "Literature" as purveyed in university English courses throughout the nation, and "Texas and Southwestern Literature" as considered, when at all, in schools of our own region, and as most often exemplified in retrospective work—histories, memoirs of old Indian fighters and traildrivers and the like, biographies of notable figures, folklore, and so on.

I have respect and affection for these regional writings, both old and new. If many of them fall short in grace of language and the exploration of human complexities, and some exhibit provincial viewpoints and plain bad writing by contemporary standards, they nevertheless give basic definition to our past and in some degree to our present. My own effort to come to terms with my origins would have been direly hampered by the absence of such a record. Whatever its artistic failings may be, it opens access to a rich background and can still move me strongly because that background is *mine*—is *ours*—and I am grateful that it's there.

I'm grateful too, however, that for generations now, awareness of wider esthetic and cultural horizons has been spreading in the region and spurring efforts by authors to publish writing that excels as writing, and not merely as a record of people and events and phenomena—excels, that is, as literature. Only a few of the results have approached "greatness," however defined, but for that matter neither have literary results elsewhere often approached it, even in those elsewheres called New York and Paris and London. What we do have these days in terms of Texas and the Southwest—and have had for longer than some critics will admit—is a varied body of talented people producing books and stories and poems and essays of real merit, writings that are well worth reading not just for what they say but for how they say it as well.

This collection, like its predecessor, presents a sampling of the prose work of some of these people past and present, and it is most pleasant to see them thus honored. They deserve it, and deserve also a sponsoring figure like Kay Cattarulla, whose intelligence and taste have shaped the two volumes of *Texas Bound* as effectively as the writers themselves have shaped their stories.

John Graves
Glen Rose, 1997

xvi

Texas Bound: Book II

DONALD BARTHELME

The School

Well, we had all these children out planting trees, see, because we figured that . . . that was part of their education, to see how, you know, the root systems . . . and also the sense of responsibility, taking care of things, being individually responsible. You know what I mean. And the trees all died. They were orange trees. I don't know why they died, they just died. Something wrong with the soil possibly or maybe the stuff we got from the nursery wasn't the best. We complained about it. So we've got thirty kids there, each kid had his or her own little tree to plant, and we've got these thirty dead trees. All these kids looking at these little brown sticks, it was depressing.

It wouldn't have been so bad except that just a couple of weeks before the thing with the trees, the snakes all died. But I think that the snakes—well, the reason that the snakes kicked off was that . . . you remember, the boiler was shut off for four days because of the strike, and that was explicable. It was something you could explain to the kids because of the strike. I mean, none of their parents would let them cross the picket line and they knew there was a strike going on and what it meant. So when things got started up again and we found the snakes they weren't too disturbed.

With the herb gardens it was probably a case of overwatering, and at least now they know not to overwater. The children were very conscientious with the herb gardens and some of them probably . . . you know, slipped them a little extra water when we weren't looking. Or maybe . . . well, I don't like to think about sabotage, although it did occur to us. I mean, it was something that crossed our minds. We were thinking that way probably because before that the gerbils had died, and the white mice had died, and the salamander . . . well, now they know not to carry them around in plastic bags.

Of course we *expected* the tropical fish to die, that was no surprise. Those numbers, you look at them crooked and they're belly-up on the surface. But the lesson plan called for a tropical-fish input at that point, there was nothing we could do, it happens every year, you just have to hurry past it.

We weren't even supposed to have a puppy.

We weren't even supposed to have one, it was just a puppy the Murdoch girl found under a Gristede's truck one day and she was afraid the truck would run over it when the driver had finished making his delivery, so she stuck it in her knapsack and brought it to school with her. So we had this puppy. As soon as I saw the puppy I thought, Oh Christ, I bet it will live for about two weeks and then . . . And that's what it did. It wasn't supposed to be in the classroom at all, there's some kind of regulation about it, but you can't tell them they can't have a puppy when the puppy is already there, right in front of them, running around on the floor and yap yap yapping. They named it Edgar—that is, they named it after me. They had a lot of fun running after it and yelling, "Here, Edgar! Nice Edgar!" Then they'd laugh like hell. They enjoyed the ambiguity. I enjoyed it myself. I don't mind being kidded. They made a little house for it in the supply closet and all that. I don't know what it died of. Distemper, I guess. It probably hadn't had any shots. I got it out of there before the kids got to school. I checked the supply closet each morning, routinely, because I knew what was going to happen. I gave it to the custodian.

And then there was this Korean orphan that the class adopted through the Help the Children program, all the kids brought in a quarter a month, that was the idea. It was an unfortunate thing, the kid's name was Kim and maybe we adopted him too late or something. The cause of death was not stated in the letter we got, they suggested we adopt another child instead and sent us some interesting case histories, but we didn't have the heart. The class took it pretty hard, they began (I think; nobody ever said anything to me directly) to feel that maybe there was something wrong with the school. But I don't think there's anything wrong with the school, particularly, I've seen better and I've seen worse. It was just a run of bad luck. We had an extraordinary number of parents passing away, for instance. There were I think two heart attacks and two suicides, one drowning, and four killed together in a car accident. One stroke. And we had the usual heavy mortality rate among the grandparents, or maybe it was heavier this year, it seemed so. And finally the tragedy.

The tragedy occurred when Matthew Wein and Tony Mavrogordo were playing over where they're excavating for the new federal office building. There were all these big wooden beams stacked, you know, at the edge of the excavation. There's a court case coming out of that, the parents are claiming that the beams were poorly stacked. I don't know what's true and what's not. It's been a strange year.

I forgot to mention Billy Brandt's father, who was knifed fatally when he grappled with a masked intruder in his home.

One day, we had a discussion in class. They asked me, where did they go? The trees, the salamander, the tropical fish, Edgar, the poppas and mommas, Matthew and Tony, where did they go? And I said, I don't know, I don't know. And they said, who knows? and I said, nobody knows. And they said, is death that which gives meaning to life? And I said, no, life is that which gives meaning to life. Then they said, but isn't death, considered as a fundamental datum, the means by which the taken-for-granted mundanity of the everyday may be transcended in the direction of—

I said, yes, maybe.

They said, we don't like it.

I said, that's sound.

They said, it's a bloody shame!

I said, it is.

They said, will you make love now with Helen (our teaching assistant) so that we can see how it is done? We know you like Helen.

I do like Helen but I said that I would not.

We've heard so much about it, they said, but we've never seen it.

I said I would be fired and that it was never, or almost never, done as a demonstration. Helen looked out of the window.

They said, please, please make love with Helen, we require an assertion of value, we are frightened.

I said that they shouldn't be frightened (although I am often frightened) and that there was value everywhere. Helen came and embraced me. I kissed her a few times on the brow. We held each other. The children were excited. Then there was a knock on the door, I opened the door, and the new gerbil walked in. The children cheered wildly.

JOHN BENNET

Flat Creek Road

It was a new house—only four years old. There was indoor plumbing—a fact of some note on Flat Creek Road—but it didn't work. Something to do with the pump, out in the well. The stones around the well had been taken down; there was just a round hole in the ground. My mother told me horrible things about that hole, and generally I stayed away from it. One day, while Mother was in the back of the house, I decided to go sneaky-peeping—to look where I wasn't supposed to look. The well was in the front yard, a few feet from the screen porch. I got down on my belly and inched across the dirt toward the hole. Even at five, I never felt completely certain of my footing, and crawling was a way of being sure I wouldn't fall now—pre-falling. I got closer and closer to the edge. Finally, very cautiously, I stretched my neck on the ground until just the top of my head and then my eyes were over the edge. The rest of my body was an anchor flat against the dirt. I looked down, saw the water, saw the bucket awash in it. That's all there was to that particular sneaky-peeping.

Because of the broken pump, my family needed the bucket to get the water into the house. To flush the toilet you had to pour a bucket of water into it, and somebody had to go outside and draw the water. I don't remember how we took baths. Hauling up the bucket wasn't easy. Mother did most of it. "I work like a *horse*, Teddy," she'd say to me. "Oh, Lord." Stuff like that. She seemed resigned to days of drawing water from a well. She had been the salutatorian at one of the largest high schools in Dallas. Class of '29. Her family, modestly respectable, had owned its own house. She played the lead and spoke French in the French Club play. Then she married a man who would turn out to be a drunk. There was more to him than that, but that was the gist of it. The Depression ruined all their plans. Then an uncle left her six unusable acres in East Texas, near Horace, and it was the only place they had to live. Three children and a worthless husband—not much to work with. But she was also to blame, because she didn't really seem to care. When *Gone with the Wind* was published, she told me later, she stayed up three nights in a row reading it straight through. She saw the movie, too. Scarlett said, "As God is my witness, I'll never be hungry again." But my mother, much as she admired that book—and she admired it more than any other—never said that, or anything like it. She'd say, "Oh, *damn!*" or "Pshaw!" and laugh at her own expense.

I don't know how they'd got the money to put up the new house. Some wartime windfall, I guess. My father, a construction worker, had finally begun getting jobs in various defense boomtowns—Galveston, Amarillo—and he'd be away for months at a time making fair money and sending part of it home. Before they built the house, they were living in a converted chicken house. I was born just before V-J Day, just before the new house. After the war, my father got a job doing construction work on Guam for the United States government, and was gone several years. He sent self-important letters saying his work was "secret" and he couldn't talk about it. This amused my mother. "You'd think he was building atom bombs over there."

Sometimes he sent money, apparently, and sometimes he didn't. The chicken house they had moved out of reverted to chickens, and as I got older my mother collected the eggs every day and every third day would walk down Flat Creek Road to the highway with a bushel basket in her arms. It was two and a half miles to town. She gave eggs to the A. & P. in exchange for groceries.

If money didn't arrive from my father, she'd say, "People aren't much." The same when neighbors didn't pick us up on Sunday morning to drive us to church. Or if my brother or sister let her down in some way.

Something was wrong with the way I talked. I would ask for a piece of cake, and my sister, who was fifteen, would say, "Not take, *cake!* Say cake."

I would say it, and my sister would tell my mother, "He keeps saying 'take' for 'cake' and 'turch' for 'church.' "

"He'll get it some of these days."

My sister's boyfriends spent a lot of time at the house. The one I liked best was Roy. He was in his midtwenties—a big guy who worked at the feed store in town—and he was very cheerful, always grinning in a pleasant way. He took me for a walk once. Just out into the back pasture, not far from the house. It was twilight. I guess my sister was still getting ready. He was smoking a cigarette. For some reason, I said, "God damn it to hell." It was probably something I'd heard my brother say. He was fourteen.

"Hold it, there," Roy said. He became serious. "Do you know what Hell is?"

I don't remember what I said.

7

"Well, you shouldn't use big words unless you know what they mean. And Hell is a big word." He bent down and held his cigarette pointed toward me. "Do you see the end of this cigarette?" he said. "See how it's glowing fiery red? See how hot it is? Well, that's what Hell is like, only it's much, much bigger—bigger even than this pasture, or even the whole town of Horace. And God is up in the sky. Sometimes you can see his face in the clouds. He has a white beard. And someday you're going to die—everybody has to die—and if you're bad God will send you to Hell, where you'll burn in pain just the way the tip of this cigarette would burn you if I were to touch your stomach with it. And you won't just burn for a little while—you'll burn forever."

Roy was ordinarily very happy-go-lucky. Other than being crazy about my sister and wanting her to marry him before she even graduated from high school, he never seemed to have much on his mind. He certainly wasn't religious. But he was serious now, and his seriousness impressed me. Today I wonder what was going on in his mind that he would talk that way to a child. Maybe somebody had once talked that way to him. Maybe he thought that by marrying my sister he would become my father, since my father was away. (This prospect thrilled me.) Maybe he was just killing time waiting for my sister.

Roy had another claim to fame. One morning I woke up and pulled open my clothes drawer in my mother's bureau and found it filled with kittens. Fiddlesticks, the mother, was with them. I yelled, "Mama, come look!"

"Well, I'll be," she said. "You can keep 'em for a while."

That afternoon, my sister took the kittens out of the bureau drawer and put them in a milk box on the screen porch. As they grew, they began to climb out of the box. Eventually, they climbed through a tear in the screen. I was always afraid one of them would fall into the well hole. My favorite was a nearly all-white kitten. My brother named her: Snow Cup. The upshot of all this is that one day when Roy came to pick up my sister and was backing his car around the side of the house one of his tires crushed Snow Cup. Because of that, my sister broke up with him. For a while, my mother would see his car going down Flat Creek Road—an out-of-the-way place for him—but he never stopped.

My mother had a thin face, but to me she seemed unusually beautiful. She was nearly forty then. She looked fifty or fifty-five. Later, relatives said she did all the aging in her life between thirty-five and forty. After that, she was so far ahead she didn't have to age anymore. She didn't seem to mind that her face was wrinkled. Her smile carried her through, I guess. When we went to church, and she was wearing her good dress, with shoulder pads, and her hair was carefully braided, she'd smile and laugh at the breakfast social after the service, but sometimes it wasn't her real smile. These socials were a big deal to her. Being with the ladies. There she didn't seem beautiful. She'd be edgy, and she'd snap at us.

One day, while I was standing on the screen porch looking at the trees down by the creek, I must have turned blue. I wasn't aware of it. My sister called for my mother to come quick.

"He looks pale," my mother said. "I can't see that he's blue."

"Well, he *was* blue," my sister said.

"Maybe he hasn't been eating. I'll get some hungry medicine at the store tomorrow."

The next day, my mother opened a bottle of brown syrup and held out a teaspoonful for me to swallow. "This don't taste good, but it's mighty good for you," she said. "It's a special medicine that'll make you hungry, so you'll have some appetite." The medicine had a bad taste.

Flat Creek Road had a blacktop surface. In the summer you couldn't really walk on it, because the tar burned your bare feet. In other seasons, it was good and hard. Somebody from the church had dropped off an outgrown tricycle, and for a long time I rode it in the house and on the screen porch while my mother sat in the kitchen during the day. When she began to take the eggs to town, after I turned five, I suddenly had more opportunities. I would drag the tricycle across the sand—our driveway, which was fifty or sixty yards, consisted of two ruts in the sand—and set it on the edge of the road and climb on it and pedal back and forth. People driving by would stop and chew me out, and I'd promise to stay off the road, but I didn't have to keep those promises. Considering that it was a country road, cars came down it fairly fast, but they always slowed when they saw me. I got to where I could hear them way back before they came into sight.

One day, a neighbor visited and chatted with my mother awhile and said, "I wouldn't let him play in the road if I was you."

I was annoyed that she was telling my mother this.

Mother took my side. "Well, he'll be starting first grade next year and catching the bus to school. He has to learn."

She must have done a lot of chores—hauling water, tending chickens—but she didn't do them early in the morning. She had to sit and have her coffee and smoke cigarettes for a couple of hours before she was awake enough to start wondering what needed to be done. She was a nighttime farmer, and was more likely to be feeding the chickens when the sun was going down than when it was coming up. In my memory, she was always sitting in the kitchen smoking a cigarette and drinking coffee. There was an old upholstered chair there, my favorite chair of all we had—the pink fabric was torn, and the cotton stuffing could be pulled out and then pushed back in again. The chair sat right in the middle of the kitchen floor, where a table would ordinarily have been. She drank coffee all day long. Years later she told me, "I was twenty-seven years old before I tasted my first cup of coffee. That was the first day of my life, really."

* * *

Our house was surrounded by huge pastures that we didn't own. Some of them had been neglected and were grown over with brush. One of the neglected fields had been an orchard, and was filled with gnarled plum trees. Those trees were easy to climb, and I'd get right to the top. Once or twice, my foot got caught in a fork in the branches and I had to wait until somebody came to find me. I always had to watch out for bull nettles—a plant that was a delicacy, provided somebody older was around to cut it open for you. I was afraid of bull nettles, because every time I got near them I would fall on them and get stuck all over with needles. I also liked something called sour dock; it had a long, grooved stem that you could insert gradually into your mouth and chew on a bite at a time. It had a lot of flavor.

I began to go farther and farther from the house. The fields that weren't neglected were planted with corn or watermelons. The summer I turned five, I probably cracked open one green watermelon for every day of the summer until, in what must have been July, I found a red one. There was nothing illicit about this. There were so many watermelons in those fields that it didn't make any difference. The cornfields weren't very interesting in early summer, but they became wonderful in July. In the beginning, I had to bend over to hide in them, but by July the stalks were taller than I was, and I could walk around in the rows until I was almost dizzy, and finally emerge with no sense at all of what side of the field I was on or even where the house was.

Once when this happened, I was completely bewildered. I was so far away, so deep in the pastures, that I couldn't hear cars on the road. I needed to find the road in order to find our house. I set off in what I thought was the direction of the road. I came to a pasture I'd never seen before. A farm machine stood in the middle of it. As I bent over to step through the barbed-wire fence, I ripped my shirt. After I got clear of the fence, I could see that the farm machine was an old plow, with rusted red disks and a bicycle-type seat without upholstery—a plow meant

11

to be dragged behind a horse, I think. It was overturned—the seat post and the hitch formed a sort of V in the air. I remember thinking, Nobody wants this plow. It could be mine. If I had a horse, I could plow with it.

I started walking again. I saw an animal on the ground—a dead fox. Ants were crawling all over its head and back. It had been dead a long time. It was just a bunch of fur, really. I thought, It looks like it's still a fox but it's not still a fox. Something strange began happening to me, and I had to stop. I sat down in the dirt. I had lost my breath. After a while, I felt better.

Now I knew where I was. I was at the lake—a lake that we passed every time we went down Flat Creek Road—but I was at the wrong end of it. The road was clear across on the other side. The lake had dozens of fingers; its shore was jagged and sometimes marshy. Getting around it took me nearly the whole afternoon. At one spot, three bamboo fishing poles were stuck in the mud at the edge of the water. The corks on their lines floated on the surface. But no one was around. In the shade of a willow was a shiny tin washtub. It was filled with water, and two fish were alive in it.

I make us sound poor, but there were niceties. We had a piano, for instance. I don't know if it was any good—it was an upright, in my sister's bedroom—but it was apparently in tune, because my sister used it for voice practice. She wanted to be an opera singer, and a woman in town who had had formal training gave her voice lessons in return for babysitting and housecleaning. At home, my sister would strike a note on the piano and sing up and down a scale.

There had once been a fancy dog in the household—a Sealyham terrier that my grandfather, a fire-truck salesman who served as judge at all the bigger Texas dog shows, had given the family years before. The dog's name was Blink, and everybody talked about it a lot, but it had run off before I was old enough to remember it.

My brother had rifles. One of them had a telescopic sight. During the summers, he worked for nearby farmers loading watermelons into trucks. When he was paid, he would go buy ammunition and stand out behind the house and shoot. He was handy with machinery.

My mother had two Hummel dolls: a boy playing a violin and a girl sitting against a truncated tree. They were on a small corner shelf in the living room, out of my reach.

We had electricity. There was a radio in the living room. But I also remember coal-oil lamps. Maybe there were times when the service was cut off. The smell of the oil was rich and filled the room. These lamps were always being tinkered with: the wicks needed constant attention. But the light was extraordinary. If the lamp was in a corner, the shadow of the glass made a statuesque pattern on the walls and ceiling. Other corners became dark and inviting.

Years later, in talking about this period, I asked my sister if she and my brother had realized that we were poor.

She answered, "What do you think?"

One day, I decided to make poison. I went first to the dump. This was a large, lion-trap-size pit back beyond the chicken house. Every year, my brother would cover the hole over with dirt and dig another. As a hole became filled, its side would erode, so that I could climb in and out. It contained mostly tin cans and broken glass, and it was blinding—reflecting an entire sky of sunshine. I was looking for a container of some kind. What I found was a huge, lidless mayonnaise jar—it must have been something meant for a diner or a school lunchroom. The neck was extremely wide. I picked the jar up and held it against my chest and climbed out of the pit. Then I looked back and saw some coffee grounds in a soggy paper bag. I went back for them and put them in the jar.

I set the jar down by the entrance to the chicken house and stepped in. This was scary. The chickens flew all around, flapping their wings and squawking. I never liked being around the chickens. I reached in amid the fluttering and grabbed two eggs for my jar.

I went into the house. "Mama, can I have some baking soda?"

She was sitting in the chair. "You making poison?"

"Yes."

"There's no baking soda. It's all gone."

I walked outside and began looking around. On the way to the creek was an old tractor shed that my brother used as a garage for his car. He had bought a shot two-seater Chevrolet for five dollars and persuaded a friend to tow it to our house. He worked on it all the time, visiting junk yards to look for parts. It had a rumble seat, which I liked to sit in, and an engine crank, which I couldn't turn. What caught my attention now was a red tin gas can. The can made a swishing noise when I tilted it. I tried to wiggle it and shake it, but it was too heavy. Pouring some of the gas—or kerosene, or coal oil, or whatever it was— into the mayonnaise jar wouldn't be easy. It must have occurred to me to put my thumb in the pouring spout of the can to get a better grip. In any case, that's what I did, and when I moved the can my thumb suddenly hurt. I tried to pull it out but couldn't, and blood seemed to be flowing upward, all over my hand.

The shed was some distance from the house. I don't know how long I shouted. Suddenly my mother was there. "Don't pull on it!" she said. "Let me try to get it out." She took my hand in her fingers and pushed down on the skin at the base of my thumb and tried to work it out. The blood just got worse— the tin of the spout, which had appeared so rounded and smooth and safe, was simply curled under; the part you couldn't see was broken in jagged points. "I can't get it," she said. "Hold on. Now, don't move it. Stand stock-still!"

She ran to the house and returned with some rags from under the sink and knotted them around my hand. She opened the main cap on the gas can and somehow held me and the can in such a way that the fuel spilled out on the ground. She picked me up and lifted me over her shoulder with one arm while she held the empty can with the other. She carried me out to the road and began walking toward the Tyler highway, nearly a mile away. You took the Tyler highway to get to Horace. It also led, in the opposite direction, to Tyler, but Tyler was so far away I'd never been there. She had to stop and put me down every little while. There were other houses along the road—neighbors, people we knew, including the woman who had mentioned my playing in the road—but my mother didn't stop at any of those houses. The lake shone blue.

Where Flat Creek Road met the highway that went to Horace, there was a big clay pit—a huge pit, as big as a farm, a place I'd always wanted to play in, with hard red earth and water-filled craters and mountainlike peaks and caves. An old steam shovel was parked in the pit, but you almost never saw anybody working there. On the other side of the road was Tilson's trailer park—another dreamy place for me, because the people there lived close together, in houses that could roll on wheels from town to town. Lots of children lived in the trailer park; I'd always noticed them whenever we went past on the way to church.

My mother set me down on the shoulder of the highway. "We're going to Dr. Hart's," she said.

"Where's Dr. Hart's, Mama?"

"On the Palestine highway."

That highway, which led from Horace to the town of Palestine (pronounced Palesteen), was on the other side of Horace. We would have to walk all the way through town. (I doubt if I understood this. All I probably knew was that town was someplace most people drove to, not walked to.)

A car pulled over. It belonged to Roy, my sister's old boyfriend. "Need some help?" he said. "Goodness gracious! Cain't get it off? Let me drop you at the doctor's." (As a result of this coincidence, my sister began going out with Roy again, and they went off to Oklahoma one weekend and secretly got married.)

My love for my mother was absolute. It had no qualifications; nothing was held back. I loved her for every aspect of her nature. She was mindless of discipline, so there were practically no hard feelings between us—almost none of the hard feelings that ordinarily occur between a parent and a young child. I loved her for everything: for the way she wore her clothes, the way she drew water from the well, the way she said, putting an old horse collar around her neck, "If I'm going to *work* like a horse, I might as well *look* like one." (Years later, someone told me that that was a line from a Ma and Pa Kettle movie; my mother had probably seen it at the Dixie, on the square in town.) I loved her for the way I could persuade her to let me do things; if I kept at something long enough, she'd always give in. The freedom she gave me was a bond of our love, not a cause for sadness. Little as I knew about other families and other lives, I was vaguely aware, even then, that this was something special between us. Other kids in other families had to mind, and had to be in the house at suppertime and had to go to bed at a certain hour every night, but I didn't have to do any of those things. It's true I carried in my head a picture of a large house in town. It was a three-story house, with stairs, and through the windows you could see that the lights were turned on in every room. And on the stairs— softly carpeted stairs—kids, lots of kids, my age and maybe just a little older, played games in their pajamas while their mother and father, in fancy dressing gowns, stood by and gave encouragement. That house was a house of play. But the image of that house was a vague image. I really didn't know enough about such houses to pine for them. I knew that my days were very long and very boring—at home alone with my mother, my brother and sister not due until the afternoon school bus, if they chose to come home. I wanted lots of things that I couldn't have; the world outside came to me in scraps, in pages from the

Sears catalogue—people in dressing gowns, kids on swing sets. But whatever I lacked, and knew that I lacked, I loved my mother. I never had bad thoughts about my mother. At least, that's how it seemed then and how I remember it now. I never thought, Mother's wrong, or Mother should have done this, or Mother shouldn't have done that. I never thought, as most children apparently do from time to time, I hate my mother.

Dr. Hart undid the rags and tried, gently, to work the thumb out. There was a large brown spot on the back of one of his hands. He spoke to his nurse: "Joyce, let's let you run over to Tom's"—a service station—"and ask him to give us some tin cutters or wire cutters. And a hacksaw." Then he turned to my mother. "How long has it been like this?"

"About an hour or so," my mother said.

"How come it took so long to get him here?"

"Well, I had to walk most of the way."

"Why didn't you call?"

"Phone's out."

"You couldn't ask a neighbor?"

My mother's voice took on a defensive tone. "I *carried* him here," she said.

When the nurse returned with the tools, the doctor took the hacksaw and began sawing through the spout on the gas can. After it was separated, he took the wire cutters and began cutting up from the base of the spout toward my thumb. It took him a long time. "I only like"—lack—"a few snips more," he said.

He washed my hand off under a faucet—it burned, and I told him so—and put in some stitches. He must have given me a local anesthetic, because I don't remember the stitches hurting. In any case, he had a very reassuring voice and he kept telling me that there was only a little bit more and it would all be over. He promised me an ice-cream cone if I would just hold still.

When he was finished and the thumb was bandaged, he told my mother, "I might as well look him over while he's here. I know you don't have a chance to get in that often."

"I don't really have any money, Dr. Hart."

"Don't worry about that."

Once more he fixed his entire attention upon me. "Open up your mouth, bub. Say *ahhh*. I guarantee that this won't hurt." He meant the tongue depressor.

Then he said, abruptly and not to me, "How long has he been like this?"

"About an hour," my mother said again.

"I mean in here. Just look in here! Keep it open, boy—it's all right. Can't you see? His whole throat has filled with adenoids. Adenoids and tonsils. They've blown up like a balloon in there. No wonder he can't talk right. I've never seen anything like it. I'm surprised he can draw breath."

"I don't know *how* it happened," my sister said not long ago. She meant this whole period of impoverishment. She was driving me from the airport to the funeral home in Dallas where my mother's body was. Two years after my sister married Roy, she had left him and gone to the junior college in Horace and then to T.C.U., where she paid her tuition by working nights as a switchboard operator at the telephone company. She is now a professor of English literature. We weren't going to have a funeral. My brother, who lives in Oregon, couldn't come down.

"What can I say?" she went on. "We should have known better, but we didn't, that's all. I was just a fifteen-year-old kid. I suspected things weren't right, but what did I know? It was Mother who should have known. But she didn't. She just tuned it all out. She didn't want to face up to it."

"Come on, that was an incredibly hard life," I said.

"She could have done something about it. She could have found a job in town. She could have divorced him and looked around for somebody else. Found a provider. My God, we were her kids."

Dr. Hart said, "He's got to go to Tyler to have all this removed. He has to go right now."

"All the way to Tyler?" my mother said. "Well, I can't take him. I'll get Dad to come down from Dallas and drive him." She meant my grandfather.

"No, he has to go right now, I'm afraid. I'll call Skip Cousins, over in the courthouse. He'll make the arrangements."

"I don't want that," my mother said. "I don't want the Welfare mixed up in it."

"You *must* agree to this." He picked up the phone.

"Thank you and goodbye!" my mother said.

Outside, she began talking to me. "Let's don't go by the square," she said. "Let's take a side street." She said a lot of other things—things I didn't really get.

To walk from the Palestine highway, on one side of the square, to the Tyler highway, on the other, without crossing the square itself involved a circuitous route. I didn't mind, because as my mother kept talking I began to realize something: if I asked her questions, she would answer in great detail and with obvious sincerity.

I asked her who she loved more—me, my brother, or my sister.

"Why, *you!* You're my *baby* boy. And, truly, I don't think much of them, either one."

I asked her why she was mad at the doctor.

"He's a big shot. Tried to high-hat us. Wants them to take you to Tyler and cut your tonsils out. Put you in with the polio kids."

I asked her if I would ever burn in Hell.

"Son, you might. But you shouldn't study it. If it's going to happen, it's going to happen."

Later, on the highway, a sheriff's car pulled up. The sheriff walked over and stood talking to my mother. He wore a gun, but he was not unfriendly. In a few minutes, a gray jeep with a canvas top pulled up. It belonged to the county, and a man and a woman got out. The man was heavy-faced and wore a white straw hat and a double-breasted suit. The sheriff called him Skip. The woman, who was a little older, was an assistant of some kind. She was thin and had a tight, pinched face. They were the Welfare. Both were gloomy; both wore pained expressions. They began telling my mother why I had to go to Tyler. I hid, enfolded in her skirts. The more they said, the more I loved her.

The Convict

for Lyle Williams

My father was a popular man in New Iberia, even though his ideas were different from most people's and his attitudes were uncompromising. On Friday afternoon he and my mother and I would drive down the long, yellow, dirt road through the sugarcane fields until it became a blacktop and followed the Bayou Teche into town, where my father would drop my mother off at Musemeche's Produce Market and take me with him to the bar at the Frederic Hotel. The Frederic was a wonderful old place with slot machines and potted palms and marble columns in the lobby and a gleaming, mahogany-and-brass barroom that was cooled by long-bladed wooden fans. I always sat at a table with a Dr. Nut and a glass of ice and watched with fascination the drinking rituals of my father and his friends: the warm handshakes, the pats on the shoulder, the laughter that was genuine but never uncontrolled. In the summer, which seemed like the only season in south Louisiana, the men wore seersucker suits and straw hats, and the amber light in their glasses of whiskey and ice and their Havana cigars and Picayune cigarettes held between their ringed fingers made them seem everything gentlemen and my father's friends should be.

But sometimes I would suddenly realize that there was not only a fundamental difference between my father and other men but that his presence would eventually expose that difference, and a flaw, a deep one that existed in him or them, would surface like an aching wisdom tooth.

"Do you fellows really believe we should close the schools because of a few little Negro children?" my father said.

"My Lord, Will. We've lived one way here all our lives," one man said. He owned a restaurant in town and a farm with oil on it near St. Martinville.

My father took the cigar out of his teeth, smiled, sipped out of his whiskey, and looked with his bright, green eyes at the restaurant owner. My father was a real farmer, not an absentee landlord, and his skin was brown and his body straight and hard. He could pick up a washtub full of bricks and throw it over a fence.

"That's the point," he said. "We've lived among Negroes all our lives. They work in our homes, take care of our children, drive our wives on errands. Where are you going to send our own children if you close the school? Did you think of that?"

The bartender looked at the Negro porter who ran the shoeshine stand in the bar. He was bald and wore an apron and was quietly brushing a pair of shoes left him by a hotel guest.

"Alcide, go down to the corner and pick up the newspapers," the bartender said.

"Yes suh."

"It's not ever going to come to that," another man said. "Our darkies don't want it."

"It's coming, all right," my father said. His face was composed now, his eyes looking through the opened wood shutters at the oak tree in the courtyard outside. "Harry Truman is integrating the army, and those Negro soldiers aren't going to come home and walk around to the back door anymore."

"Charlie, give Mr. Broussard another manhattan," the restaurant owner said. "In fact, give everybody one. This conversation puts me in mind of the town council."

Everyone laughed, including my father, who put his cigar in his teeth and smiled good-naturedly with his hands folded on the bar. But I knew that he wasn't laughing inside, that he would finish his drink quietly and then wink at me and we'd wave goodbye to everyone and leave their Friday-afternoon good humor intact.

On the way home he didn't talk and instead pretended that he was interested in Mother's conversation about the New Iberia ladies' book club. The sun was red on the bayou, and the cypress and oaks along the bank were a dark green in the gathering dusk. Families of Negroes were cane fishing in the shallows for goggle-eye perch and bullheads.

"Why do you drink with them, Daddy? Y'all always have a argument," I said.

His eyes flicked sideways at my mother.

"That's not an argument, just a gentleman's disagreement," he said.

"I agree with him," my mother said. "Why provoke them?"

"They're good fellows. They just don't see things clearly sometimes."

My mother looked at me in the back seat, her eyes smiling so he could see them. She was beautiful when she looked like that.

"You should be aware that your father is the foremost authority in Louisiana on the subject of colored people."

"It isn't a joke, Margaret. We've kept them poor and uneducated and we're going to have to settle accounts for it one day."

"Well, you haven't underpaid them," she said. "I don't believe there's a darkie in town you haven't lent money to."

I wished I hadn't said anything. I knew he was feeling the same pain now that he had felt in the bar. Nobody understood him—not my mother, not me, none of the men he drank with.

The air suddenly became cool, the twilight turned a yellowish green, and it started to rain. Up the blacktop we saw a blockade and men in raincoats with flashlights in their hands. They wore flat campaign hats and water was dancing on the brims. My father stopped at the blockade and rolled down the window. A state policeman leaned his head down and moved his eyes around the inside of the car.

"We got a nigger and a white convict out on the ground. Don't pick up no hitchhikers," he said.

"Where were they last seen?" my father said.

"They got loose from a prison truck just east of the four-corners," he said.

We drove on in the rain. My father turned on the headlights, and I saw the anxiety in my mother's face in the glow from the dashboard.

"Will, that's only a mile from us," she said.

"They're probably gone by now or hid out under a bridge somewhere," he said.

"They must be dangerous or they wouldn't have so many police officers out," she said.

"If they were really dangerous, they'd be in Angola, not riding around in a truck. Besides, I bet when we get home and turn on the radio we'll find out they're back in jail."

"I don't like it. It's like when all those Germans were here."

During the war there was a POW camp outside New Iberia. We used to see them chopping in the sugarcane with a big white P on their backs. Mother kept the doors locked until they were sent back to Germany. My father always said they were harmless and they wouldn't escape from their camp if they were pushed out the front door at gunpoint.

The wind was blowing hard when we got home, and leaves from the pecan orchard were scattered across the lawn. My pirogue, which was tied to a small dock on the bayou behind the house, was knocking loudly against a piling. Mother waited for my father to open the front door, even though she had her own key, then she turned on all the lights in the house and closed the curtains. She began to peel crawfish in the sink for our supper, then turned on the radio in the window as though she were bored for something to listen to. Outside, the door on the tractor shed began to bang violently in the wind. My father went to the closet for his hat and raincoat.

"Let it go, Will. It's raining too hard," she said.

"Turn on the outside light. You'll be able to see me from the window," he said.

He ran through the rain, stopped at the barn for a hammer and a wood stob, then bent over in front of the tractor shed and drove the stob securely against the door.

He walked back into the kitchen, hitting his hat against his pants leg.

"I've got to get a new latch for that door. But at least the wind won't be banging it for a while," he said.

"There was a news story on the radio about the convicts," my mother said. "They had been taken from Angola to Franklin for a trial. One of them is a murderer."

"Angola?" For the first time my father's face looked concerned.

"The truck wrecked, and they got out the back and then made a man cut their handcuffs."

He picked up a shelled crawfish, bit it in half, and looked out the window at the rain slanting in the light. His face was empty now.

"Well, if I was in Angola I'd try to get out, too," he said. "Do we have some beer? I can't eat crawfish without beer."

"Call the sheriff's department and ask where they think they are."

"I can't do that, Margaret. Now, let's put a stop to all this." He walked out of the kitchen, and I saw my mother's jawbone flex under the skin.

It was about three in the morning when I heard the shed door begin slamming in the wind again. A moment later I saw my father walk past my bedroom door buttoning his denim coat over his undershirt. I followed him halfway down the stairs and watched him take a flashlight from the kitchen drawer and lift the twelve-gauge pump out of the rack on the dining-room wall. He saw me, then paused for a moment as though he were caught between two thoughts.

Then he said, "Come on down a minute, Son. I guess I didn't get that stob hammered in as well as I thought. But bolt the door behind me, will you?"

"Did you see something, Daddy?"

"No, no. I'm just taking this to satisfy your mother. Those men are probably all the way to New Orleans by now."

He turned on the outside light and went out the back door. Through the kitchen window I watched him cross the lawn. He had the flashlight pointed in front of him, and as he approached the tractor shed, he raised the shotgun and held it with one hand against his waist. He pushed the swinging door all the way back against the wall with his foot, shined the light over the tractor and the rolls of chicken wire, then stepped inside the darkness.

I could hear my own breathing as I watched the flashlight beam bounce through the cracks in the shed. Then I saw the light steady in the far corner where we hung the tools and tack. I waited for something awful to happen—the shotgun to streak fire through the boards, a pick in murderous hands to rake downward in a tangle of harness. Instead, my father appeared in the doorway a moment later, waved the flashlight at me, then replaced the stob and pressed it into the wet earth with his boot. I unbolted the back door and went up to bed, relieved that the convicts were far away and that my father was my father, a truly brave man who kept my mother's and my world a secure place.

But he didn't go back to bed. I heard him first in the upstairs hall cabinet, then in the icebox, and finally on the back porch. I went to my window and looked down into the moonlit yard and saw him walking with the shotgun under one arm and a lunch pail and folded towels in the other.

Just at false dawn, when the mist from the marsh hung thick on the lawn and the gray light began to define the black trees along the bayou, I heard my parents arguing in the next room. Then my father snapped: "Damn it, Margaret. The man's hurt."

Mother didn't come out of her room that morning. My father banged out the back door, was gone a half hour, then returned and cooked a breakfast of *couche-couche* and sausages for us.

"You want to go to a picture show today?" he said.

"I was going fishing with Tee Batiste." He was a little Negro boy whose father worked for us sometimes.

"It won't be any good after all that rain. Your mother doesn't want you tracking mud in from the bank, either."

"Is something going on, Daddy?"

"Oh, Mother and I have our little discussions sometimes. It's nothing." He smiled at me over his coffee cup.

I almost always obeyed my father, but that morning I found ways to put myself among the trees on the bank of the bayou. First, I went down on the dock to empty the rainwater out of my pirogue, then I threw dirt clods at the heads of water moccasins on the far side, then I made a game of jumping from cypress root to cypress root along the water's edge without actually touching the bank, and finally I was near what I knew my father wanted me away from that day: the old houseboat that had been washed up and left stranded among the oak trees in the great flood of 1927. Wild morning glories grew over the rotting deck, kids had riddled the cabin walls with .22 holes, and a slender oak had rooted in the collapsed floor and grown up through one window. Two sets of sharply etched footprints, side by side, led down from the levee, on the other side of which was the tractor shed, to a sawed-off cypress stump that someone had used to climb up on the deck.

The air among the trees was still and humid and dappled with broken shards of sunlight. I wished I had brought my .22, and then I wondered at my own foolishness in involving myself in something my father had been willing to lie about in order to protect me from. But I had to know what he was hiding, what or who it was that would make him choose the welfare of another over my mother's anxiety and fear.

I stepped up on the cypress stump and leaned forward until I could see into the doorless cabin. There were an empty dynamite box and a half-dozen beer bottles moted with dust in one corner, and I remembered the seismograph company that had used the houseboat as a storage shack for their explosives two years ago. I stepped up on the deck more bravely now, sure that I would find nothing else in the cabin other than possibly a possum's nest or a squirrel's cache of acorns. Then I saw the booted pants leg in the gloom just as I smelled his odor. It was like a slap in the face, a mixture of dried sweat and blood and the sour stench of swamp mud. He was sleeping on his side, his knees drawn up before him, his green-and-white, pin-striped uniform streaked black, his bald, brown head tucked under one arm. On each wrist was a silver manacle and a short length of broken chain. Someone had slipped a narrow piece of cable through one manacle and had nailed both looped ends to an oak floor beam with a twelve-inch iron spike. In that heart-pounding moment the length of cable and the long spike leaped at my eye even more than the convict did, because both of them came from the back of my father's pickup truck.

I wanted to run but I was transfixed. There was a bloody tear across the front of his shirt, as though he had run through barbed wire, and even in sleep his round, hard body seemed to radiate a primitive energy and power. He breathed hoarsely through his open mouth, and I could see the stumps of his teeth and the snuff stains on his soft, pink gums. A deerfly hummed in the heat and settled on his forehead, and when his face twitched like a snapping rubber band, I jumped backward involuntarily. Then I felt my father's strong hands grab me like vice grips on each arm.

My father was seldom angry with me, but this time his eyes were hot and his mouth was a tight line as we walked back through the trees toward the house. Finally I heard him blow out his breath and slow his step next to me. I looked up at him and his face had gone soft again.

"You ought to listen to me, Son. I had a reason not to want you back there," he said.

"What are you going to do with him?"

"I haven't decided. I need to talk with your mother a little bit."

"What did he do to go to prison?"

"He says he robbed a laundromat. For that they gave him fifty-six years."

A few minutes later he was talking to mother again in their room. This time the door was open and neither one of them cared what I heard.

"You should see his back. There are whip scars on it as thick as my finger," my father said.

"You don't have an obligation to every person in the world. He's an escaped convict. He could come in here and cut our throats for all you know."

"He's a human being who happens to be a convict. They do things up in that penitentiary that ought to make every civilized man in this state ashamed."

"I won't have this, Will."

"He's going tonight. I promise. And he's no danger to us."

"You're breaking the law. Don't you know that?"

"You have to make choices in this world, and right now I choose not to be responsible for any more suffering in this man's life."

They avoided speaking to each other the rest of the day. My mother fixed lunch for us, then pretended she wasn't hungry and washed the dishes while my father and I ate at the kitchen table. I saw him looking at her back, his eyelids blinking for a moment, and just when I thought he was going to speak, she dropped a pan loudly in the dish rack and walked out of the room. I hated to see them like that. But I particularly hated to see the loneliness that was in his eyes. He tried to hide it but I knew how miserable he was.

"They all respect you. Even though they argue with you, all those men look up to you," I said.

"What's that, Son?" he said, and turned his gaze away from the window. He was smiling, but his mind was still out there on the bayou and the houseboat.

"I heard some men from Lafayette talking about you in the bank. One of them said, 'Will Broussard's word is better than any damned signature on a contract.' "

"Oh, well, that's good of you to say, Son. You're a good boy."

"Daddy, it'll be over soon. He'll be gone and everything will be just the same as before."

"That's right. So how about you and I take our poles and see if we can't catch us a few goggle-eye?"

We fished until almost dinnertime, then cleaned and scraped our stringer of bluegill, goggle-eye perch, and sacalait in the sluice of water from the windmill. Mother had left plates of cold fried chicken and potato salad covered with wax paper for us on the kitchen table. She listened to the radio in the living room while we ate, then picked up our dishes and washed them without ever speaking to my father. The western sky was aflame with the sunset, fireflies spun circles of light in the darkening oaks on the lawn, and at eight o'clock, when I usually listened to "Gangbusters," I heard my father get up out of his straw chair on the porch and walk around the side of the house toward the bayou.

I watched him pick up a gunny sack weighted heavily at the bottom from inside the barn door and walk through the trees and up the levee. I felt guilty when I followed him, but he hadn't taken the shotgun, and he would be alone and unarmed when he freed the convict, whose odor still reached up and struck at my face. I was probably only fifty feet behind him, my face prepared to smile instantly if he turned around, but the weighted gunny sack rattled dully against his leg and he never heard me. He stepped up on the cypress stump and stooped inside the door of the houseboat cabin, then I heard the convict's voice: "What game you playing, white man?"

"I'm going to give you a choice. I'll drive you to the sheriff's office in New Iberia or I'll cut you loose. It's up to you."

"What you doing this for?"

"Make up your mind."

"I done that when I went out the back of that truck. What you doing this for?"

I was standing behind a tree on a small rise, and I saw my father take a flashlight and a hand ax out of the gunny sack. He squatted on one knee, raised the ax over his head, and whipped it down into the floor of the cabin.

"You're on your own now. There's some canned goods and an opener in the sack, and you can have the flashlight. If you follow the levee you'll come out on a dirt road that'll lead you to a railway track. That's the Southern Pacific and it'll take you to Texas."

"Gimme the ax."

"Nope. You already have everything you're going to get."

"You got a reason you don't want the law here, ain't you? Maybe a still in that barn."

"You're a lucky man today. Don't undo it."

"What you does is your business, white man."

The convict wrapped the gunny sack around his wrist and dropped off the deck onto the ground. He looked backward with his cannonball head, then walked away through the darkening oaks that grew beside the levee. I wondered if he would make that freight train or if he would be run to ground by dogs and state police and maybe blown apart with shotguns in a cane

31

field before he ever got out of the parish. But mostly I wondered at the incredible behavior of my father, who had turned Mother against him and broken the law himself for a man who didn't even care enough to say thank you.

It was hot and still all day Sunday, then a thundershower blew in from the Gulf and cooled everything off just before suppertime. The sky was violet and pink, and the cranes flying over the cypress in the marsh were touched with fire from the red sun on the horizon. I could smell the sweetness of the fields in the cooling wind and the wild four-o'clocks that grew in a gold-and-crimson spray by the swamp. My father said it was a perfect evening to drive down to Cypremort Point for boiled crabs. Mother didn't answer, but a moment later she said she had promised her sister to go to a movie in Lafayette. My father lit a cigar and looked at her directly through the flame.

"It's all right, Margaret. I don't blame you," he said.

Her face colored, and she had trouble finding her hat and her car keys before she left.

The moon was bright over the marsh that night, and I decided to walk down the road to Tee Batiste's cabin and go frog gigging with him. I was on the back porch sharpening the point of my gig with a file when I saw the flashlight wink out of the trees behind the house. I ran into the living room, my heart racing, the file still in my hand, my face evidently so alarmed that my father's mouth opened when he saw me.

"He's back. He's flashing your light in the trees," I said.

"It's probably somebody running a trotline."

"It's him, Daddy."

He pressed his lips together, then folded his newspaper and set it on the table next to him.

"Lock up the house while I'm outside," he said. "If I don't come back in ten minutes, call the sheriff's office."

He walked through the dining room toward the kitchen, peeling the wrapper off a fresh cigar.

"I want to go, too. I don't want to stay here by myself," I said.

"It's better that you do."

"He won't do anything if two of us are there."

He smiled and winked at me. "Maybe you're right," he said, then took the shotgun out of the wall rack.

We saw the flashlight again as soon as we stepped off of the back porch. We walked past the tractor shed and the barn and into the trees. The light flashed once more from the top of the levee. Then it went off, and I saw him outlined against the moon's reflection off the bayou. Then I heard his breathing—heated, constricted, like a cornered animal's.

"There's a roadblock just before that railway track. You didn't tell me about that," he said.

"I didn't know about it. You shouldn't have come back here," my father said.

"They run me four hours through a woods. I could hear them yelling to each other, like they was driving a deer."

His prison uniform was gone. He wore a brown, short-sleeved shirt and a pair of slacks that wouldn't button at the top. A butcher knife stuck through one of the belt loops.

"Where did you get that?" my father said.

"I taken it. What do you care? You got a bird gun there, ain't you?"

"Who did you take the clothes from?"

"I didn't bother no white people. Listen, I need to stay here two or three days. I'll work for you. There ain't no kind of work I can't do. I can make whiskey, too."

"Throw the knife in the bayou."

"What 'chu talking about?"

"I said to throw it away."

"The old man I taken it from put an inch of it in my side. I don't throw it in no bayou. I ain't no threat to you, nohow. I can't go nowheres else. Why I'm going to hurt you or the boy?"

"You're the murderer, aren't you? The other convict is the robber. That's right, isn't it?"

33

The convict's eyes narrowed. I could see his tongue on his teeth.

"In Angola that means I won't steal from you," he said.

I saw my father's jaw work. His right hand was tight on the stock of the shotgun.

"Did you kill somebody after you left here?" he said.

"I done told you, it was me they was trying to kill. All them people out there, they'd like me drug behind a car. But that don't make no nevermind, do it? You worried about some no-good nigger that put a dirk in my neck and cost me eight years."

"You get out of here," my father said.

"I ain't going nowhere. You done already broke the law. You got to help me."

"Go back to the house, Son."

I was frightened by the sound in my father's voice.

"What you doing?" the convict said.

"Do what I say. I'll be along in a minute," my father said.

"Listen, I ain't did you no harm," the convict said.

"Avery!" my father said.

I backed away through the trees, my eyes fixed on the shotgun that my father now leveled at the convict's chest. In the moonlight I could see the sweat running down the Negro's face.

"I'm throwing away the knife," he said.

"Avery, you run to the house and stay there. You hear me?"

I turned and ran through the dark, the tree limbs slapping against my face, the morning-glory vines on the ground tangling around my ankles like snakes. Then I heard the twelve-gauge explode, and by the time I ran through the back screen into the house I was crying uncontrollably.

A moment later I heard my father's boot on the back step. Then he stopped, pumped the spent casing out of the breech, and walked inside with the shotgun over his shoulder and the red shells visible in the magazine. He was breathing hard and his face was darker than I had ever seen it. I knew then that neither he, my mother, nor I would ever know happiness again.

He took his bottle of Four Roses out of the cabinet and poured a jelly glass half full. He drank from it, then took a cigar stub out of his shirt pocket, put it between his teeth, and leaned on his arms against the drainboard. The muscles in his back stood out as though a nail were driven between his shoulder blades. Then he seemed to realize for the first time that I was in the room.

"Hey there, little fellow. What are you carrying on about?" he said.

"You killed a man, Daddy."

"Oh no, no. I just scared him and made him run back in the marsh. But I have to call the sheriff now, and I'm not happy about what I have to tell him."

I didn't think I had ever heard more joyous words. I felt as though my breast, my head, were filled with light, that a wind had blown through my soul. I could smell the bayou on the night air, the watermelons and strawberries growing beside the barn, the endlessly youthful scent of summer itself.

Two hours later my father and mother stood on the front lawn with the sheriff and watched four mud-streaked deputies lead the convict in manacles to a squad car. The convict's arms were pulled behind him, and he smoked a cigarette with his head tilted to one side. A deputy took it out of his mouth and flipped it away just before they locked him in the back of the car behind the wire screen.

"Now, tell me this again, Will. You say he was here yesterday and you gave him some canned goods?" the sheriff said. He was a thick-bodied man who wore blue suits, a pearl-gray Stetson, and a fat watch in his vest pocket.

"That's right. I cleaned up the cut on his chest and I gave him a flashlight, too," my father said. Mother put her arm in his.

"What was that fellow wearing when you did all this?"

"A green-and-white work uniform of some kind."

"Well, it must have been somebody else because I think this man stole that shirt and pants soon as he got out of the prison van. You probably run into one of them niggers that's been setting traps out of season."

"I appreciate what you're trying to do, but I helped the fellow in that car to get away."

"The same man who turned him in also helped him escape? Who's going to believe a story like that, Will?" The sheriff tipped his hat to my mother. "Good night, Mrs. Broussard. You drop by and say hello to my wife when you have a chance. Good night, Will. And you, too, Avery."

We walked back up on the porch as they drove down the dirt road through the sugarcane fields. Heat lightning flickered across the blue-black sky.

"I'm afraid you're fated to be disbelieved," Mother said, and kissed my father on the cheek.

"It's the battered innocence in us," he said.

I didn't understand what he meant, but I didn't care, either. Mother fixed strawberries and plums and hand-cranked ice cream, and I fell asleep under the big fan in the living room with the spoon still in my hand. I heard the heat thunder roll once more, like a hard apple rattling in the bottom of a barrel, and then die somewhere out over the Gulf. In my dream I prayed for my mother and father, the men in the bar at the Frederic Hotel, the sheriff and his deputies, and finally for myself and the Negro convict. Many years would pass before I would learn that it is our collective helplessness, the frailty and imperfection of our vision that ennobles us and saves us from ourselves; but that night, when I awoke while my father was carrying me up to bed, I knew from the beat of his heart that he and I had taken pause in our contention with the world.

ROBERT OLEN BUTLER

Jealous Husband Returns in Form of Parrot

I never can quite say as much as I know. I look at other parrots and I wonder if it's the same for them, if somebody is trapped in each of them, paying some kind of price for living their life in a certain way. For instance, "Hello," I say, and I'm sitting on a perch in a pet store in Houston and what I'm really thinking is Holy shit. It's you. And what's happened is I'm looking at my wife.

"Hello," she says, and she comes over to me, and I can't believe how beautiful she is. Those great brown eyes, almost as dark as the center of mine. And her nose—I don't remember her for her nose, but its beauty is clear to me now. Her nose is a little too long, but it's redeemed by the faint hook to it.

She scratches the back of my neck.

Her touch makes my tail flare. I feel the stretch and rustle of me back there. I bend my head to her and she whispers, "Pretty bird."

For a moment, I think she knows it's me. But she doesn't, of course. I say "Hello" again and I will eventually pick up "pretty bird." I can tell that as soon as she says it, but for now I can only give her another "Hello." Her fingertips move through my feathers, and she seems to know about birds. She knows that to pet a bird you don't smooth his feathers down, you ruffle them.

But, of course, she did that in my human life, as well. It's all the same for her. Not that I was complaining, even to myself, at that moment in the pet shop when she found me like I presume she was supposed to. She said it again—"Pretty bird"—and this brain that works the way it does now could feel that tiny little voice of mine ready to shape itself around these sounds. But before I could get them out of my beak, there was this guy at my wife's shoulder, and all my feathers went slick-flat to make me small enough not to be seen, and I backed away. The pupils of my eyes pinned and dilated, and pinned again.

He circled around her. A guy that looked like a meat packer, big in the chest and thick with hair, the kind of guy that I always sensed her eyes moving to when I was alive. I had a bare chest, and I'd look for little black hairs on the sheets when I'd come home on a day with the whiff of somebody else in the air. She was still in the same goddam rut.

A "hello" wouldn't do, and I'd recently learned "good night," but it was the wrong suggestion altogether, so I said nothing and the guy circled her, and he was looking at me with a smug little smile, and I fluffed up all my feathers, made myself about twice as big, so big he'd see he couldn't mess with me. I waited for him to draw close enough for me to take off the tip of his finger.

But she intervened. Those nut-brown eyes were before me, and she said, "I want him."

And that's how I ended up in my own house once again. She bought me a large black wrought-iron cage, very large, convinced by some young guy who clerked in the bird department and who took her aside and made his voice go much too soft when he was doing the selling job. The meat packer didn't like it. I didn't, either. I'd missed a lot of chances to take a bite out of this clerk in my stay at the shop, and I regretted that suddenly.

But I got my giant cage, and I guess I'm happy enough about that. I can pace as much as I want. I can hang upside down. It's full of bird toys. That dangling thing over there with knots and strips of rawhide and a bell at the bottom needs a good thrashing a couple of times a day, and I'm the bird to do it. I look at the very dangle of it, and the thing is rough, the rawhide and the knotted rope, and I get this restlessness back in my tail, a burning, thrashing feeling, and it's like all the times when I was sure there was a man naked with my wife. Then I go to this thing that feels so familiar and I bite and bite, and it's very good.

I could have used the thing the last day I went out of this house as a man. I'd found the address of the new guy at my wife's office. He'd been there a month, in the shipping department, and three times she'd mentioned him. She didn't even have to work with him, and three times I heard about him, just dropped into the conversation. "Oh," she'd say when a car commercial came on the television, "that car there is like the one the new man in shipping owns. Just like it." Hey, I'm not stupid. She said another thing about him and then another, and right after the third one I locked myself in the bathroom, because I couldn't rage about this anymore. I felt like a damn fool whenever I actually said anything about this kind of feeling and she looked at me as though she could start hating me real easy, and so I was working on saying nothing, even if it meant locking myself up. My goal was to hold my tongue about half the time. That would be a good start.

But this guy from shipping. I found out his name and his address, and it was one of her typical Saturday afternoons of vague shopping. So I went to his house, and his car that was just like the commercial was outside. Nobody was around in the neighborhood, and there was this big tree in back of the house going up to a second-floor window that was making funny little

39

sounds. I went up. The shade was drawn but not quite all the way. I was holding on to a limb with my arms and legs wrapped around it like it was her in those times when I could forget the others for a little while. But the crack in the shade was just out of view, and I crawled on till there was no limb left, and I fell on my head. When I think about that now, my wings flap and I feel myself lift up, and it all seems so avoidable. Though I know I'm different now. I'm a bird.

Except I'm not. That's what's confusing. It's like those times when she would tell me she loved me and I actually believed her and maybe it was true and we clung to each other in bed and at times like that I was different. I was the man in her life. I was whole with her. Except even at that moment, as I held her sweetly, there was this other creature inside me who knew a lot more about it and couldn't quite put all the evidence together to speak.

My cage sits in the den. My pool table is gone, and the cage is sitting in that space, and if I come all the way down to one end of my perch I can see through the door and down the back hallway to the master bedroom. When she keeps the bedroom door open, I can see the space at the foot of the bed but not the bed itself. I can sense it to the left, just out of sight. I watch the men go in and I hear the sounds, but I can't quite see. And they drive me crazy.

I flap my wings and I squawk and I fluff up and I slick down and I throw seed and I attack that dangly toy as if it was the guy's balls, but it does no good. It never did any good in the other life, either, the thrashing around I did by myself. In that other life I'd have given anything to be standing in this den with her doing this thing with some other guy just down the hall, and all I had to do was walk down there and turn the corner and she couldn't deny it anymore.

But now all I can do is try to let it go. I sidestep down to the opposite end of the cage and I look out the big sliding glass doors to the back yard. It's a pretty yard. There are great, placid live oaks with good places to roost. There's a blue sky that plucks at the feathers on my chest. There are clouds. Other birds. Fly away. I could just fly away.

I tried once, and I learned a lesson. She forgot and left the door to my cage open, and I climbed beak and foot, beak and foot, along the bars and curled around to stretch sideways out the door, and the vast scene of peace was there, at the other end of the room. I flew.

And a pain flared through my head, and I fell straight down, and the room whirled around, and the only good thing was that she held me. She put her hands under my wings and lifted me and clutched me to her breast, and I wish there hadn't been bees in my head at the time, so I could have enjoyed that, but she put me back in the cage and wept awhile. That touched me, her tears. And I looked back to the wall of sky and trees. There was something invisible there between me and that dream of peace. I remembered, eventually, about glass, and I knew I'd been lucky; I knew that for the little, fragile-boned skull I was doing all this thinking in, it meant death.

She wept that day, but by the night she had another man. A guy with a thick Georgia-truck-stop accent and pale white skin and an Adam's apple big as my seed ball. This guy has been around for a few weeks, and he makes a whooping sound down the hallway, just out of my sight. At times like that, I want to fly against the bars of the cage, but I don't. I have to remember how the world has changed.

She's single now, of course. Her husband, the man that I was, is dead to her. She does not understand all that is behind my "hello." I know many words, for a parrot. I am a yellow-nape Amazon, a handsome bird, I think, green with a splash of yellow at the back of my neck. I talk pretty well, but none of my words are adequate. I can't make her understand.

And what would I say if I could? I was jealous in life. I admit it. I would admit it to her. But it was because of my connection to her. I would explain that. When we held each other, I had no past

41

at all, no present but her body, no future but to lie there and not let her go. I was an egg hatched beneath her crouching body, I entered as a chick into her wet sky of a body, and all that I wished was to sit on her shoulder and fluff my feathers and lay my head against her cheek, with my neck exposed to her hand. And so the glances that I could see in her troubled me deeply: the movement of her eyes in public to other men, the laughs sent across a room, the tracking of her mind behind her blank eyes, pursuing images of others, her distraction even in our bed, the ghosts that were there of men who'd touched her, perhaps even that very day. I was not part of all those other men who were part of her. I didn't want to connect to all that. It was only her that I would fluff for, but these others were there also, and I couldn't put them aside. I sensed them inside her, and so they were inside me. If I had the words, these are the things I would say.

But half an hour ago, there was a moment that thrilled me. A word, a word we all knew in the pet shop, was just the right word after all. This guy with his cowboy belt buckle and rattlesnake boots and his pasty face and his twanging words of love trailed after my wife through the den, past my cage, and I said, "Cracker." He even flipped his head back a little at this in surprise. He'd been called that before to his face, I realized. I said it again, "Cracker." But to him I was a bird, and he let it pass. "Cracker," I said. "Hello, cracker." That was even better. They were out of sight through the hall doorway, and I hustled along the perch and I caught a glimpse of them before they made the turn to the bed and I said, "Hello, cracker," and he shot me one last glance.

It made me hopeful. I eased away from that end of the cage, moved toward the scene of peace beyond the far wall. The sky is chalky-blue today, blue like the brow of the blue-front Amazon who was on the perch next to me for about a week at the store. She was very sweet, but I watched her carefully for a day or two when she first came in. And it wasn't long before she nuzzled up to a cockatoo named Willy, and I knew she'd break my heart.

But her color now, in the sky, is sweet, really. I left all those feelings behind me when my wife showed up. I am a faithful man, for all my suspicions. Too faithful, maybe. I am ready to give too much, and maybe that's the problem.

The whooping began down the hall, and I focused on a tree out there. A crow flapped down, his mouth open, his throat throbbing, though I could not hear his sound. I was feeling very odd. At least I'd made my point to the guy in the other room. "Pretty bird," I said, referring to myself. She called me "pretty bird," and I believed her and I told myself again, "Pretty bird."

But then something new happened, something very difficult for me. She appeared in the den naked. I have not seen her naked since I fell from the tree and had no wings to fly. She always had a certain tidiness in things. She was naked in the bedroom, clothed in the den. But now she appears from the hallway, and I look at her, and she is still slim and she is beautiful, I think—at least I clearly remember that as her husband I found her beautiful in this state. Now, though, she seems too naked. Plucked. I find that a sad thing. I am sorry for her, and she goes by me and she disappears into the kitchen. I want to pluck some of my own feathers, the feathers from my chest, and give them to her. I love her more in that moment, seeing her terrible nakedness, than I ever have before.

And since I've had success in the last few minutes with words, when she comes back I am moved to speak. "Hello," I say, meaning, You are still connected to me, I still want only you. "Hello," I say again. Please listen to this tiny heart that beats fast at all times for you.

And she does indeed stop, and she comes to me and bends to me. "Pretty bird," I say, and I am saying, You are beautiful, my wife, and your beauty cries out for protection. "Pretty." I want to cover you with my own nakedness. "Bad bird," I say. If there are others in your life, even in your mind, then there is nothing I can do. "Bad." Your nakedness is touched from inside

43

by the others. "Open," I say. How can we be whole together if you are not empty in the place that I am to fill?

She smiles at this, and she opens the door to my cage. "Up," I say, meaning, Is there no place for me in this world where I can be free of this terrible sense of others?

She reaches in now and offers her hand, and I climb onto it and I tremble and she says, "Poor baby."

"Poor baby," I say. You have yearned for wholeness, too, and somehow I failed you. I was not enough. "Bad bird," I say. I'm sorry.

And then the cracker comes around the corner. He wears only his rattlesnake boots. I take one look at his miserable, featherless body and shake my head. We keep our sexual parts hidden, we parrots, and this man is a pitiful sight. "Peanut," I say. I presume that my wife simply has not noticed. But that's foolish, of course. This is, in fact, what she wants. Not me. And she scrapes me off her hand onto the open cage door and she turns her naked back to me and embraces this man, and they laugh and stagger in their embrace around the corner.

For a moment, I still think I've been eloquent. What I've said only needs repeating for it to have its transforming effect. "Hello," I say. "Hello. Pretty bird. Pretty. Bad bird. Bad. Open. Up. Poor baby. Bad bird." And I am beginning to hear myself as I really sound to her. "Peanut." I can never say what is in my heart to her. Never.

I stand on my cage door now, and my wings stir. I look at the corner to the hallway, and down at the end the whooping has begun again. I can fly there and think of things to do about all this.

But I do not. I turn instead, and I look at the trees moving just beyond the other end of the room. I look at the sky the color of the brow of a blue-front Amazon. A shadow of birds spanks across the lawn. And I spread my wings. I will fly now. Even though I know there is something between me and that place where I can be free of all these feelings, I will fly. I will throw myself there again and again. Pretty bird. Bad bird. Good night.

SANDRA CISNEROS

Barbie-Q

for Licha

Yours is the one with mean eyes and a ponytail. Striped swimsuit, stilettos, sunglasses, and gold hoop earrings. Mine is the one with bubble hair. Red swimsuit, stilettos, pearl earrings, and a wire stand. But that's all we can afford, besides one extra outfit apiece. Yours, "Red Flair," sophisticated A-line coatdress with a Jackie Kennedy pillbox hat, white gloves, handbag, and heels included. Mine, "Solo in the Spotlight," evening elegance in black glitter strapless gown with a puffy skirt at the bottom like a mermaid tail, formal-length gloves, pink chiffon scarf, and mike included. From so much dressing and undressing, the black glitter wears off where her titties stick out. This and a dress invented from an old sock when we cut holes here and here and here, the cuff rolled over for the glamorous, fancy-free, off-the-shoulder look.

Every time the same story. Your Barbie is roommates with my Barbie, and my Barbie's boyfriend comes over and your

Barbie steals him, okay? Kiss kiss kiss. Then the two Barbies fight. You dumbbell! He's mine. Oh no he's not, you stinky! Only Ken's invisible, right? Because we don't have money for a stupid-looking boy doll when we'd both rather ask for a new Barbie outfit next Christmas. We have to make do with your mean-eyed Barbie and my bubblehead Barbie and our one outfit apiece not including the sock dress.

Until next Sunday when we are walking through the flea market on Maxwell Street and *there!* Lying on the street next to some tool bits, and platform shoes with the heels all squashed, and a fluorescent green wicker wastebasket, and aluminum foil, and hubcaps, and a pink shag rug, and windshield wiper blades, and dusty mason jars, and a coffee can full of rusty nails. *There!* Where? Two Mattel boxes. One with the "Career Gal" ensemble, snappy black-and-white business suit, three-quarter-length sleeve jacket with kick-pleat skirt, red sleeveless shell, gloves, pumps, and matching hat included. The other, "Sweet Dreams," dreamy pink-and-white plaid nightgown and matching robe, lace-trimmed slippers, hairbrush and hand mirror included. How much? Please, please, please, please, please, please, please, until they say okay.

On the outside you and me skipping and humming but inside we are doing loopity-loops and pirouetting. Until at the next vendor's stand, next to boxed pies, and bright orange toilet brushes, and rubber gloves, and wrench sets, and bouquets of feather flowers, and glass towel racks, and steel wool, and Alvin and the Chipmunks records, *there!* And *there!* And *there!* And *there!* and *there!* and *there!* and *there!* Bendable Legs Barbie with her new page-boy hairdo. Midge, Barbie's best friend. Ken, Barbie's boyfriend. Skipper, Barbie's little sister. Tutti and Todd, Barbie and Skipper's tiny twin sister and brother. Skipper's friends, Scooter and Ricky. Alan, Ken's buddy. And Francie, Barbie's MOD'ern cousin.

Everybody today selling toys, all of them damaged with water and smelling of smoke. Because a big toy warehouse on

Halsted Street burned down yesterday—see there?—the smoke still rising and drifting across the Dan Ryan expressway. And now there is a big fire sale at Maxwell Street, today only.

So what if we didn't get our new Bendable Legs Barbie and Midge and Ken and Skipper and Tutti and Todd and Scooter and Ricky and Alan and Francie in nice clean boxes and had to buy them on Maxwell Street, all water-soaked and sooty. So what if our Barbies smell like smoke when you hold them up to your nose even after you wash and wash and wash them. And if the prettiest doll, Barbie's MOD'ern cousin Francie with real eyelashes, eyelash brush included, has a left foot that's melted a little—so? If you dress her in her new "Prom Pinks" outfit, satin splendor with matching coat, gold belt, clutch, and hair bow included, so long as you don't lift her dress, right?—who's to know.

MATT CLARK

The West Texas Sprouting of Loman Happenstance

Loman Happenstance's ancient gold Cadillac died finally, sputtering, spasming next to a green road sign which read "Sweetum." Loman climbed out of the car and drank in the surroundings. The skies over the low mountains around him, egg-carton blue purpling up into squid-inky blackness, were nonplussed to witness the steamy demise of a once-regal highway yacht. The short sweet aria of a whippoorwill prodded Loman to begin his eulogy. "You picked a strange graveyard, my love," he said to his failure-belching auto. "Nobody will come to visit you way the hell out here." He stalked to the trunk of the car, gravel crunching underfoot, and removed two suitcases. In one resided his traveling wardrobe. In the other, heavy shifting sighs and whispers, his wares, his life, his trade: seeds. He peddled exotics and domestics of the vegetable and flowering varieties all over the grand expanse of Texas. "Loman Happenstance," he would introduce himself to strangers in cafes and five and dimes from El Paso to Gladewater. "Seed salesman extra-extraordinaire."

I report this to you as if I was there, because, of course, I was. Watching Loman from my front porch.

There was nowhere else for Loman Happenstance to go, really, except toward the dilapidated two-story building in front of him. Everything else was obviously abandoned. The drugstore, the gas station, the old city hall/post office/fire station—all those buildings were shadowy-still and barn mouse quiet. Only the feed store showed signs of life: 1) a light bulb, bare, harvest moon yellow, mermaid-charming moths to its heat; 2) the soft, cricket-purr creak of a rocking chair stroking the time-worn boards of the porch; and 3) a man—me—caught up in that rocking chair's pulse. Loman Happenstance aimed his lily-white bucks toward this new oasis. The two suitcases pack-mule slapped against his seersuckered legs.

"How de do!" the seed peddler announced with zest. "Loman Happenstance: seed salesman extra-extraordinaire."

"Evening," I responded. "Vehicular apocalypse?"

"Yessir," Loman sighed. "The end of a great one, I'm afeared. We've been together for a long while, but I regret to say that our relationship has come to a hot asphalt stop. If I could just borrow your phone, I'll call for a wrecker to come remove Ol' Beulah and myself from your beautiful little town. Do you garden?"

"No phone."

"I beg your pardon?" Loman Happenstance's long-lasting perma-smile faltered for a moment. Lips quivered and met, then reparted to form a disbelieving O. "No phone?"

"Nope. You're in the famed Middle of Nowhere, friend. Communication out here is a thing of terrible uncertainty. My perceptions of time and distance are equally shaky. It's the landscape, you see. Desert meets mountain. Metaphysical borderland."

"Well, how in the name of . . ." Loman paused until he regained his beauty pageant smile. "I suppose if you need something, then you just drive to the nearest town, right?"

"Nearest town is seventy-five miles that way." I pointed my whole hand, empty glass and all, eastward. "And I don't own a car."

Loman Happenstance swooned to a seat on the larger of his two cases.

"Nosiree," I said. "Got shed of it thirteen years ago. On the mutual birthday of Shakespeare and Nabokov. Sold it to a football player on his way to college. He gave me a brand new thesaurus inscribed, 'Love, Aunt Enid,' and I tossed him my key ring, feeling a little guilty, knowing full well I'd come out ahead in the deal. Understand the boy has done all right for himself, despite the curse of my Ford. He owns a nightclub in Dallas. Hoss's Beerateria. Sends me a Christmas card each December with a picture of his boy in it. Pup was conceived in the spring-sprung seat of the same truck I drove my daddy's coffin out to the cemetery in. Fathers and sons. Pappies and their midget reflections."

Loman Happenstance did not know how to react to my weird little soliloquy. There was a West Texas pause that a bobwhite rushed to fill with a litany of monotonous, questioning squeaks. Loman rubbed the back of his neck and produced his biggest, bedsheet-whitest grin. "I don't believe I caught your name," he ventured.

(Now, this was a moment of great strife in the roadrunner life of Loman Happenstance. I had thrown him the at-least-partially-true crazy country coot act, and he was at a crossroads. He knew there was no way he could walk seventy-five miles in those dad-blamed shoes. So how would he handle me? He was a salesman, a people person par excellence. Did he have any ready-made plans for being trapped in a ghost town with a lunatic? No. "This will be my greatest performance," he must have thought to himself.)

"Cayman Bliss," I said. "Pleased to meet you."

"Well, Cayman," Loman began. He was back on his feet, ready to try again now that he had a name to play with. "You're a sort of Robinson Crusoe out here it appears. Do you have a Friday-man bring your groceries or how do you get on?"

There was a patronizing tone in Loman's trombonish voice. Like maybe he was humoring a loony woman until her husband wrote out the check for a shipment of squash seeds. I didn't like it one bit. Decided to pull out all the organ stops.

"My childhood was full of balloons and gladiolas," I said. "Daddy was a balloonist, of sorts, and Momma damn near became a gladiola herself. She lived and breathed the blossomy things. Both these hobbies came about in a summer I can remember like my last gulp of wine. The train station over there was constantly getting strange items dropped off with no reason at all. And after letting the mysterious boxes—ill-addressed and full of secrets—sit on the dusty platform a week or so, Daddy would drag home the treasure chests, and we would all hold our breath while his Old Timer cut the cardboard wide open. The lids Jack-in-the-Can popped up, and we leaned forward, then backward while Daddy reached in slow, picked up cautious and raised high and proud a new prize courtesy of God or the Southern Pacific or maybe—as I used to dream—some long lost aunt trying to contact us from elsewhere.

"Daddy, knife bright in his left hand, knelt before a big green box. Momma went and fetched her pinking shears so she could neatly unravel the second package's well-traveled enigma.

"Here's what was inside Momma's package: gladiola bulbs. Twenty-eight thousand eight hundred of them. All colors, we would later find out.

"Here's what was inside the trunk that Daddy sliced into: balloons. Seventy-two thousand. All round. In these colors: blue, orange, green, red, yellow.

"Momma looked at Daddy. Daddy looked at her. I looked at the new treasures and wondered, What on earth will come of this?"

While I spoke, the hours passed, until it was almost midnight and Loman Happenstance sat bolt-upright, half-drunk and wide-eyed in Momma's wicker porch swing. He had taken to the apple wine with some enthusiasm, punctuating my story with gulps, belches and the occasional "Golly." So, I knew I had his fullest attention when I cleared my throat one last time and launched—finally—into the finale.

I said, "The October night we buried Daddy under six feet of soil and a whole layer of gladiola bulbs Momma fell asleep at the kitchen table and refused to wake up. Her poor old heart was broke open like a peacock egg. She'd written 'Fly Me To The Moon,' on the back of *The Farmer's Almanac* in her last lucid moments, and that's exactly what I did. It took two thousand balloons (the orange ones were all there was left) and a whole night of helium pumping, but at dawn—fingernails splintered from tying knots—I was ready to cut the ropes. Momma's old four-poster lifted off like a dream. A princess being carried away off into Mexico by a whole flock of pumpkins. It was a Viking funeral, of sorts, the way Jules Verne might have reported it."

"I'll be damned," Loman said, swaying off into slumber.

The night was velvet-painting smooth and quiet. I could hear Happenstance's breathing, deep and relaxed, an air-conditioner addict coming down off his freon high to find that the natural ether of the night was a trip well worth taking.

"I'll be," Loman mumbled in his sleep.

The next morning, over breakfast, I explained to Loman that he might could catch a ride to town with the postman if he should happen to come by in the next couple of days. "Or sooner or later a train is sure to ratchet by and you could hobo a ride to Dryden. Then again, you are perfectly welcome, sir, to bunk here for as long as you like. I so rarely have the luxury of a visitor. And by the jelly-fish blue bags swimming under your eyes, I can tell you are in most dire need of a week or a month of do nothing vacation time."

"A vacation!" Loman exclaimed. "Never in my life have I been wont to shirk my responsibilities! Do I seem to you, sir, a slacker?" Loman eyed me hurtfully.

"Responsibilities," I mimicked Loman's voice unintentionally, weighed the word on the tip and sides and rear of my tongue. "Who are you responsible to besides yourself? You got any family?"

"No."

"That company you work for gonna holler 'BANKRUPTCY!' if they miss an order or three of pansy flats?"

Loman remained quiet. He listened carefully.

"You'll be a better salesman, boy, if you take a breather and regroup your synapses."

Loman cleared his throat and hummed the first few bars of "Anything Goes."

"A *vacation*. Magic word for most. A mystery to me." Loman wrinkled up his eyebrows. "What in the bejeezus would I do out here to vacation?"

"Wonderful things, amigo," I said. "A sloppy parade of wonderful things."

The chameleons—all 131 of them; I'd tell you their names, but I'm no good with names—the chameleons watched attentively while I thumbed through a stack of postcards. Loman Happenstance's gaze darted ping-pong style between my rustling and the lizards' tongue-flick patience. "*These* were left at the depot?" he asked, pointing at the reptiles underfoot. "*These* came on a train?"

"Indeed. The box in which they arrived," I told Loman, "was addressed to SVEN GARLIC'S VAUDEVILLE HOEDOWN, but it ended up here. Stamped LIVE ANIMALS and poked full of holes. I couldn't endure Pa's traditional week-long 'somebody-might-come-claim-it' wait, you know. I just opened her up and there they were. Four dozen little baby dragons is what they looked like. They've grown quite a bit since then. I reckon this is their full size.

"Now," I continued, "I have always been a lover of art, you see. It has been a hobby of mine to write museums and galleries the world over requesting postcards of their more famous and dramatic pieces. For instance, here's a little 'Guernica.'"

The chameleons, a lime-green, sized-ten tennis shoe army, leaned toward me, their eyes fixed on the postcard I held. I noticed their attention and shielded the card from their hungry stares, slowly put it back—face-down—on the tabletop.

"I didn't realize what they were good for for the longest time. I just let them run around the house like a reptilian Our Gang. Then one day I got a postcard of Van Gogh's 'Starry Night' and just held it up for them to look at. As a sort of joke, you know. Bam! As soon as they saw what I was holding they junebug-quick—well, here's that 'Starry Night' now," I said, fishing the battered card out of a pile of Warhol soupcans. "Watch this," I whispered.

I turned the postcard around so that the chameleons could get a good look at it. Without hesitation they began to scurry around the floor, tails sliding and claws scratching maniacally. Then, door-slam resolute, they stopped moving and Loman Happenstance had to suppress the urge to holler.

"It may take them a couple of seconds to get the colors absolutely right," I explained. In a whisper, I added, "Some of them are a little slow."

Gradually the lizards' hides began to change, becoming bumpy brushstrokes of blue and black, sunbursts of yellow. A moment or two later Mr. Van Gogh's far-away suns and swirling cosmic airs sat right before our eyes, a "Starry Night" more perfect than any your average museum guard has ever frowned upon. "Oh my god," said Loman, dumbfounded.

"This? Oh, this is relatively easy. They do a knockout 'Washington Crossing the Delaware.' And this," I confided, "is my most favorite one."

I held another postcard in my right hand. This time, though, I kept the artwork a secret from Loman. After I flashed the card at the chameleons, I couldn't help but laugh out loud at their jumping-bean deconstruction. Whilst my laughter subsided, so did the lizards' wild contortions.

"The Mona Lisa!" Loman yelled.

"Living and breathing," I pointed out.

The last one to get it right was—as always—the mouth one. He had to readjust his tail several times before the new creation was Xerox-perfect, the tail-turned-mouth blushing, curving ever-so-slightly into . . . what is that? a smirk? a smile? a just-kissed smacker?

After the lizards successfully stacked themselves into a bone-white facsimile of the Venus de Milo, I felt the need to stretch my legs a bit. "Let's give them a rest and take a little stroll," I suggested to Loman.

We meandered out back by the windmill and water tank. It was a hazy, wasp-thirsty midmorning, and our feet squishing around the wet grass sounded like a bunch of cows molesting a field of bubblegum.

Squish, squish, squish, our shoes went.

For about the millionth time, Loman said, "But—But—"

"Oh, hell, Happenstance," I said. " 'Is it art? Is it not art?' Who gives a damn? I didn't make the lizards, but I gave them the inspiration to paint. If I'm not the artist, then at least I'm the artists' patron. Fact is, it doesn't matter. They're happy. I'm happy. We're both happier for knowing each other."

Then it hit me. "Loman Happenstance," I said, "what on earth did you ever make? Did you at any time fingerpaint or mold your Pa an ashtray for Christmas? Build a birdhouse in shop class or spray paint your best girl's name on a train trestle? Have you once cooked a good meal from scratch or sung Puccini in the shower? Surely some summer you lifeguard-tanned at the community pool or beer-dizzy bunny-hopped your way around a Valentine dance? What have you made, Loman Happenstance, with your hands or your mouth or the waggling of your limbs? What's your momma got magnet-stuck on her Frigidaire that you can call your own?"

Loman, head bowed, admitted, "I don't think I did any of those things." His feet were muddy up to his ankles.

"Well, this is a first for me," I announced to the spiraling buzzards above. "I can't remember ever having had a conversation with a corpse before. And them shoes are ruined."

Loman Happenstance sat at the kitchen table all night long. He had a roll of paper towels, a cigar box full of Crayolas and a bottle of Southern Comfort to keep him company through the night's blackest hours and the farm report on my radio to occupy his eardrums at dawn.

He spent the whole of the day out by the water tank, measuring with a yardstick and lugging his largest suitcase around.

He spent the next day doing the same.

The postman came by on the third day, and I hollered out the window to Loman that he might be able to catch a ride into town, but he ignored me and went right on crawling around in the short, mushy grass.

That evening he came in for dinner and said, "Voila!"

I rushed to the window and looked out, but the backyard looked the same as ever to me. "Is it something minimalist?" I asked.

"Your perceptions of time and distance are shaky," Loman reminded me. "It's the landscape, remember? Anyhow, the thing to do now is wait." He sat down at the table and began to spoon green beans onto his plate. Shamrock green green beans, Alaska white plate.

For weeks I watched out the kitchen window to see what Loman had wrought. He'd planted a whole bunch of stuff, sure, but it looked kind of haphazard, the sprouts, the sky-pushing green stalks. I never questioned him, though, and he never offered any explanations. In truth, *he* himself never looked out back to see what was growing there. He spent his days like I did. Playing with the lizards. Reading from the family library. Rocking on the front porch with a glass of apple wine and an every-evening earful of coyote choir recital.

Finally, one misty A.M. Loman asked me if I kept a ladder about the place and I showed him out to the chicken shed. We dragged the ladder over to the house and leaned it fully extended up against the rain gutter. It reached the roof and a little bit more.

Without a word Loman began his precarious ascension and—equally silent—I followed.

Ladder tops, as you may well know, are tricky things to handle. The whole of this feat required a slow and muscular patience. At last I stood (warily) on the dewy shingles and looked at where Loman was directing his gaze, to the mysterious backyard garden of one seed salesman extra-extraordinaire.

"Sweet mother of pearl," I whispered. I was surprised and surprised at myself for being surprised.

"Edward Hopper's 'Nighthawks,'" Loman announced un-necessarily. For this reproduction of the lonely night cafe was exquisite beyond belief. A giant, perfect copy of Hopper's famous painting done brilliant in gardenias and mums and lilies and orchids and daisies and enough bluebonnets to make the Daughters of the Alamo Fighters blush in their coon-skinny gift shop. It was a one-better-than the Rose parade would never come close to.

"Loman," I said. "It's beautiful."

Loman took a deep breath and sighed. "It's a picture that has always made me feel like I wanted to be home. I just hate it that they have to be so lonely, those people in that diner. Those poor, lonely souls."

Then Loman, without so much as a sigh, left my side and climbed down the ladder. I heard him go into the house. A few minutes later, he emerged carrying his suitcase and a cardboard sign which read, "MILLER'S POINT." He walked to the side of the road and stood there, not more than ten yards from his dead automobile. I'd never noticed it before, but from up here, I could see that he was a little bald on top.

I started to holler something down to him, but before I could work up the breath, a train came bulleting around the mesa and stopped to drop off my monthly grocery supply. Calmly and deliberately Loman walked to the engine and pulled himself up into the driver's cabin. The train departed with a long, happy whistle.

Every day I climbed roof-top and marveled at Loman's masterpiece, wished that he might have stayed on a while longer. You see, I thought for a time that Loman had left mad at me for my attack on his artless life.

Then, slowly, I began to realize the picture was changing, and it became obvious in leaves and blooms that Loman had left me with a gift of enormous faith and thanks. Maybe even love. Hopper's night diner was magically filling up with customers. They grew into a laughing crowd of nurses and gangsters and symphony conductors and firefighters and astronauts and telephone operators. Eventually, daylight overtook the diner and the people began to leave, going home in pairs and groups of four.

And when it was gone, all of it, the people and the diner, every last hint of the wonderful West Texas Sprouting of Loman Happenstance, I went back to the lizards. They were crawling on the ceiling doing their best to reproduce the Sistine Chapel. But there wasn't enough of them to complete the whole. God reached out to touch Adam, but Adam wasn't there.

As it was, Our Scaly Father Above ended up pointing a wiggling finger at yours truly.

Uncle Norvel Remembers Gandhi

I'll tell you one goddamn thing, Mahatma Gandhi was a sonuvabitch. You want your oral history, you turn that tape machine on and I'll give you some oral history. Sure, I saw the movie on television. What a crock. During World War Two my army unit was sent over there to try and get the goddamn Indian railroads back to running. The food was not fit to eat. Damn cows all over the place and not a decent steak to be had anywhere. Ever once in a while one of us would shoot some skinny old cow and cook it over a bonfire.

The Indians were more interested in fighting the British than whipping Tojo. They could tear up more rail in one day than we could lay in a week. They didn't give a plug nickel if it killed fifty train crew as long as it pissed the limeys off. And all the time that little half-naked Gandhi was running around in a diaper making *Life* magazine think he was holier than any bleeding Catholic saint.

I guess religion is the same everywhere, at least in some ways. My daddy used to say that many a man had been trudging along behind a mule and plow in the blazing heat when he got called by God to go preach somewhere in the shade.

Anyway, ever now and then the British command would send over a case or two of potted meat that tasted like soap. I was hungry the whole time I was over there. Even the cafes that was supposed to be for the English served up some of the most peculiar stuff I had ever seen set on a table. I dreamed of a river of cream gravy, and when I come home my momma stood at that old wood-burning stove for four solid days cooking, trying to fill me up. Finally she told Daddy to take me to town and buy me steaks until I couldn't eat no more.

We would get one rail-line running and have to go back and fix the line we fixed the month before. The Mahatma was preaching peace and some of his followers was tearing up track nonstop. The most you could hope for about the food was that it didn't have maggots in it. The people were hostile little brown bastards, and the weather was something else. I mean, I grew up in Texas and I know something about hot weather, but India was hotter than a two-bit whore on nickel night. I like to have died from the heat. One old boy from Vermont or one of them places asked the chaplain where he would go if he got sent to military prison. When the chaplain told him San Francisco, he jumped up and slapped the living fire out of a major sitting next to him at the bar. Of course, a couple military police beat the crap out of him and he had to come to work the next morning just like everybody else. No San Francisco for him or any of us. I tell you it was hot.

We had ten old steam locomotives shipped over from the States. Typical army deal. Had to nearly rebuild them from the ground up to put them into service. Whenever we got one of them to run on a few yards of track, a general would show up to have his picture made hanging off the cow-catcher, grinning and saluting the camera.

So, you kind of get an idea of how I formed my opinion of Gandhi. A year after I got home from the war I married Hazel and she finally told me that nobody wanted to hear my opinion of Mahatma Gandhi anymore. I knew she was right. She generally was right about things. She knew before the doctor told her that she couldn't have kids, and she knew when she was dying before her doctor told either one of us.

So, I kind of quit talking about Gandhi and the war. Ever now and then I would run into somebody and talk about it a little. One time they hired six of us welders to put up the new mill south of town and one of those guys had fought in Europe. He told me about the Battle of Bastogne and I told him about India. But mostly I just quit mentioning any of it. I'd hear other guys talking on the job about Adlai Stevenson, inflation, or Viet Nam, and, of course, communism was real popular for a while. I even worked on a job that old man Vogel poured the foundation for and one of his boys talked nonstop about movie stars. Somebody told me that boy later run off to Oklahoma to become a homosexual, and I can believe it because I've met people from Oklahoma. But the point is, I quit talking about the war I knew about.

I moved to this nursing home after I had a little stroke. They don't like you to call it a nursing home. They say it is a "retirement village." That word village reminds me of India and I say this place is a nursing home.

One afternoon right after I got here, a little brown man in a blue suit toured through the place. When I asked who he was, one of the nurses said, "That's Mr. Patel. He is thinking of buying this place."

"Is he a Mexican?" I asked. I knew he didn't look like any of the Mexicans around here except for being brown, but I thought maybe he was from deep down in old Mexico or something. She didn't answer me. I had forgot her oldest girl married one of the Ortiz boys. She just walked back in the office and set at the desk eating out of a big gold box of candy which she really didn't need since her whole family runs to the fleshy side.

Turns out Manjit Patel did buy this place, and he owns two more. Also turned out he was from India. Well, I thought I might talk with him about India if the right chance come along.

In the mornings I like to sit on the east porch in the sun and listen to Zettie Thompson tell stories about her family. If she's making those stories up, she is a by-god genius. If they are true, she has had the saddest and funniest life of anybody I ever met. Anyway, one morning Zettie was off getting her hair done and I was settin' there by myself just kind of wondering how long I was gonna live, and Patel comes walking by. Now, by then I had figured out a couple of things about him. For one, he is pretty good at his job. This place don't smell bad like it did when Pinky Willis owned it. Pinky has always been so damn tight his balls grind together when he walks. He acted like buying a quart of disinfectant would send him to the poor-house. Now this place smells like some different kind of spice, something foreign but nice. The first day I walked in here I thought the whole place smelled like a beer-joint outhouse on a hot summer afternoon. Patel fixed all that.

He was headed out to his car. When he passed me he said, "Good morning. How is everything?"

I knew he wouldn't slow down enough for me to work up to a real conversation. I just blurted it out. "Mahatma Gandhi was a sonuvabitch."

"What?"

"Mahatma Gandhi was a sonuvabitch."

He started laughing. He said, "My grandfather would agree with you if he were alive."

Now that kind of surprised me. I hadn't even thought about somebody from India not liking Gandhi. I told Patel about the trains in India.

He laughed again and said, "You did good work. Did you know Gandhi was a lawyer?"

I said, "Don't a little detail like that just write you a whole damn book?"

64

He was still laughing when he went to climb in his big car and take off. Now, ever time he sees me, he says, "What about that Gandhi?"

"Sonuvabitch," I answer, and he laughs. Sometimes we talk a little if Zettie's not around. Manjit is actually a pretty good old boy. He even got me to thinking about whether Gandhi had a good reason to be a sonuvabitch, and even whether I should have been more of one in my life.

I'm all talked out. You can shut that tape machine off. I believe I'm fixing to take a little nap right about now, but if you'll come back next Thursday, I'll tell you about Harry Truman.

TOM DOYAL

Sick Day

Lester blew a quantity of mucus out of his head Tuesday morning and knew he was sick. He called Doctor Felps. "Doc, the snot is kind of a neon green and got solid chunks in it big as pinto beans."

"Don't be disgusting, Lester," said Dr. Felps. "I'll call a prescription down to Farley at the drugstore. Can you go to pick it up?"

"Myrna will pick it up. She's supposed to call me before she comes home for lunch," said Lester.

After Lester hung up the phone, he wandered through the dark house. He turned on the television in the living room and lay down on the couch. His boss at the car dealership was on a commercial hollering about "uptown service at downtown prices" and he turned the set off. Red Phillips was happy to act a fool as long as the money kept rolling in. Lester's title was

Business Manager, although he knew he didn't really manage anything; he just kept the books at the dealership. Not a bad job, he thought, for somebody with just two years of college. Although at forty he knew that he would never finish the degree, he still occasionally checked the night class schedule at Alamo Community College in San Antonio.

Lester called Myrna at the high school. "Can you come home, Baby?"

"For godsakes, Lester, it is only nine-fifteen. I just can't run home when I feel like it, and if I take a vacation day, I'd have to hire a substitute or Coach will have a fit."

"It's just lonesome here by myself. I got the quack to call me a prescription down to Farley at the drugstore. Can you pick it up on your way home?"

"Yes. Now, you watch a little television or take a nap. You're supposed to be resting. There is a bottle of vitamin C tablets in the kitchen window next to the ivy. Go in there and take about four of them."

"Do you love me, Myrna?"

"Yes, but it is difficult when you're whining. Neither one of our kids was ever as bad a patient as you are. Thank god."

"I'm not too sick to show my appreciation to you."

"Lester, don't talk dirty on the school phone. Now, goodbye."

At ten o'clock Red called to ask where the key to the petty cash box was. "It's in my middle desk drawer on an orange dealership key ring," said Lester.

"That doesn't seem safe, keeping the key in the drawer next to the locked cash box," said Red.

"That's what I told you when you decided to do it that way."

"Oh," said Red. "Well, I've got a couple of *mojados* out here wiping down cars and I wanted to pay them out of petty cash."

"Put a note in there that you paid cash for donuts for the boys in the service department."

"How you feeling?"

"Red, I feel like I been eat up by a wolf and shit off a cliff."

"Well," said Red, laughing. "Long as it ain't serious. I won't make a bank deposit today. If you're still sick tomorrow, I'll bring the stuff up to your house and you can make the deposit out."

Lester hung up the kitchen phone, took the vitamin C tablets, and looked in the refrigerator. He ate a piece of left-over fried chicken and a sliver of lemon meringue pie. Then he went down the hall to the bedroom, got in bed and fell asleep immediately. He dreamed he was painting the interior of a big mansion that he had never seen before. He kept painting the same room over and over again. Each time he was almost finished, someone would come in and tell him that the color was all wrong. Sometimes the color was just off by a couple of shades and sometimes it was not even close. Once, he had painted the walls pink and Myrna came in to tell him that she wanted the room painted "a tranquil gray." When Red came in, he just said the color was wrong, but he wouldn't tell Lester what the right color was. His late mother wanted "a pale aqua, something Esther Williams would have liked." Everybody had an opinion: his first wife whom he hadn't seen in years, his high school football coach, the overly friendly choir director he met when he was seventeen, and a bunch of strangers.

Finally, Lester's dream-self was standing in the middle of the big room just mixing paint in huge buckets, paint puddling in the floor around his feet, great splotches of red, white, yellow, and blue. The instructions about the color were changing so fast there was no time to actually paint the walls. Finally, his late Grandmother Hooper came in and asked him what he was doing. As he explained about trying to get the color right, he started crying. "Honey, you're the one doing the painting. Just please yourself. Tell these other folks to go off and paint their own rooms. You're just getting your bowels in an uproar over nothing. Go on and do it the way you want to," she said, patting him on the back. As she walked out of the dream room, Lester woke, sweating and panting.

He went to the kitchen and drank a glass of water. It was only eleven-thirty. Myrna should be home soon with the prescription. He took a shower and put on a clean T-shirt and sweat pants. The phone rang. He expected it to be Myrna, but it was Hardy Willis calling about the Business Development Committee of the Mahler Chamber of Commerce. Hardy always tried to get somebody on the committee to do something before the regular monthly meeting so he would have something to report on at the meeting.

"I called out to the dealership, but they said you were home sick," said Hardy.

"They were right, Hardy. You going to have to get somebody else to do whatever it is that you're trying to get done," said Lester.

"I'm just calling to check on you, see if you need anything."

"No. Myrna's bringing me a prescription here in a little while."

"By the way, did you ever send off for that brochure on manure-burning power plants?"

"You asked Harvey to do that. It was the two of you who thought cow-shit could put this town on the map," said Lester.

"Yeah. I remember now. I'll call Harvey. I still think those cattle feedlots east of town could be a major asset if we could just think of them in a new way."

"Maybe the wind will change and blow some of that inspiration over to your house, Hardy. I just don't view cow-shit as a development opportunity. Marie James has opened a craft shop out on the highway toward Rio Verde. You could report a new business."

"Hell's bells, Lester. You know Frank left her enough life insurance to provide everybody in this town with a plaster toadstool for their yard every year for the rest of her life. That place don't look like a real business proposition to me," said Hardy.

"You could be right, but it's something to report."

70

"Maybe you're right. Well, get better. I was wanting you to go up to San Antonio with me for the Small City Association meeting. They are having a convention and bringing in some economists and development experts. I thought we could get some ideas. It's on Friday and Saturday of next week. Put it on your calendar."

Lester thought Hardy Willis had a greater ability to bullshit himself than any man Lester had ever known. Hardy once wrote to the people at Disneyland trying to get them to build a theme park in Mahler, Texas. His letter went on and on about the "abundant sunshine and clean water." He got back a form letter which thanked him for his interest in Disneyland. Hardy talked for two years about his "negotiations with the people at Disney."

When Myrna came in at noon, Lester met her at the kitchen door. "Want to fool around?" he asked.

"I guess you're feeling better," she said. "And, no, I don't want 'to fool around,' as you so seductively put it. I've got to pick up a sheet cake for Alta Faye Willis's birthday party in the office this afternoon at three."

"Will her yard man be there?"

"Don't be a gossip, Lester," she said, laughing. "I'm going to heat some soup for you. Farley said for you to take these pills with some food. Do you want some toast with your soup?"

"Yes. With cheese melted on it. Do you think it would be okay for me to call Melissa this afternoon?"

Their daughter Melissa attended the University in Austin where she studied elementary education. Lately, she had told them that she was dating "somebody special."

"I guess so," said Myrna. "Just don't make her mad by prying into her business."

"You mean I can't ask her if she is sleeping with that little pencil-necked geek?"

"That's exactly what I mean."

"Do you think she is?"

"You're starting to annoy me, Lester."

"We didn't."

"No thanks to you," she said, and they both laughed.

After Myrna went back to work, Lester got in bed and started reading a story in one of Myrna's magazines about a woman who was having an affair with her boss, a man her husband despised. To the question "can this marriage be saved" Lester answered who cares. He dropped the magazine beside the bed and rolled over, hugging Myrna's pillow to him. The pillow smelled like her perfume. He breathed deeply a couple of times and dozed off.

The phone woke him. It was Red Phillips again wanting to know why the invoice to the *Mahler Anvil-Herald* hadn't been paid. Inky Stotts had called wanting his money.

"I didn't pay it because the invoice is wrong. They overcharged us. I talked to Inky about it over the phone and he was supposed to send a corrected invoice. The little sumbitch must have heard that I'm not at work today."

"Well, I don't have to call him back today," said Red. "Sorry to bother you at home while you're sick."

"That's okay. It's kind of boring around here anyway," he said and hung up the phone.

Lester dialed Melissa's number, but her machine answered. He hung up without leaving a message.

He watched a quiz show for a while. Not only could he not answer the questions, he didn't even recognize some of the categories. I need to read more, he thought. He took more pills with a piece of pie and dialed Melissa again.

When she answered, she sounded out of breath. "I was just bringing some groceries in from the car," she said. "Kimberly and I are giving a party Friday night. Want to come?"

"I don't think so. I'm too old for it. I just called to say hi. I've got a sinus infection so I stayed home from work today. Are you doing okay? Is your money holding out?"

"I'm fine. I got a raise at the bookstore and I worked some overtime during registration. Don't worry about it, Dad. I'll ask if I really get in a bind."

"You still dating that guy?"

"Didn't Mom tell you not to ask about that?"

"She mighta said something about it. I'm just being your father. It's my job, you know."

"Roger and I are still dating, but he has applied to graduate school in California. It is cool, Dad. You don't need to worry."

"Damn, I was just getting used to Roger. Now there will be somebody else."

"I love you, but I have to go. There is ice cream in the car."

"Love you too. Bye."

At two Lester called Myrna at school. "Do you think we ought to paint the inside of the house?"

"Lester, can't you sleep? I can't talk to you on the phone all day."

"This is only the second time I've called today. What do you think about painting the inside of the house a nice tranquil gray?"

"Have you been drinking?"

"No."

"What ever gave you the idea to call a color "tranquil gray."

"I just thought you might like it. Pardon me for being a thoughtful husband."

"Lester, I will leave right after we cut the cake for Alta Faye. Right now, I want you to go back to bed. We'll talk about painting the house tonight. Now, don't call me back unless it's an emergency."

"Yes ma'am," he said.

He watched Hoss Cartwright fall in love with a girl who got killed at the end of the show. He turned off the television and wondered whether a request for more tissues was an emergency or not. Probably not, he decided. He was feeling better and thought maybe he should go in to work for a couple of hours, just to keep everything from being such a mess tomorrow. On the other hand, having Red Phillips scurry around on his own a little bit was kind of a satisfying thought. Lester decided to wait for Myrna to come home.

DAGOBERTO GILB

The Prize

Mondays I won't go to Chino's because he's too crudo, hung-over, to cut hair. I won't go on Fridays after four because that's Bud time and he can't concentrate. Saturday and Sunday he's drinking, and though I get to have a beer along with him, I worry too much about my hair looking good when he's done with it, vain as that sounds or not. I've learned these lessons about Chino through close to ten years of personal experience. I call him for an appointment any of the remaining hours and days, never too early, not too late. When the whites of Chino's eyes aren't veined pink, when he's talking about the catfish he pulled from his personal spot on the river—he'll show me the fish, wrapped loosely with foil in the freezer section of his refrigerator—that's when Chino's an artisan. I can run my fingers through my hair when he's done, pleased, and walk out like I stole a twenty-dollar haircut for the seven he charges.

Facing the mountains, Chino's shop is in a Southwestern-theme motel called El Río Bravo—textured white plaster, fake vigas, red tile overhangs, long-hinged wooden doors painted turquoise, the same color, peeling off and fading away, as the window trim and the drained pool in the center of the court. Big made-in-America cars still puddle oil in the slots in front of room doors, but, just as the motel is in a decline, and old, they too are without hubcaps, dented, mud and dust slung all over them.

Chino's is the only business operating in his row; a tailor shop next door was abandoned a year ago, and management never has tried to clean it out inside. Chino recently moved from down the line some to a larger motel room, and he's been in the process of moving out or moving in since he's been here. Not that you can tell the difference. There are two broken wooden chairs on the porch, one good though rusting chrome one, and cardboard boxes, and a gutted stereo speaker, and a pushbutton car radio and portable TV set, their innards exposed to the elements. A life-size cut-out of a blond girl in a bikini, her backing a little bent by abuse and crinkled by damp weather, leans underneath Chino's handpainted—his own hand—black sign in small letters: barbershop.

It's Wednesday, minutes before one o'clock.

The sign in the window says closed, and his motel door is shut securely, but I park next to Chino's white convertible anyway. The sign never changes, and though its ragtop still goes up and down, the convertible doesn't run, and even though I don't see the car he drives, I'm confident because Chino's never stood me up.

I squint through the cloudy glass, and he's there, lights off, by the coffee table, above some steaming food. He's waving me in, but he goes to the door as I'm opening it anyway.

"I almost didn't have time for lunch," he explains.

"I'm glad somebody I know's got so much business," I say. "But you're gonna have to knock down a wall to make room for all your customers pretty soon." It's a tight squeeze inside. Half the motel room, now partitioned off, is his bedroom, and this narrow, visible part is for his business. He's been doing the remodeling himself, and has been for months. Pieces of wood and plastic molding jut and poke, carpenter's tools are piled and heaped. I sit on the frayed, lumpy couch in a tangle of an extension cord, which is on top of a few sections of a Juárez newspaper, which is underneath a pile of more recent editions. Rumpled newspapers and magazines inhabit his shop like cats in an old maid's home. You have to dig yourself some space.

"I'll only be a minute," Chino says, his mouth full. "You hungry?"

"No, no, you eat, take your time."

In the darkness, Chino looks even blacker than he is. His teeth and eyes illuminate his face like automobile grillwork at night, and the white plumber's outfit he wears radiates against his skin, as though a testament to laundry detergent. Chino has on a black hat—"I'm the one your mother always warned you about"—and the bill of it dips and sweeps around his hands. These hands balance half a Big Tex hamburger bun, folded like a tortilla, loaded with barbeque meat, the whole of it scooped into a see-through tub of pico de gallo.

"You're sure?" he asks again.

Watching his enjoyment I'm not, but I say I am. I root around for his naked-girl magazines. It's the only place I get to see them anymore. Though most are the well-known ones, occasionally I encounter speciality mags like this one called *Bottoms Up*. Its centerfold is a line of young women—twelve, I count them—bent away from the camera, their hands pressed to their symmetrically parted knees, their shapely moons ruler straight across the glossy double page. My imagination soars to the process, as a photographer, and it's such a bizarre, comic fantasy—line them up just right, framing the shot, talking it over, squeezing them together—"Candy, sweetheart, could you bend your knees just a little bit . . . a *little* more . . . there it is!"—it puts me into a good mood.

"My God, Chino," I say, "how do they find them?"

Chino's gotten up and switched on the lights and drinks soda from a two-liter bottle in the refrigerator. He comes back to see what I'm talking about with the indifference of experience. "They're everywhere," he tells me sagely. "You only have to know where to look." He seals the foil around the meat, picks up the bag of extra-large buns, and goes over to the pressed-wood vanity, opens a drawer, its paper mahogany veneer revealed, and shoves around its contents to make room. He stuffs the puffy bag of burger buns there, and then the meat. Then he looks over at me, shaking his head, stares at what he's done, and takes back the meat from the drawer.

"One of those days, eh Chino?"

"One of those last nights," he says. He slides the foil package into the refrigerator. He tosses his hat on top, turns on the 24-inch console color television between the vanity and the refrigerator, and stares blankly into it as it warms up.

I decide to visit the toilet before I get under his bib. This room is as packed with his life's junk as the rest of the motel room. The sink next to where I stand has overflowed cigarette butts and stained food wrappers and empty beer cans—must be a case or so—but it doesn't really look remarkably messy in the context. I've left the bathroom door open. "Last night?" I say, nodding at the sink.

"Oh no, I only save them."

After I flush, Chino spins the barber's chair in my direction so I can sit. Then he turns me toward the television. It's such a tight fit in the narrow space that he's had to cut a V out of the vanity so the metal footrest can clear. He snaps the bib at the back of my neck.

"So what'll you have today?" he asks me. He lights a cigarette.

On the mostly purple TV screen, a couple from the Mexican novela are manicly kissing. "A little of her. She looks pretty good at it. Wait. Now that I think about it, I guess as long as you're asking, let me have two of her style, one for each arm. That'll be just fine, I wouldn't wanna get greedy."

"I'll see what I can do," Chino says. "You know, sometimes
. . ." Chino's smile is sly, his pause like a drag off his cigarette.
"Let me tell you something," he starts. Now he does take a hit
on the cigarette. "This morning I was cutting a customer's hair,
and I was thinking, after this I'm not supposed to have nobody
for an hour."

I check Chino's homemade, cork appointment board. It's laid
out Monday through Sunday on the vertical, and, starting at nine
A.M., stretches across in half-hour segments until six P.M. Chino
has fuzzy polaroids of most of his customers sitting in his barber
chair, and he tacks them in the spaces they call for. He has blanks
from 11:30 to 12:30. Otherwise, the spaces are filled from 9:00.

"And you know, I'm glad about it today, because I'm tired.
But I also know I am wrong. I can feel it, you see? I see in my
mind I have another customer after this one, a walk-up, and I'm
thinking how I should get out of here five minutes sooner so he
won't come and ask. I can't turn down a customer if he asks. In
my mind, I already see him standing there. But this customer, he
likes to have his time here. Gets the shave, the whole thing. So
I can't leave early, but I tell my customer, 'You watch, a man will
be at my door wanting the next appointment. Any minute now,'
I tell him. He laughs at me, thinks I'm making it up. But then
there he is, like I said. And he's asking me if he can be next.
'See?' I tell my customer."

Chino's clipping my hair now. I'm getting my usual. He cuts
between sentences. It's dramatic, and I see him as a character in
his story. He's thin and tiny, Indio-like. I notice the elegant sil-
very streaks through his black hair, tied back into a chic, two-
inch ponytail. He has gray, unshaven stubble all over his face. I
notice how his palms are almost as dark as the back of his hands.
His color amazes me because he's indoors all day.

"Now when I'm cutting this customer's hair, in my mind I see
another one about to come, another walk-up. I can't believe it. I'm
thinking how if I finish this one more fast, I can get out, eat, and
then, after you at one, I don't got nobody til three-thirty. But then
I realize no matter when, he'll come when I'm about to finish . . ."

"Shaking the hair off the apron!" I jump in, excited. "Brushing little hairs off his neck!"

". . . Yes, I know there'll be another customer, no matter if I hurry or go slow, this other walk-up will be here. And just like I knew, when I'm finishing, I look up, and there he is standing at the door."

I laugh. "You're a brujo, Chino, admit it!"

"It's what I'm saying. La brujería. Sometimes my mind can make something happen."

It's not really very logical what he's saying. Maybe he knows it too. But it's fun going along. "Shit, Chino, if that's how it is it shouldn't be no trouble for you to arrange those pretty women for me. With all your powers, at least *one* of them, a couple of margaritas with crushed ice on the side—it should be *easy*."

His laugh is more controlled by other thoughts. He grips the top of my head while he snips my sideburns and around my ears. Afterwards, he steps in front of an impassioned TV dialogue about incest. Chino has equally passionate eyes.

"Let me tell you this other one. Last year I was in Juáritos, at a baseball game."

"You were pitching?"

"No, I was hurt, and I don't pitch anymore." Chino and I shared baseball stories since we both had played in league fast-pitch softball, me here, him over there. I'd gone to a couple of games in Juárez a few years ago to watch his team play in a championship tournament against a team from Chihuahua.

"Too bad. What happened?"

"Forget that! Listen to what I'm telling you!"

I want to laugh at him for being so serious, but I resist.

"I was sitting with my friend, behind home plate, and we were losing three to one. Two guys had gotten on . . . well, it doesn't matter what their names are . . . they got on first and second, a bunt and an error, but, well, their pitcher, he's been doing too good since he settled down, and he's at the bottom of the order now, and the infield's in and ready, and he's struck out the last two."

80

I think I already know what's going to happen. Anybody would. But since it's so obvious, and he's telling it like it isn't, I'm listening for some unique twist. "It's bottom of the ninth, right?"

Chino nods his head, appreciative of my interruption this time. "We only got two hitters on the team, and that's how we got the run, two doubles in the first, but these guys, well nobody else has come close, and Heri, he's up, he can't hit. My friend, Jorge, sitting next to me, he says, 'That's it, it's three outs, let's get some beers.' And I say, 'You wanna make a bet?' He laughs at me."

"You saw it on the time delay, like a horserace, eh Chino?"

"I tell him he gives me fifty dollars and I put up five. I'm figuring that I'm gonna spend it on the beer anyway, you know?"

"Andale, Chino!"

"But really it's that I'm having this feeling. You know, like I been telling you about, So Jorge takes it. And so I'm sitting there, and I close my eyes."

Chino nods his dark head downwards and squeezes his dark eyelids, a hint of a frown, and touches his dark hands to his dark temples. I hear the TV above his silence. He looks up again.

"Jorge's laughing at me while I'm doing this, when *poosh!*, there it goes." Chino smiles big and proud.

"An easy fifty bucks. Or did he pay up?"

Since I appear to be missing the point, Chino hesitates to answer me. "I didn't make him." He goes back to cutting the rest of my hair.

I'm glad he's cutting my hair again too. I really have to be somewhere by two, and I don't want to get hung up here. "I'll tell you what, Chino. I'm broke, I need money. Make some money for me, all right? Make a big sack of money for me. You think you could do that?"

"Sure!" he says.

"Well, you just do that then, and then we can split it. Just one sack, man. It's enough."

"It's a deal," he says. He steps away for a second, and he squints with his eyes closed again.

"Andale, Chino! Big bills, no smaller than twenties!"

He shushes me quiet, puts his hands to his temples. It seems to me he's also got a grin, but maybe I'm interpreting. After some long seconds, he comes back to my hair.

"I'm talking a big sack, Chino. Like those ones for bushels of onions."

"Okay, you got it," he says. "But don't forget, we split it right down the middle, even."

"You can count on it," I say. "I wouldn't cheat you."

Chino's clipping the top of my hair right now, and I can't really see him, not even in one of the mirrors. "You can't cheat me," he tells me. "It makes bad things happen. You can't play with la brujería."

"Of course, I know."

He's just about finished. "I'm gonna do it everyday for you. It might take me a few weeks, say by the next time you have to come in."

"A few weeks is nothing for a sack of twenties."

"Good," he says. "I promise, I'm going to concentrate on it everyday for you. And if you get the money, you let me know. I'm going to trust you to tell me too. I'm not saying where it's going to come from. Only someplace like you've never gotten it before. It might be by a check in the mail, some relative you haven't thought of, something like that, but you have to tell me, we have to split it."

I don't even think about it, I'm so sure. No easy money's ever come to me, and if Chino can make it happen . . . even though I know he can't, he won't, it won't happen. "Andale, Chino. Make us both rich. I know you can do it." He hands me a small mirror. "Looks great," I say, checking the back from its reflection in the big mirror behind me. He unsnaps the bib and lets my cut hairs roll down the front and onto the floor. Then he picks up the powdered brush and sweeps my neck. I stand up, dig in my pockets, and count out seven dollars. "Thanks. We'll see you next time."

"Everyday I'm going to concentrate," he reminds me. "You call me when it gets there."

"Everyday I'm gonna look outside my front door, Chino. I'm already counting on it. We'll both buy new cars."

I get in my current one. Looking in the rear-view mirror, I run my fingers through my hair, pleased. I pull out, I drive away. Then I remember something. The prize. I applied for a prize. I did it so long ago, seven, eight months ago, I'd forgotten. I didn't expect to win. Not because I shouldn't, because I arrogantly believe I should, even pisses me off to think I won't. Except the prize isn't only about the work, how deserving. It's more about being in the right places, knowing the right people, doing the right things. I live in El Paso, and Chino, who I like, cuts my hair for seven bucks, and most of the time I scrounge for any work I can get. I'm not appropriate, I am not winner material. For years I've suggested to myself that I move. Then, not living here anymore, living in the right place, knowing the right people, living the right life, my past here would become exotic and exciting, like I'd been in the wilderness. Of course, I don't entirely believe that either, which is why I'm afraid to leave. It's my home, where all my family is, and it's comfortable.

But then again I do expect to win. Maybe they'll get it right, I'll get lucky and this time someone out there will choose me, make an exception, because I *don't* live in the right place and the rest, or despite the fact, or because they like my work. It's what I believe in, what I depend on. That's how I'd do it, if I were giving the prize.

I'm driving down Mesa Street, and I'm turning on Rio Grande, then I'm on Copia, and I'm thinking I can call Chino. I'll tell him the prize doesn't count.

I don't have to do that though. It *doesn't* count. I know it, and I don't have to explain myself. If I win, it won't be because of Chino but me.

And probably I won't win. Chino can't make me win.

I should hear about it any day now though. If I win, I have

to make sure that Chino doesn't find out. And if he finds out, screw him. He drinks too much, and my hair's easy to cut, and I'm easy to please.

I think I'm going to win. I really could use the money.

A week later, on Wednesday, Chino calls me at home. Chino hasn't called my house in years. Not since around the time when I went to those ballgames in Juárez with him. "I've been concentrating everyday," he says, "and I wanted to know if anything happened yet."

"Not yet," I say. Do I tell him to relax, not work so hard? But I don't want him to think I'm hiding something. Do I tell him about the prize, how it doesn't count? But I don't want to tell him something he won't find out about if I don't bring it up at all. "You're not doing a good enough job of it, Chino. You're losing your touch."

"I'll keep trying," he says. "Let me know if something happens."

"Andale, Chino. Hey but if I find a dime on the street, I ain't reporting it to you."

It upsets me that Chino called. I think I won't get my haircut at his motel room anymore. I want to win the prize, but I hate all this worry. When I'm out in the day, I rush home to see what's in my mail.

On Friday night of the next week, Chino calls again. His eyes are pink, his ponytail is falling apart, the tails of his white shirt are hanging out, he's working on a twelve-pack of Budweiser in his refrigerator. I see all this through the phone, without squinting. "If anything, I'm losing money, Chino. Now that I think about it, maybe you're sucking money from me, not to me."

"I try to remember everyday."

"Well, there you go! Whadaya mean you *try to remember*?"

He laughs unreasonably. Then he gags, coughs, catches his breath, and his voice comes back deeper. "You better tell me. You have to split it with me, you know. You can't get it all and not let me have my share."

This really pisses me off. I can't think of anything funny or clever. "Chino," I say, "I gotta go right now. I'll get back to you." I hang up the phone.

I'm sure I will win the prize now. Nothing in my life has ever been simple, I've never gotten any easy money, so it makes sense.

Or I can put it in terms other than money. Most of the people who have won the prize think of it this way since they're already rich, own houses and new cars, and they've never had to scrounge for a job.

My best hope is that the news comes late. That I don't find out for a few more weeks. Then I won't have anything to explain to Chino. So when the letter arrives, my heart whimpers. Here I am, I tell myself, supposed to be excited about winning this prize, and instead I feel sick to my stomach. Suddenly, I've made a decision. Or it comes to me. I don't know which, but it's mine, from the inner me or from the out there, and it's got me, it's my liberation from Chino's spell: I won't tell him, and if he finds out, I'll tell him I didn't hear about it until later.

I open the letter. We regret to inform you. I'm not really surprised, I tell my cynical self. As they like to say over and over to us, Who ever said life was fair? All I have to do is go across the river, imagine how miserable everyone over there is, and realize how lucky I am. Or I could go blind, I could be paralyzed, I could be wandering the streets hungry, cold, filthy, muttering and paranoid. Those people don't even complain. It's all true, I know it. I could be dead. Life is too short to worry about petty prize politics, and I'm doing what I'm doing anyway. I also think of Chino. I could call him and point out to him how he didn't make it happen. But I remember those few minutes earlier. My decision. What if I had decided to go along with Chino? Would the letter inside have read differently?

No way. No.

A week later, I call Chino. "Nothing, not even some scratched-up pennies in a parking lot. You're not doing your job. Are you concentrating right?"

"I can't understand it. I'm doing the best I can."

I feel him smiling through the phone. I see him. "Shit, Chino, I'll tell you what, think smaller. Could be that's the problem, you know? Maybe if you like just go for a box of ones."

"It's an idea."

"Or I'll tell you what. Remember the pretty woman I asked for? Just one of those. With a good body though."

He laughs. "So you want an appointment?"

"I can't even afford you now. Not for another week or two at least."

"Let me know," he says.

"Andale, Chino. We'll see you."

★

DAVE HICKEY

I'm Bound to Follow the Longhorn Cows

"I'm bound to follow the longhorn cows until I get too old;
It's well to work for wages, boys, I get my pay in gold.
My girl must cheer up courage and choose some other one,
For I'm bound to follow the longhorn cows until my race is run."
—*A Cowboy Song*

When the white sun had spun into the pupil of the sky, as it hung at the top of its trajectory between the two horizons and then began to fall into early afternoon, the old man found himself trapped in a bathtub of tepid water on the second floor of his ancient house. He flailed about for a few moments and then he became quiet and listened to the long winds shushing through the empty corridors and rooms of his house, which was Victorian in design, having two stories, an attic, a storm cellar, spires, lightning rods, weather vanes, cupolas, traceries and an occasional leaded window; it rested on the plain like a child's block dropped on an immense crazy quilt patched with green and yellow, an old house, but the interior had been completely modernized, and the bathroom in which the old man sat was paneled with cool blue tile.

He had seen ninety summers, as the Comanches, who were gone now, would say, and he was the only person in the surrounding country who was older than the house. On the old man's first birthday his father had driven four stakes into a bald ridge on the prairie, and begun to lay the foundation, and the old man had grown up with the house. It was part of all his memories, the nucleus of his childhood, the point of departure and the point of return for the many journeys of his youth and manhood, for, during his first half-century, the old man had been a rambler and a heller. But, unfortunately, unlike his house, the old man could not be modernized, except by the use of what he called "contraptions": his false teeth, his electric wheelchair.

He was just a shriveled man with gray eyes whose sight was still keen, with a yellowish white mustache drooping below a swollen pockmarked nose that still smelled well enough. He had only a few fringes of white hair on his head, and there was more growing out of his ears than around them, but his hearing was still better than most since he knew what to listen for. He still had the use of his senses, but ninety is an age when senses can be a burden, for your body no longer responds to them. It would have been a blessing if the old man had been a little deaf, or a little blind; then he could not hear the hooves clopping beside the stable, or see the Mexican cowboys ride out toward the pastures where the white-faced cattle dipped their heads slowly in the heat.

At the age of sixty-five he had lost his teeth and his virility, and hadn't mourned his teeth for an hour; he put them in a bottle on his desk. At the age of eighty his right arm was crippled with arthritis, and at the age of eighty-six his legs gave out. They refused once and forever to clench a horse's side, or even to support his weight, though he was a small man. When this happened his son, who was born when the old man was fifty, bought an electric wheelchair for his father and, after several interviews, hired a pretty blond nurse with heavy breasts and a slow smile to care for him. For the next four years the old man spent most of his time resting on a couch in his second-floor bedroom, watching his land, watching the seasons and the sun change its face. Sometimes the nurse, whose name was Roberta May Kuykendall, would read the newspaper to him, and once a week she bathed him.

Roberta May had left the old man's face covered with a lather of soap, and it dried into a crust in the first few minutes, while he sat there, immobile, not knowing what to do. Finally he decided to remove the soap by lifting his knees and sliding down into the clear water. His buoyant heels and buttocks leisurely rose and fell as he let the water creep over his chin and climb in a prickly line across his cheeks. He lifted his good arm and freed the dried soap by rubbing his sand-grained face. His skin felt better, but the taste of soap still hung about his gums. Roberta May had let one soapy finger slip into the old man's mouth as she fell. He sucked his saliva into a cud and spat vehemently into the bath water.

Roberta May lay where she had fallen. She had been scrubbing the old man's neck when her eyes had widened. Her hand jumped, a soapy finger slipped into the old man's mouth, and she had collapsed. She sat for a moment shaking convulsively. Then she had cried something in surprise and fallen back, her head striking the tile like a clay jar. And she had died, so quickly it wasn't even sad, sprawled on the blue tile with her blue eyes looking upward, her skirt caught up around her thighs, and one white arm extended so that the hand rested on a crumpled pile of clothes.

The clothes belonged to the old man's son. As Roberta May had wheeled him down the hall they had met him coming out of the bath. "I have to fly to Dallas, Pa. I'll see you tomorrow afternoon," he had said and run down the steps three at a time. Now his jeans, his denim work shirt and his wide-brimmed straw hat lay in a little pile between the toilet and the bathtub, and the girl's hand seemed to be pointing to them. A scrap of a breeze lifted Roberta May's skirt, revealing another inch of her thigh.

The bathroom curtains billowed white above the old man's head, and the smell of alfalfa, incredibly sweet, swam into his nostrils, only to be cut by the lingering fumes of the soap. The alfalfa wind died quickly, like a breath sucked in, and becalmed the curtains. The old man heard the starched linen crackle faintly as it collapsed. Then he became aware of grasshoppers clicking in the hot grass of the lawn. Outside the window the lawn sloped down to a barbed-wire fence where the hayfields and pastures began and continued into the horizon, but the sill was two feet above the old man's head. All he could see by looking upward was a rectangle of blue sky.

It irritated him to be able to move with such relative freedom in the buoyancy of the water, and yet not be able to climb out of the tub and into the wheelchair, which stood by the bathroom door, but he knew he couldn't. He pulled in his lower lip and clamped it with his gum. Before him the pale image of his body undulated on the surface of the water. His legs were thin and hairless, and the skin on his ankles and thighs had a yellowish cast; his narrow chest was covered with white hair that bristled in patches out of the water, creating little patterns of surface tension. His body, which in its time had mounted many good horses, and many women as good as Roberta May, was just a stringy bag of flesh. He glanced at Roberta May's nylon-sheathed legs, and then slowly looked away.

Just a few minutes before she died, they had heard the Estansas' Chevrolet clatter by the house, had heard Manuel's special honk which he gave every Saturday when he and Señora Estansa headed for town.

"I can tell you two Mesicans gonna be drunk tonight," the old man had said.

"Oh, Mr. Cotton," Roberta May had said, "now how do you know that?"

"I tell you, punkin'. I done a little cowboyin' in my time, and whenever I got to town, it sure wasn't for no tea party."

"Mr. Cotton, I bet you were a wild one."

"That I was, in my way. I drank a little whiskey, and chased me a few girls might' near as pretty as you." He had winked at her. "I ain't gonna tell you if I caught 'em or not."

Roberta May had laughed as she bent over and scrubbed the old man's neck. He looked down the V of her blouse and watched her hanging breasts quiver as she laughed. What a sweet hussy you would have been, he thought, and cast a furtive glance down into the water, where everything was still. And if the old man had ever cried, which he hadn't, he would have then; he would have clenched his fists and let the hateful tears, squeezed like vinegar from his clenched eyelids, crash down over his cheekbones; he would have dropped his toothless jaws and howled, then or any of a thousand times when Roberta May with her soft hands was bathing him or changing his clothes. He would watch her narrowly as she went about her business, as a newly broken horse will watch the wrangler approaching with the bridle dangling from one hand, trailing in the dust. He would decide that she was teasing him, that she was flaunting herself, but closeted in the back of his mind he marked a secret calendar from Saturday to Saturday, when he was bathed by Roberta May Kuykendall who bent forward so casually. Then he would try to convince himself that it was a good thing, nature's law, that old men and young girls could not get together, but he was never completely successful, and now the heart beneath those breasts had stopped, the valves had sucked closed, stopping the surge of blood that flushed her cheeks and made little patterns of red on her neck, and the darkness in her veins, where her blood eddied into stillness, had closed around her sight. She had fallen very heavily, not at all as a girl should fall, onto the blue tile, with her blonde hair sprayed around her head . . .

And so he sat there for a long time, not thinking anything, knowing all along that the day was Saturday and that the Estansas had gone to town to get drunk, that his son was relaxing in flight somewhere between Sonora and Dallas, in the blue air, and that he, like some goddamned relic, had been left in Roberta May's care and that she was stiffening on the chilly tile, but not formulating these thoughts in his mind, not admitting their consequences, until the room began to fill with golden light that poured through the bright window like water from a sluice. It was only then, when he knew the sun was falling, that he accepted the fact that the tub was a prison. Its slick white sides described his boundaries and confined him. He, who owned three hundred sections, who had ridden to Montana and back, might as well have been in a life raft in the middle of a golden ocean, or in a coffin.

But deep in his marrow it was not fear that the old man felt, it was inconvenience; the habits of his last four years, the last fifteen hundred days, plucked at him more urgently than any terror. More than anything on God's green earth he wanted, desired even, to be on his couch by the window, dry, in soft pajamas, his knees covered with a Navajo blanket. He wanted Roberta May to rise up and read him the newspaper while he watched the prairie change colors, or he wanted his son to come into the room and talk to him, a little dully, about a new cattle deal, or oil deal, or the prospects for the cotton crop. His warm bedroom was twenty steps away from the bathtub. Behind the blue-tiled wall, one door down the upstairs hall, his couch was being warmed by the falling sunlight, the Navajo blanket folded at its foot. He shivered.

It startled him for a moment because he thought he was afraid of dying there, ending his century in the bathtub, but it just irritated him. The whole idea filled him with indignation: to have to spend the night in the bathtub! He wasn't afraid, but he was very nearly mad. He lifted his good hand and tugged at his mustache, twisting the damp hairs and poking the end into his mouth. "Crap!" he said aloud.

Then, when he dropped his hand, making a little splash, he realized that the water had become chilled. Three hours. With a little effort he lifted his left leg, watched it appear like a continent bursting from the sea, draining, and with his toe he turned on the hot water faucet. The burst of water burned his heel and so, maneuvering his foot, he turned on the cold faucet and settled back to enjoy the warm surge of water around his feet and up his legs, the tingling when it reached his crotch.

When the edge of the water's surface began to sting like the touch of a hot razor, he turned off the water, and no sooner had the last drop pinged into the tub than a muffling silence settled around him. It pressed against his eardrums and drew sweat from his bald scalp. But the silence, in itself, wouldn't have bothered him, for he had spent a large portion of his life in silence. It was the noiselessness, the noiselessness of an empty house, and different from the silence of the High Plains. Out there there were distances in the silence, crystalline depths; it had size, magnitude, but it didn't make a man, or a man on a horse anyway, feel small. Somehow the two feet between the stirrup and the ground put a man's head among the stars, if he was young, and made the silence right. But in the house, where the silence was cut into dusty cubes, divided into a thousand little silences . . .

He grasped the side of the tub, pulled himself into a sitting position, and to the golden room, the dead girl and the cavernous house he shouted:

"I'm big and I'm bold, boys, and I was big and bold when I was but nine days old. I'm the meanest son of a bitch north, south, east and west of Sonora, Texus. I've rode everything with hair on it and a few things that was too tough to grow any hair. I've rode bull moose on the prod, she-grizzlies and long bolts of lightning. I got nine rows of jaw teeth and holes bored for more, and whenever I get hungry, I eat stick dynamite cut with alkali, and when I get thirsty, I can drink a risin' creek after a goose-drowner plumb dry and still have a thirst for a little Texas whiskey cut with cyanide. Why, when I'm cold and lonesome, I nestle down in a den of rattlers 'cause they make me feel so nice and warm!"

He took a long breath and continued at the top of his lungs. "And when I'm tired, I pillow my head on the Big Horn Mountains, and stretch out from the upper Gray Bull River clean over to the Crazy Woman Fork. I set my boots in Montana and my hat in Colorado. My bed tarp covers half of Texus and all of old Mesico. The Grand Canyon ain't nothin' but my bean hole. But boys, there's one thing for sure and certain, and if you want to know, I'll tell ya: that I'm a long way short of being the Daddy of 'em all. 'Cause he's full growed. And as any fool can plainly see, why boys, I ain't nothin' but a youngun!"

Ho! Drunk in Tascosa or Abilene with your hands behind you holding to the bar, bellied out and hell-raisin', stinkin' of two weeks' sweat, bad whiskey, Bull Durham and cow dung, with a whole skillet of mountain oysters under your belt . . . The echoes of his voice wandered for a few moments down the halls and into some of the empty rooms of the old house; then, one after another, like pebbles falling into a stream, they dropped into silence. (Shards and flecks of the yellow light glittered in Roberta May's eyes.) There was the silence again, but the old man felt better for having shouted.

He had composed that brag, and a lot more of it he couldn't remember, when he was a boy, seventeen, nineteen, he couldn't remember now, but when he had followed the last of the big herds up the trail through the Indian Territory into Wyoming and Montana. It was something to do while you rode in the drag and chewed on the cloud of dust that billowed from the herd of long-striding cattle who walked steadily with their heads down and their wide horns dipping rhythmically. But most of all it passed the time on night watch after the herd had been thrown off the trail. The old man could remember himself, young Jerry Cotton, sitting in the saddle, there in the tall darkness, feeling his pony breathing, its barrel expanding and contracting regularly between his thighs, listening to the sleeping cattle snort and bluster in their dreams of new grass. There was nothing to do but lean on the saddle horn and compose brags, or rather compile them, adding an occasional flourish of your own, putting them in the order in which the words fell right. It was the kind of thing to do in silence. Or he could count the stars which hung like diamonds on fire around his head. (And he counted the stars so often, and in such detail, that he used to tell his wife: "Judy, I got so I could tell you the date, tomorrow's weather and who your grandmother was, just by looking at the stars." And she would always ask him what if it was cloudy? "Then I could only tell you tomorrow's weather and let you worry about the date and your grandmother, which you ought to know anyway.") Or he could sing songs, which he did, in a thin voice that was a little unsteady, but good enough for himself and the cattle. In his prime he had known eighty-five verses to "The Texas Rangers," some of which he had composed himself.

And so, as the surface of the water grew placid around him, old Jerome Cotton shuttled these memories through his mind, selecting the ones he liked and discarding those he didn't (and also those dealing with women, in respect for, or at least because of, Roberta May, whose feet, encased in sandals, stood up awkwardly at the ends of her exposed legs). He reflected that he liked these memories, but he was not such a damn fool as to say that there was anything good about those days except that they were the days when he was a young bull and on the prod. He had sold his Longhorns and bought white-faced cattle when they produced more beef, and when the railroads came, and hadn't wept one tear for the old rangy cattle who could live on anything and tasted like it. He and Judith had nearly starved when the drought came and the Depression on top of it. He had taken Mr. Roosevelt's money, gladly. When the oil came, he found some, more or less on his property, a good deal of it, and when irrigation was practical he irrigated and planted cotton and alfalfa, but by then George was running the land. His son, though, being his son, didn't get too excited about leaving land fallow and taking Mr. Truman's money or, though he was a Republican, Mr. Eisenhower's or Mr. Kennedy's either.

Whenever some old coot would get to talking around the table about the "good old days," Jerome Cotton would lean forward out of his wheelchair and say: "I'll tell you what, sir, there is not one good thing about eatin' dust all day and gettin' rained on at night unless you're young." But by damned if you were young . . .

It became dark in a moment, as it always does when the air is clear, and a square of moonlight appeared on the door opposite the window as if a switch had been snapped. The wreath of white hair around the back of his skull dripped onto his neck, and little droplets traced cold paths down onto his narrow shoulders. He slid again down into the tepid water and, resting his chin on his shoulder, watched the square of moonlight on the door until he could perceive it moving downward toward Roberta May, who was stretched in the shadows.

It was an exercise in patience. It kept his mind off his stomach, which was tightening painfully, excreting unusable acid, waiting for food, wanting food. He watched the square moving and finally he thought about food: enchiladas covered with cheese, frijoles, tortillas with steam rising from them, which you picked up gingerly, smeared with butter, salted, poured hot sauce on, folded, bent so the sauce would not run out and stuffed into your mouth while they were still hot. There was an art to folding tortillas, you had to do it quickly or the thin circles of cornmeal would cool, and dexterously, or the hot sauce would pour into your lap. And when the sauce burned your throat, when you could feel it burning all the way down to your stomach . . . He could see Señora Estansa silhouetted in the kitchen door holding a big plate of enchiladas and chili con queso . . . His chin fell forward into the water and awakened him. It frightened him a little that he had fallen asleep, so he reached up with his toe and flipped the handle which let the water out of the tub.

This amused him for a few minutes: listening to the gurgling water and watching his dark body appear like islands growing out of a sea of mercury. But then he felt his weight returning to press him into the bottom of the tub. His head became hard to manage; it seemed to roll erratically on his white shoulders, and his good arm, when he reached up to pull three towels from the rack above his head, was as heavy as a log. But he laboriously dried himself and the inside of the tub as well as possible. His elbows and knees made thumping and clanging noises as they collided awkwardly with the porcelain, sometimes causing little pinches of pain and making red flowers bloom and fade before his eyes. But as he worked in the darkness he was not altogether unhappy; he enjoyed being without his contraptions, controlling what he did, even if it was only drying a bathtub from which he might never escape, in which he might wake up dead. "This is a hell of a thing for a man ninety years old!" he said to the dark, and a hilarious vision of himself being buried in the tub built itself before his eyes: there he was, arms folded, in a blue suit, resting in the tub. He chuckled.

When the tub was as dry as he could get it, he folded a towel and placed it beneath his head. As he closed his eyes he reflected that the towel was a damn sight softer than some saddles. But it was no good. There is no one in the world, he realized, as naked as a naked man in a damp empty bathtub, and there is no place which is more uncomfortable to sleep in when you are naked. His shoulder began to ache, as did his arthritic arm. His hipbone was thrust cruelly against the stone-hard bottom of the tub. But worst of all, his manhood—his "gentleman," his Granny had called it (*It ain't no gentleman now,* he thought. *Wouldn't stand up for nobody.*)—lay damply against his leg. When he rolled over, if it touched the porcelain, he awoke with a start; if he rolled the other way it became uncomfortably wedged between his legs. *If he could only get out!* He grasped the side of the tub with both hands and, with a wrenching movement, began to lift the dead weight of his body. Flares of pain pulsed through his bad arm and the flowers returned whirling before his eyes. But he was almost up, he had almost raised himself high enough to flop forward out of the tub, when he saw poor dead Roberta May Kuykendall, and his bad arm slipped. He fell, striking his chin on the edge of the tub and slithering and squeaking back into its dark maw. He curled in the bottom of the tub with his eyes closed and his breath coming in cries. He knew the side of his chin would be black with a bruise in the morning. On the other side of the white wall, Roberta May rested with her pale face framed in the moonlight, lips slightly parted. Her hair flared out to one side, as if windblown, and her eyes flickered in the silver light.

In an hour he moved: he held his bad arm to his side and rolled over onto his back; then, with his toes, he turned on the water full force and closed the drain. The roar of the water laughed in his ears; it laughed down the halls of the empty house and out into the climbing night. The water was fine; it brought heat, buoyancy, freedom, everything a man could want. He arranged a wet towel around his neck so he would not drown himself, turned off the water and relaxed. Involuntarily he glanced at Roberta May. The moonlight had moved again and now it fell across her breasts. Only her chin and her half-smiling mouth were visible above the V of her blouse. Her brassiere held her breasts upright and they flowed together on her bare neck. But the old man pushed thoughts of the dead girl behind curtains in his ancient mind. Before he went to sleep, he lowered his chin and quenched his thirst, then he leaned his head back comfortably, his "gentleman" floating blessedly free . . .

In his dream the old man was a part of a story which he hadn't believed when he had heard it. Marsh, who had had his nose cut off, squatted just inside the circle of light thrown by the bitter-smelling mesquite fire and spoke with a Colorado twang. "By God it was raining catfish and nigger babies, and we was so drunk you would have had to sober us up to kill us . . ." They were all drunk and running through the back streets of Tascosa in the rain. Jerome Cotton could feel the deep mud gurgling over the instep of his boot every time he took a step. They ran past bright windows, whose light bled in this vision like yellow paint. There were four or two of them running together, and he could see Marsh's noseless profile rising and falling beside him as they ran through the downpour. Finally, after hours it seemed, he realized that they were looking for a special whore.

Suddenly Marsh, without saying a word, dodged into a lighted doorway, and Jerry followed. He burst into dryness and light just in time to see Marsh draw his pistol and shoot a Mexican who was climbing out of a high window. (*I don't believe this story,* the old man thought, but the Mexican fell with a splash outside the window.) Then Marsh, the two nostrils on his face bubbling because he had a cold, turned the pistol on the whore who was curled on the bed staring at them. She was a tall black-headed woman, slightly pretty. Marsh lowered the barrel of his pistol, as if he were shooting a bottle off a fence post, and shot her.

"You want her in here or out in the street?"

"Out in the street," Jerome Cotton heard himself say in a young voice.

"Good enough," Marsh said, and slung the whore over his shoulder and carried her into the rain. Jerome Cotton heard the splash as Marsh threw her into the mud; it seemed to come from down on the river . . .

But then it was daylight, dry beautiful daylight, and they were on the trail. He was sitting on his pony on a grassy slope overlooking the Platte River; its wide sandy bed twined away into green distance. Down on the river the boys were trying to free about ten head of cattle who were being sucked into a bed of quicksand. He noticed one particular steer who was caught near the bank. A cowboy had waded out and slipped a rope around one of the steer's hind legs. The rope was tied to the saddle horn of another cowboy who was trying to pull the steer free, and the steer was bawling to the sky. In a moment there was a sucking noise as the leg to which the rope was tied popped up out of the sand and lay at an odd angle in the water. The man on the horse continued to pull but he couldn't free the other three legs. Two men were with the steer in the water now.

99

Jerry Cotton took off his hat and swatted a fly. There was a nice breeze and it was a pretty day. He seemed to be hearing the shouts of the cowboys and the bawling of the cattle from a great distance. When he looked again down into the riverbed, the boys had tied the rope that was attached to the steer to the chuckwagon, and the grubspoiler was trying to drive the team up the slope and out of the riverbed. There was a clatter of harness and a shout from the cookie as the wagon shot forward. Young Jerry Cotton had to look very closely to see that the steer's hind leg was bouncing behind the wagon, trailing water and blood.

The old man was awake during the last few seconds of this dream, but he didn't open his eyes; he let the phantasma play themselves out on the back of his eyelids until the team and the driver disappeared behind a melting bluff, but still he did not open his eyes. He knew that the room was lit by the gray gallows-light that crept like smoke before the dawn. He lowered his chin and took some of the bitter water into his mouth and spat it out. He had relieved himself during the night. His face itched with its damp morning bristle, which Roberta May would—which Roberta May *used to* shave with his electric razor. Still without opening his eyes, he raised his foot and let the polluted water out of the tub; then, feeling with his feet, he turned on the faucets, admitting fresh water. The water crackled like new fire as it spattered on the porcelain. "Just like a goddamn goldfish," he mumbled to himself, but he drank great quantities of the new water.

He opened his eyes, looking straight ahead. His hands were grotesquely shriveled, and his entire floating body was logged and puckered. The old man felt that if he grasped his arthritic arm tightly, he could slide the skin right off the bone. All of his joints ached and hunger sent pains sliding up under his ribs. *Ninety years old,* he thought, and found the dangling tip of his mustache with his tongue and sucked on it. To avoid looking at the girl he closed his eyes again and waited for the sunlight; Sunday morning . . .

But even after the light shone dark red through the blood vessels in his eyelids, and an occasional flash fell through his lashes like dawn through a forest, the old man kept his eyes clenched against it. He lifted his hand from the water and pressed two fingers into his eye sockets until they hurt. But finally he had to; it became, in the darkness of his morning thoughts, a test of courage. He opened his eyes and deliberately looked at the body stretched on the tile. He stared at her for a moment and then, strangely, the vision liquified. He blinked his eyes fiercely to clear his vision only to discover that there were tears in them. Children, women, cowards and men in pain may cry, but the old man who had nearly turned a century wept.

He wept because during the night some immodest wind had blown her skirt completely up, exposing her legs, her blue garters and her blue panties; wept for the silliest thing: a heart sewn on the panties just above the left leg, and *Saturday* embroidered just below it. He wept because he had desired her so overtly and called her the names of his frustration. But most of all, and this is why he wept and didn't cry, the tears topped his lower lids and streamed down because she was dead. His own life had only been a furious explosion of days, a mad clock that ran the seasons round, a flash in the eye of time. What a flicker hers must have been, who had touched and seen and tasted only one year for his five. And he wept because he was ashamed and brave enough, or old enough, to be.

But he didn't weep for long at all with his forehead pressed to the side of the tub. The sobbing in his throat relaxed. His eyes dried quickly as he stared down into the turquoise water. He was ninety years old, and it seemed to him a little sacrilegious for a man ninety years old to weep for very long, and a little silly for anyone to be weeping in a bathtub where he was preserved like a snake in a fruit jar; too much weeping renounces too many things. And so he raised his head and looked at the girl again, giving her the respect which, perhaps, is due the dead. He looked at her closely and dispassionately, wishing the body could be taken to a funeral home, noticing again her hand which seemed to be pointing to his son's clothing which lay between the toilet and the bathtub. With his good hand the old man reached over . . .

George Cotton arrived from Dallas in the late afternoon. He entered the front door and called and when he heard the muffled answer he ran up the stairs three at a time. He threw open the bathroom door and saw his father sitting in the bathtub pulling at his mustache, wearing the wide-brimmed hat he had left on the floor.

"You take care of that poor dead girl," his father said.

"Here, Pa, let me get you out of that tub," George Cotton said, and he started to step over Roberta May Kuykendall.

"You get that girl," his father said. "I just may never get out."

BARBARA HUDSON

The Arabesque

Sometimes Arden's mother would get them up in the middle of the night to clean the house. The first time Arden was four. The room was dark and her mother stood in the light from the hall.

"It's time to get up," she said and turned on the overhead light, and Arden saw the crack that began above the door and ran across the ceiling. Her sister Kate rose from the other bed. The ceiling was blue and their beds were white. Her mother wore an old print dress and tennis shoes. "We're going to clean. Before your father gets home." She turned and moved away, her feet soft on the carpet, heavy against the stairs. Soon *The Firebird* by Stravinsky filled the house.

"Come on," said Kate, pulling at her arm. "Get out of bed. Get out."

"What is Mommy doing?" Arden asked.

"Hell," said Kate, who was nine. "I don't know."

Arden had never heard her say that word, and she was scared.

Later, when the beds were made and the baseboards dusted, they sat at the kitchen table eating cornflakes; their mother was talking. "I'm going to paint the living room today. Kate, when you get home from school, Arden and I will have painted the entire living room. What color shall we paint it?" She turned to Arden. "My little angel, what color shall we paint it?"

Arden was worried. She had no idea how to paint. "I don't know," she whispered.

"Think," her mother said and rose from the table.

Arden heard the car door slam and she slipped out of her chair.

"Sit down," her mother said. "I'll greet your father."

"This is terrible." Kate twisted a piece of her long blond hair tighter and tighter. "Maybe you should go with me. Maybe I should take you to school."

Their father, who was a doctor and who had been up all night working in the emergency room, walked into the kitchen. His fine light hair fell across his forehead, his shoulders sagged, his eyes slipped past theirs and dropped to their shoes. He touched them on their heads. "How are my girls?"

"Fine, Daddy," Arden said.

"Yeh," said Kate. "Just fine. We've been listening to *The Firebird*."

"Oh?" He raised his head and looked at their mother.

She smiled, her face radiant, one hand pushing her dark hair from her oval face. "Go upstairs and get in bed and I'll bring your breakfast. Whatever you want. Just tell me. Whatever. Waffles, strawberries, whipped cream."

He reached out his arm and drew her to him and she laughed. "Your mother is crazy," he said and kissed her nose.

They painted the living room that day, while her father slept upstairs. First they stood in the cold gray outside the paint store until the man with the key came. "Colors!" her mother said. "Show me all your colors!" Arden chose white for the walls—Silver Butterflies, or something like that—and a very light pink for the molding. Fairy Pink, she called it. And later when they were almost finished and her father was at the top of the stairs, asking if he could come down, her mother shouted, "Wait," and said, "Here, Arden, right here. Paint a fairy." And Arden painted a little pink fairy on the wall where the edge of the desk would cover it.

It was a strange and wonderful day. And a horrible night. When her father left again for the hospital, her mother wouldn't let them go to sleep. Arden was so tired, but her mother kept shaking her or slapping her face. Kate was supposed to be dancing to *Swan Lake*—she wore pink tights and a black leotard and her black ballet shoes.

"Wake up," her mother said. "You're being rude. Kate is dancing for us." And Kate would lift her arms into a big circle one more time. Arden couldn't help it. She had never been so tired.

Finally the phone rang and their mother went away, long enough for them to climb the stairs and crawl into their beds, still clothed. Kate locked the door.

It wasn't the first day her mother had been like that, Arden was sure—people don't go mad overnight—but it was the first day she could remember. A whole day. From the beginning to end.

Later she would ask Kate when it started, and Kate would say, "I don't want to talk about her."

One day Arden tried to tell her father. She was six and had walked out of her first-grade class, where Mrs. Engelhardt spoke softly and looked at her with steady eyes. Arden was going to clench her teeth and catch the bus and ride home with children who yelled. But there he was, all by himself, waiting in the old Chevrolet, and she didn't even ask why.

"Bright Arden," he said and touched her hair. "How are you?"

"I'm fine, Daddy," she answered.

"Are you always fine?" he asked. "Are you always bright and fine?"

"Yes," she said and rolled down the window to feel the warm air. "Did you save anyone last night?"

"Yes," he said. "We saved a mommy who took too many pills."

"What kind of pills?" she asked and watched the trees go by. They were covered with pale green buds.

"Sleeping pills," he said. "She thought she wanted to sleep a long time, but maybe she really didn't. Maybe she wanted something else." He put on his sunglasses. "To be happy. Happy people don't take too many pills."

Arden didn't say anything for a while. They passed the yard with the willows and the creek bank covered with late daffodils. "I don't think I would have saved her," she finally said, thinking of her own mother.

"What do you mean?" he asked, raising his sunglasses.

"Then I could sleep at night."

"What's the problem, Arden?"

"I have nightmares," she said. It was always one hand. Always going for her face. Sometimes with talons. Sometimes changing at the last into something else: a bird that would light on her shoulder, a butterfly that would brush her nose. On the bad nights she would crawl into Kate's bed and Kate would let her stay.

"Have you told your mother?" her father asked.

She shuddered. He didn't understand.

He said it again. "Have you told your mother?"

"No." She looked down at her dress. They had picked it out last week and it was wonderful, finding the dark blue with pink flowers. But now she had to wear it every day and she didn't like it anymore. Every morning her mother sent her back upstairs to put it on. She wanted to tear it into pieces.

"Maybe I should tell her," he said.

"No," she said. "I think I made it up. I sleep fine at night."

He put out his arm and she moved across the seat and let him hold her until they got home. Then she kept her distance. It was safer.

Some days their mother didn't even get up, and they would tiptoe down the stairs and into the kitchen. No chaos. Order and peace. Heaven. They would eat their cereal and smile. Once Kate leaned over and kissed Arden's cheek for no reason. Arden started to cry. Then she began to laugh, then they were both laughing, loud and hard, and Kate took the cereal box and dumped the cornflakes on the table, and they began to throw cornflakes in the air, all over everything. They smashed them on the floor. Arden climbed on the table and let them fall through her hands like rain, and Kate pretended she was taking a shower. Then they got out the brooms and swept them around the kitchen and finally out the back door, where Brothers Grimm, the dog, began to eat them.

On those days their mother might still be in bed when they came home from school, the house just as it was when they'd left—curtains drawn, her door still closed, no music, none of her smells. Suddenly Arden would miss her and want to sneak into her room, but Kate would say no, not when Daddy's in there. He would come out later, his hair rumpled, and take a shower. They didn't bother him. He would speak when he wanted to. And later they would eat potpies together, and he would tell them about his patients. Very sick people, sometimes children, who would probably die unless he was there, and sometimes even that didn't work. He would leave for the hospital, and they would do their homework and go to bed, and still their mother wouldn't get up.

When Arden was eleven and Kate was sixteen they moved into a new house with all new furniture. Arden's bedroom was white with blue trim, no cracks in the ceiling, and Kate's was pale green like an aquarium. Their mother hired a housekeeper who came twice a week, and they thought that maybe she wouldn't get them up anymore. Besides, if Kate locked her door, then Arden couldn't get in when she had a nightmare. In the old house, locking the door had sometimes worked. Arden would hear her mother's hand on the knob, then the pull on the door that wouldn't open. Sometimes she went away and never said anything. Other times she banged until Arden opened the door. "Get your sister up," she'd say. "We have work to do."

One night in the new house Arden woke up because Kate was yelling.

"I'm not going to get up anymore," she shouted. "You can't make me. Something's wrong with you."

"What's wrong with me?" her mother yelled, her voice growing until it swallowed all sound.

"Nobody's mother does this," Kate shouted but her voice quivered.

"How do you know?" her mother yelled. "How do *you* know?" Arden could imagine her reaching for Kate's shoulders, and she began to tremble.

"Don't touch me," Kate yelled. Then Arden heard the slap, and Kate was silent.

Someone moved down the hall and stood in the doorway, but Arden didn't move. She tried to breathe as though she were asleep. One breath in. I can change this into a dream. Hold it. Slowly let it out. I can make this person disappear. Hold it. Slowly let it out. But maybe it was Kate. Maybe she had slapped their mother. Suddenly Arden wanted to open her eyes, to whisper, Kate come here. But no. It wouldn't be this quiet. Slowly let it out.

After a while, her mother turned on the light. She moved into the room and sat on the edge of Arden's bed and ran one hand over her eyes, again and again. "I'm sorry," she whispered. "I'm sorry." She sat for a long time looking down, that hand passing over her eyes. "I'm so sorry." Finally she stood and straightened her dress. Her eyes brightened and she lifted her long fingers to touch her brow, as though to remember something. "We have work to do. Before your father gets home. I'll put on the music." She moved down the hall. Stopped. Came back. "Maybe you could tell Kate." She was gone again, her feet on the stairs.

Arden could hardly get out of bed, but she crept down the hall and found Kate on the carpet, face down, crying.

She knelt and whispered in her ear, "She says she's sorry."

"I don't care," mumbled Kate.

The music was coming up from downstairs. Arden whispered louder, "I think she really means it."

"Go away," said Kate. "Go away forever."

Arden got up and left the room. She didn't know what to say. Even now it was hard. Pushed out into the cold where it was dark with no moon. No one left. A door slammed shut and a note shoved beneath it. Don't come back. You've taken the other side. Find your friends among the traitors.

She went downstairs and their mother left Kate alone and Arden polished the silver.

Later that morning Kate talked to their father, and after a few days, he put their mother into the hospital for a while. Arden missed her in the afternoons when she came home from school. At night she had the same dreams. In the morning she wasn't sure how she felt. Their father's mother came and cooked runny scrambled eggs and talked to herself as she moved about the house. Arden worried that she might suddenly discover she wasn't talking to anyone. Kate loved her and broke into her murmurings to chatter on and on as she followed her from room to room. Their father kept to himself; he went to the hospital and he went to visit their mother. Never again would he laugh and say that she was crazy.

When their mother left it was fall. When she came home it was winter, and they were all waiting for her—Kate, Grandmother,

Arden. They sat on the sofa and watched the late afternoon snow fall, the squirrels at the birdfeeder. Kate was talking to their grandmother, using a name she'd heard. "Mema, I saw this boy again yesterday."

Arden was trying to decide what she would do when her mother walked through the door. Would she stand and say, "I'm so sorry, Mother. What have they done to you?"

"He walked me to my locker, you know, kind of slow, like he wanted to ask me something."

Maybe she would yell from the sofa, "Why have you come back? I don't want you here."

"Finally I just said, 'Do you want to ask me something?' He looked me straight in the eye and said no. I was so embarrassed." Their grandmother coughed.

She could run up the stairs, into her room, lock the door, crawl under the bed.

"But later he came back and said, 'Yeh, do you want to go out?' "

Or she could stay on the couch and not move and not say anything.

Their grandmother lifted a wrinkled hand and picked a piece of lint from the sofa. "Ask your mother about it, Kate. Give her a day and then ask her. I think she'd want to know."

Kate took her grandmother's hand and squeezed it. "You tell me. *You* tell me what I should do. Should I go out with him? Should I call him up on the phone and tell him to pick me up across the street? At the Stanways across the street?"

Their grandmother lifted her other hand and touched Kate's hair. "Ask your mother, dear. You don't need to send him across the street."

"Hell I don't. She doesn't give a damn." Kate stood up, and Arden moved over and put her head on their grandmother's lap. She didn't know her grandmother that well, but when she saw her touch Kate's hair, that was what she wanted to do. Her grandmother began to stroke her head, and Arden began to cry.

She couldn't help it. Then Kate began to cry. She sat down and put her head on Arden's back and Arden could see their grandmother's arm come around to touch Kate while she stroked Arden's head, and their grandmother began to hum softly, nothing Arden knew, but it was a wonderful song.

Then the car was in the driveway and they all straightened up and sniffed and smoothed their dresses, and it was almost like nothing had happened, nothing with their grandmother, that is; too much of the other had happened to forget now.

Two car doors opened and closed. The trunk slammed. Boots crunched through the snow on the stone path. Then onto the porch. The door opened and Arden's father stepped in with a suitcase. He looked taller than he had that morning, his shoulders more broad. Her mother followed, dressed in new clothes: a long red coat, a brilliant scarf, strands of her dark hair electric in the dry air. She paused for a moment, her eyes uncertain, her hands at the scarf. Then she laughed and threw her arms wide. "I almost went crazy," she said. Arden ran to her—she couldn't help it—and her mother pulled her close and whispered, "Do you still love me, little angel?" And she smelled as she always had.

"Yes," Arden whispered back. She did in that moment. It was a true answer but not complete.

"And Kate, what about you?" She extended an arm. Their father was beaming. Their grandmother rose from the sofa. Kate didn't move.

"Do you want me to lie?" Nobody said anything. "I think you are the most wonderful mother in the entire world. You are such a wonderful mother I think you should teach classes, and I will personally invite all my friends who have never been here— all my friends who ask, 'Why don't we go to your house?' and I say, 'It smells bad. A cat died underneath it.' Do you know how many cats have died underneath our house?"

Arden began to scream. That's all she could remember. Screaming as her father took her outside where the snow was falling. He picked her up and began to swing her slowly around and around, like he'd done when she was five, when she would laugh and ask for more. She was small and thin for eleven, and he swung her until she was quiet. Then he stopped and held her for a while. Finally he said, "It's time to go in now," and they went in together, and nothing more was said about it.

Life together was too much for them. Arden could see that now. Too intense. People cannot live like that for long.

When their mother came home from the hospital, she was different. She had fooled Arden that first afternoon, but gradually Arden began to see that her mother's mountains and valleys had been stretched by some hand, maybe her own, into one long thin line. She rose in the morning at 7:00; she went to bed at 10:00. The housekeeper came three days a week and did all the cleaning. She attended the Medical Auxiliary luncheons and ran a few errands. She and Arden went to Kate's ballet recitals, where she sat quietly and clapped with no sound. Sometimes she would say, "Arden, why don't you have a friend over to spend the night," and she asked nice questions of Kate's boyfriends—what they liked to do instead of what their parents did. She and their father went to the symphony once a month, and Arden watched them leave, her father's arm wrapped around her mother.

Arden was happy; she slept well at night. Sometimes she would sit on Kate's bed and they would talk about those bad days when their mother was mean, the good days now that she was nice, and oh yes tell me and smile big, isn't it easier, especially for our father, who has to work so hard anyway. And for us, too, because we're young and have to navigate such a complicated world. And for our grandmother, who won't have to worry so much anymore. Yes and giggle, our heads together, murmuring, muttering, trying to make her sounds of wandering through the house. And for our mother, too. It must be easier. Of course we can't ask her; how do you ask someone, "Are you happy now that you're not crazy? Do you know what a bitch you were?" But surely she was happy, or she wouldn't be so nice. Yes, Mother, we want so much for you to be happy.

Finally one night after Kate had gone away to college, to a small school in North Carolina where she could study dance, their mother sat down at the kitchen table and lowered her head into her hands. "I have a terrible headache," she whispered. "Please call your father." Arden ran to the phone, her whole body shaking, and she dialed as fast as she could, but when she came back her mother had lost consciousness, her head on the table, her hands limp. The ambulance came, and she was gone.

Later her father called. "Arden," he said, "your mother died on the way to the hospital."

"I see."

"We think she burst an aneurysm."

"Thank you for calling, Dad." She put down the phone, walked into her bedroom, crawled under the bed, and went to sleep.

During the service, her father leaned over and whispered, "I always knew she would die before me." Then he leaned the other way and said something to Kate, who smiled, a grim sort of smile, their grandmother beside her, but Arden could only see her black hat. She was overwhelmed with relief; they had escaped, all of them. The past would die with their mother, and Arden would live on as somebody else, not trapped on a wall behind the edge of a desk. She could be anyone. Her mother could be anyone. They were all free.

And for a while it worked—that vigorous suppression of history. But eventually she wore out—what with all the energy it took just to live—and her mother came rumbling back. In women who laughed too hard, who were too kind, who had long fingers and dark hair. In the middle of the night when she couldn't sleep and finally rose to put on *The Firebird*, sitting with her ear to the speaker so as not to wake her father, who worked during

the day now. In the department store that sold her mother's perfume, buying some, standing too long, forgetting why she was
there and how to get out, until her friend Abby found her. In a
boy who held her hand, whose mouth was thin like her
mother's, and she wouldn't let him kiss her. In her father, who
took her to the symphony, his arm on the back of her chair, not
touching her shoulder.

Then it was summer and Kate was home. She was nineteen and
Arden was fourteen, and one day Arden was sitting in the
bathtub, clothed and dry, trying to remember the song her
grandmother hummed. She looked up, and Kate stood in the
doorway, dressed in her leotard and tights.

"It's gone," Arden said. "I can't remember."

Kate walked into the room, bent low, and peered into her
eyes. "How long have you been in the bathtub?" she asked.

"I don't know." She looked down at her clothes and
couldn't remember when she'd put them on.

"Don't let her do this to you," Kate said and grabbed her
shoulders.

"What?"

"She's making you crazy. Do you hear me?" Kate shook her.
"Do you hear what I'm saying?"

Arden pushed her hands away and stood up. "She's dead."

Kate rolled her eyes. "Can't you see?" She lifted her long fingers and touched Arden's forehead. "You can't get rid of her
without destroying your mind."

Arden sat down again in the bathtub and put her head on
her knees. "Sometimes I want her back."

"You miss somebody else," Kate said. "Somebody else's
mother," and Arden began to cry.

"Maybe you miss me." Kate climbed into the bathtub and
sat facing Arden, her knees pulled to her chest. "We had the
same mother." Kate took one of her hands. "She was a strange
woman."

"Not always," Arden said.

"But we didn't know her long enough," Kate answered.

"I was alone with her when she died."

"She died in the ambulance."

"But I thought I'd killed her, that I'd done it without realizing, and Dad was calling to ask why."

Kate pressed her hand.

The words kept coming. "Then he told me and I was so happy. She was dead and I hadn't killed her. I could love her always and things would be better, but they're not. They're worse."

She looked at Kate, who was quiet for a moment, before she released Arden's hand and rose from the bathtub. "This is what you do," she said, and Arden followed her into the living room, where Kate stood in the middle of the Oriental rug, in first position, her shoulders back, her chin lifted, her heels, calves, and fingertips meeting. "This is what you do. You take your mother," and she pushed onto her toes and turned, stepping with the leg that would become her base, one arm moving forward, lifting her upper body, the other leg and the other arm rising slowly behind her. "You take your mother and you turn her into something else."

It was the most beautiful arabesque Arden had ever seen: one long smooth arc stretching from Kate's fingertips to her pointed toe, and the leg on the carpet so straight and sure. "Do you see?" Kate asked.

"Yes," Arden whispered. "I think I do."

ARTURO ISLAS

The King of Tears

I always get real teary in this exercise, man, I can't help it. Seems like I'm telling you that a lot tonight, ain't I, about crying all the time I'm remembering things. I've thought about that crying stuff a lot, cause if the gang ever saw me cry I'd have been teased into the next century. But I ain't no sissy, you can tell that. And the tears, seems to me, they're just like the desert rains I was telling you about before, that clean everything up and make the air smell like itself again and get the plants to blooming. I don't let many people see me do it, of course, but I was alone there in the alley and I figured, what the hell? Nobody knew me around there so I could let it all hang out, except anything about Evelina which I had to keep erasing cause thinking about her is too much for me to take anytime and just makes me wanna go self-destruct like a car in a James Bond movie.

"The King of Tears" is an excerpt from Arturo Islas's posthumously published novel, *La Mollie and the King of Tears*.

So what comes to me first is this picture of this dude with a gimp leg and a shoe with a mile-high heel who I got to know at the V.A. Hospital down the Peninsula not too far from here after I was shipped outta Korea and back to the States for going bonkers when my buddy Juan de la Torre got blown up. We thought we were lucky, man, we were part of the trip-wire forces along the 38th parallel there in Korea and nobody expected much action cause the really hot place was starting to be Vietnam. We were just supposed to do this maintenance police work but that meant we was bored and on alert at the same time. It was the not knowing when something, anything, was gonna happen that got on my nerves and then when I seen Juan blown up into a million pieces by accident cause the crate of grenades he was loading onto a truck blew up and scattered him to the four winds that did it to my head once and for all and the curtain came down over my eyes. Instant cremation, man.

After that I couldn't pretend not to be bored and I couldn't pretend not to be scared. Them grenades were made in America, man, and I seen that mosta the guys over there were Mexicans or blacks and all the heroes had split to wherever they go after the world reconnizes 'em and pins a lotta medals on 'em and there was my buddy Juan all over Korea we don't know where exactly. I started shaking all the time and getting nosebleeds that made me think I was the Red Sea.

They gave me this physical but the only thing the doctor asked me was if I slept with the window open. I told him it depended. He told me to open it if I slept with it shut and to close it if I slept with it open.

"That's it?" I asked him.

"For now," he said and put some check marks on my chart.

The next time it happened the doctor asked me if I picked my nose. I told him I did sometimes.

"Oh," he said.

A coupla nosebleeds and two whole days of shaking later, some other doctor decided I had malaria. Then when they couldn't find no bug, they came to the conclusion that I was just plain wacko. I coulda told 'em that from the start, man. So I got sent back to the States where I was supposed to be shipped back to El Chuco for some outpatient something but the Army being what it is I wound up at the gaga V.A. Hospital to recover for another six months.

For about half my time in that hospital I was real loonie tunes cause that trip-wire had tripped my switches towards haywire. They were moving patients all around then and my group was the last of what the powers that be liked to talk about as the non-hopeless to be mixed up with the ones they labeled hopeless before they finally split up the two gangs and gave each of them their own turf. I wouldn't of been able to tell the difference then, man. I was too out of it to care.

Mr. Johnson, this King Kong Swede they kept in maximum security mosta the time, was definitely one of the hopeless, though. You know, man, hope is a real scary thing. Most everybody always thinks it's so great and it really ain't. I think it's the other side of the coin to guilt. Only hope looks forward insteada backward and both of 'em are staring into darkness. Just like Mr. Johnson.

I never did find out his first name cause we only got called by our last names in the Educational Therapy classes they put us through every morning except Saturdays and Sundays when they let us give our Jell-O brains a rest. Mr. Johnson came to them E.T. classes twice a week only and attached to a big Black Momma aide in her thirties who looked like a fullback for the Green Bay Packers, man. They was connected by a two-foot chain that started at her wrist and ended in a metal ring that was part of the harness Mr. Johnson had to wear. It wasn't no strait-jacket cause his hands were free but it looked like one and probably felt worse than that to him.

Mr. Johnson was huge and never opened his mouth except once that I know about. He sat there them two hours of E.T.— even in a chair he looked six-foot high—with his eyes all watery and drool oozing outta the corners of his mouth. He was so tranqued out, the aide had to wipe his face every five minutes. She did it real automatic but with a kinda tender movement that got my heart going again.

I can still see that poor E.T. teacher—his name was Mr. Angel, man, and he told us he was a graduate student trying to get through Stanford. The Kid was all ears, this real skinny guy with radar dishes at the sides of his head who picked up on everything. And he had these real delicate hands with long crooked fingers. I can still see 'em writing things on the board real fast like they had a minda their own. He was a strange looking Mexican cause even though he said he was, he didn't look like no Mexican to me.

I remember that time there and them people in that place like we was all part of some cartoon that's showing on some channel of my brain that I don't wanna turn to or lost somewheres and find again every once in a while and then lose like I don't wanna keep it all that much or see the show too often but gotta once in awhile. When I do find it again it's like it's all happening right now. I never seen so many white rabbits in my life, man. A coupla young, early Vietnam kids were in there already who'd gone off the deep end on some pretty tough weed and kept to themselves and looked real hateful at the rest of us. But my favorites were the old guys, the World War I and II vets cause they had some interesting stories to tell and made out like they knew how come they killed other guys.

One dude who I started thinking about standing there leaning on Tomas's car with my leg about as useful as one of them sticks they give you to mix your drinks was in the Pacific during World War II. When I met him, he had only half a face. The other half was burned away during a shelling attack on one of them islands not too far from the Japanese mainland. This happened to him about the same time the first A-bomb was dropped and the guy woke up a coupla weeks later convinced he was the first atom that split in two.

Well, man, what else can you tell yourself if you're that guy looking into a mirror for the first time and seeing what happened to your face? And this ain't no horror movie. This is real life. Years later, when I first saw him, he walked over sideways—the good side—to where I was melting into the seat cause they just gave me a shot, and said real secret so's I'd know he meant it, "There's two of us, you know."

"Please to meet you both," I said. I was ready to play along. After all, I was in there too and not real sure what I was seeing or not seeing. And that's when he told me that he was the first atom to split in two and stop the fighting. That was the end of our first talk cause the tranque was working and I fell asleep right after he said that and when I came to still in the same chair he was gone, like he'd dissolved into the mushroom cloud.

About three weeks later, he came up to me in the TV room and said, "You passed out before I could tell you my names. I'm Larry and Bryant. We're black and shine shoes for a living at the Albuquerque airport. It's been restored to what it was in the old days."

"Hey, Larry! Hey, Bryant!" I said, shaking his hand twice, naturally. "I'm from that parta the country, too. El Paso, Texas." I'm really starting to get into it, man, but I see that Larry and Bryant wanna get on with the speech they memorized.

"Before I split in two, I was a blonde lesbian from Little Rock, Arkansas. All my friends called me Marilyn." He gave me a look straight outta *Gentlemen Prefer Blondes* when he said it.

Well, this was getting to be too much—even for me—and I interrupted him and said, "Hey, man, face it. You're not seeing it the way it is."

"Way it is? Way it is?" he said, almost normal. "How do you know the way it is? You're just an ugly little spic with no manners from some hick Texas border town and you can't even speak English. Isn't that the way it is?"

Well, I don't wanna get started beating up on the guy cause what's to beat up? So I try the rational approach and tell him that in this country being two black guys is not much better'n being a dyke. "How come you didn't split up into two rich Anglo guys?" I asked him in a serious way.

121

"Don't bother me," he says. "I got enough on my minds," and he turns that side of his face that got erased so's he can't even see me.

About a month later, like nothin' happened and we were friends forever, he does his crab walk over to where I was pitching horseshoes by myself and started giving me his "I can't decide what kind of 'bi' I am, Louie, help me out" routine. He was still into twos, man. Was he bicultural—Mexican and Anglo, of course? Bilingual? "Shouldn't you just speak English in this country?" he asked me over and over. Bisexual? "I can't decide who has more fun f—ing, men or women, Louie, what do you think?" Even binomial, man, like he was some math problem. "Can zero be part of a binomial, Louie?"

The guy was a real mess, man, with lotsa brains and lotsa education. He was good at words and paralyzed by language. Which one should he speak, he wanted to know. He like had all them memories and he jumbled 'em all up in his brain trying to find patterns that made sense. He said something and then took it away at the same time.

It was weird following him into his "bi" world where most everything was either this or that just cause he said it was. He was always hungry, too, and ate while he talked and talked outta one side of his mouth. The other side was too burned to move.

I finally got real tired of hearing him say the same shit over and over and one day I said, "You know what, dude? or dudes? or whatever the f— you are? I think you're just hungry for mammary. Why don't you go get laid by anyone, man, and leave me alone?"

Insteada getting mad that time, he laughed and kept saying "hungry for mammary" again and again. The next day he told me that's what he was gonna call his collection of personal essays soon as he got around to writing 'em down. I said, "Great. Just remember you're gonna talk about you and not me." I wonder now if he ever got around to putting his bi-world down on paper.

* * *

One of them mornings about halfway through my time there the Kid brought two grocery bags fulla spices, fruits and vegetables to E.T. Already, I was suspecting the Kid himself was a fruit but I was still too out of it to tease him about that.

Instead, cause I had to do something to keep him busy, the first coupla months I was there, every time he called my name during the roll call—and he said my name right cause he told me he was also a "Mexican American" from El Paso—I raised my hand and said, smiling like the idiot they all thought I was, "He's not here." I said it with a real thick Mexican accent, spraying h's all over everyone two feet away.

But during the class of the spices, fruits and vegetables, Mr. Angel got to me. He told us he wanted us to touch and smell what he was gonna pass around. He asked us not to taste— already, I took a big bite outta the apple and was chewing away—or to tell him what we heard, just in case any of us schizos heard anything. He said that after I announced out loud that the cantaloupe wanted me to do something nasty to it. The Kid was smiling so much, I figured he musta got laid the night before.

That day, he was talking about poetry and telling us that our five senses were the beginning of poetry. I knew then and there for sure he was studying something totally useless and was gonna remain a poor Mexican from El Chuco the rest of his life. But I gave him the benefit and just let him go on about poetry.

He told us that if we really put our minds to it, we could come up with the essence of whatever it was we were smelling or touching. Man, I started getting the chills in my back cause it was like old Leila P. Harper my high school English teacher was in the room grinning away and warning me to pay good attention to what was in front of my nose.

"Everyone can be a poet," the Kid was telling us suckers. "But most of us are too tired or too sick or too lazy to find the poet inside us and so we spend our lives in a doormat stage waiting for something outside ourselves to give us life."

"I ain't no doormat," I said real loud.

"No, you're not, Mr. Mendoza," he said real bright. "You may be many things, but you are definitely not a doormat." I'm grinning and looking around to see if the guys are appreciating the fact. "But I didn't say 'doormat,'" the Kid goes on. I said 'dormant.'" He told us what that meant and I had to agree that in that room anyways, most everyone was pretty much asleep.

Somewhere in the farthest, smallest cell of my wacko brain, I heard Don Manuel, he's this blind vibes player from Juárez, don't ask me how, and the shivers started coming in waves. Well, naturally I pretended nothin' was going on and that what the Kid was saying was just a big loada caca. I made like I didn't wanna play along, but when the bottle of sage got around to me, the whole desert in bloom came into the room—I could actually see it, man, no lie—and I was six years old again telling my mother I was gonna go out and play.

"Tell us what you're feeling, Mr. Mendoza," the Kid said in a real quiet voice not wanting to interrupt what he musta seen was happening to my brain.

Me, I was Mr. Dumb, not able to say nothin' and just staring at the sage all purple against the wall that separated the projects from the Border Highway. "That's all right, Mr. Mendoza. Just hold on to that feeling and when you can think of the words to describe it, tell us about it."

When I told la Mollie my girlfriend this story, she said I was lying cause Freud said that kinda thing was impossible and that no one could bring up an entire childhood outta just one smell, or any smell, for that matter. I told her I didn't care about what no weenie doctor said cause the inside of his nose was all enameled on coke by the time he came to that conclusion, anyways. But I know what I was smelling and how I felt and for the first time since I got to that forgetting place, the feeling was real.

But real ain't easy, man, ever, and I wasn't gonna let no Stanford fairy know he could get to me with some spice in a jar. "I know," I said, making myself come outta my desert dream. "It smells like Texas Ranger armpit juice," and everybody laughed that unreal laugh except the Kid who didn't say nothin' and just went on passing stuff from the bags. Next to me, Mr. Johnson was holding on real tight to an avocado and not letting no one take it away from him. It's a good thing it weren't ripe or Mr. Johnson woulda had guacamole all over his hands. The guy on the other side of him kept elbowing him to pass it on. Nobody ever touched Mr. Johnson, man, he could kill.

"Leave him alone," the Kid said real authoritative. "Keep passing around the other things and tell us what you feel." He started writing down what the guys said like they was lines of poetry on the blackboard.

There we were—a buncha grown crazy dudes—feeling fruits and vegetables, putting our noses into spice bottles like they was poppers, oohing and aahing away, and saying things like, "This peach feels like April—April Dawn, the stripper at Prince Machabelli's topless club" and "This carrot is my d—, hard and dirty" and like Mr. Emerson, who was holding onto a tomato and a zucchini, "I'm going to squash this tootsie tomato, get it, boys?" and all kindsa other lines that were getting funnier and funnier 'til we were all laughing—even the Kid—*real* laughter. Probably for the first time since they got back from wherever some of these guys done their killing or seen men they cared about get slaughtered. All of 'em laughing except, of course, Mr. Johnson. He sat there with great big Thorazine tears rolling down his pitted, greenish face and with the avocado in both his hands like he was holding an egg now, real gentle I could feel it. So could the aide cause she stopped wiping his face.

Then, right in the middle of the hubbub, a silence—like the kinda silence you get when it snows in the desert and there ain't no wind—fell on one man after another when each of us seen that Mr. Johnson was trying to say something. He finally got it out in a real high-pitched voice like some phantom from an old, long and tragic opera, spacing out each sound in the word like it was the last sound on earth.

"Ah. Voh. Cah. Doh. Ah-voh-cah-doh!" He made it seem like each syllable was a Mayan god and he did it once, real slow and quiet like he knew what he was holding in his hands, and the second time, real loud and quick in a shriek like he was finding gold.

For one long moment, all the guys woke up and nobody moved or talked—not even me—'til some smart aleck new to the joint started clapping in a real sarcastic way and the rest of us sheep joined in and the spell was broken for all eternity and a extra day. The Kid was trying not to cry outta frustration or happiness, I couldn't tell which, and Mr. Johnson went back into himself like a giant turtle that never stuck its head outta the shell cause someone was always there to whack it hard. But it was a great moment, man, and I gotta admit that I choked up a lot and cried later for all the coo-coos in that place, specially Mr. Johnson. And I was crying again, standing there in that cream of mushroom night waiting for my leg to get back on friendlier terms with my brain, and wishing that Big Swede were there so's he could carry me home to la Mollie and wondering what he really saw through those bleached blue eyes of his.

Naturally, when I see an avocado now, I thinka that Big Swede. They finally locked him up for good cause the Big Momma aide that took care of him quit during a wage dispute and nobody else wanted to risk being chained to him.

A coupla years later, the Angel Kid got asked to leave cause he spent one whole class playing Bob Dylan songs for the men and the Head Nurse decided he was a communist. If you ever wanna do some guy dirt, let it out that they're commies or queers—even if it ain't true—cause in this country, that's the worst thing anybody can be. So that was the end of him and the E.T. classes at the V.A. Hospital for the Hopeless.

I also found out the Kid had to have a operation that saved his life but left him with a bag of shit at his side for the rest of his stay in this world. Man, I'm telling you, them poetry teachers sure get the fuzzy end of the lollipop. I love it when Marilyn says that line in *Some Like It Hot*. It makes me wanna protect her forever.

CAROLYN OSBORN

The Accidental Trip to Jamaica

It was an accident, our going to Jamaica, and you had to prove you'd been there by crawling around on the bottom of the too-blue sea to snitch a piece of coral I carried home. When I got back my students asked me, "Where have you been?" They demanded to know because I'm not Mrs. Somebody-or-Other but somebody they know. That's the way they are these days, knowing. I did not tell them. Not many school teachers go to Jamaica in January or any other month, and they would not have understood. I put the coral next to a papier-mâché dinosaur made by my middle child. It's a striped blue and green dinosaur as blue and green as the water at Ocho Rios. I thought it fit, made a pair of things. The shape of the dinosaur and the coral finger are the same. They are both disasters, one belonging to a prehistoric past, one belonging to a month ago. Yet the dinosaur still inhabits the earth—SEE GIANT DINOSAUR TRACKS FIVE MILES

127

OFF THIS HIGHWAY—and the coral is the unmoving finger which wrote FOLLY.

Why did we go? Why didn't we stay here? The weather was just as peculiar at home. It snowed twice that week for the first time in seven years. I wonder and you float. You always float, not in my dreams, in my wakefulness.

AUSTIN DENTIIST DROWNS IN JAMAICA

Is it real? Yes, as real as birds in trees or gritty bits of sand in shoes.

There's blood in the sad-dul.
There's blood on the ground.
And a great big pud-dul of blood all around.

Cowboys don't go to Jamaica. They go home on the range. But we went, you in your white linen cowboy suit and me looking like a well-kept go-go girl though the go-go girls have all gone. A woman has to have some sense of history to be a well-kept anachronism. You always wanted to be a cowboy and I always wanted to be anything but a school teacher. We met dressed in our disguises, our everyday clothes worn over our everyday lives.

Two secrets are clawing each other inside my head: 1) you are dead; 2) we went to Jamaica together. I have told the most cunning lies. Mother lives in Florida, which accounts for my tan. She believes I was in New York seeing plays every noon and being pursued by murderous addicts every night. My husband believes I went to New York, then to Florida. They do not talk to each other often, but if they ever do Mother is so forgetful now that I can convince her I was in Florida in January and she forgot.

Why did we go to Jamaica?

We were going to Sun Valley. Skiing. At least you were.

We had to buy all new tropical clothes. Mine are still hidden in a locker at the Dallas airport. The Goodwill Store or the Sisters of Charity or whoever gets clothes left in airport lockers is going to get a mess of batik, two bikinis, and lots of black nylon panties and bras, your fetish, not mine.

You are floating on a whim.

That's what took us there. My whim. I had never been to Jamaica. I had never been to Sun Valley either. You said why not and I said I don't go places like that. You said I was an over-sheltered academic intellectual. We nearly parted then. I said don't speak to me of shelter. I worked my way through under-graduate school as a waitress.

There is an ancient rule written in the back of every woman's head: Don't go anywhere with a strange man.

I erased the rule.

You had some rules of your own. You tucked them in and pulled the covers over their heads.

Whim ruled.

The first whim you had was the white cowboy suit. We laughed all the way to Neiman-Marcus in the taxi and all the way back. Then we got on lots of planes and flew to Jamaica. The last one had a black stewardess with a British accent. She was so exactly right we made her talk as much as we could. She told us about Blue Mountain Coffee, Appleton Rum, the tiny beaches of Ocho Rios and Dunns River Falls.

Please quit floating!

She was a treasure, that girl. She also told us about the kinky Englishman's restaurant on the way to Ocho Rios. You re-mem-bah him, don't you, the one who tied the cardboard flowers on his almond tree to fool the *National Geographic* photographer. His name was Clive, or Cliff, or Clown. The centers of his flowers were inverted pop-bottle tops sprayed orange. The *National Geographic* man was not fooled; we were, I would have liked a picture of the almond tree in bloom, but we'd sworn off cameras.

At Ocho Rios I wanted to stay in one of those immense, immaculate, secluded hotels, and you insisted I had to see how the other half lives so we had to go to the one with bunny rabbits on the carpet. Miles and miles of ears—someone's idea of how the middle class would like to sin, walking on rabbits' heads. The bathtub was black, seven feet long, three feet deep. It was big enough for copulation, large enough for sleeping, deep enough for drowning if you were drunk and you were not. That bathtub was meet, and fit, and right for the scene, a lovely prop. The couch was all right too, even to its pretend leather cover, but the beds were twins. Very strange. I should have packed up and gone to Florida the minute I laid eyes on those beds.

You said, "That is not how a kept woman behaves."

I said, "Dear Amy Vanderbilt, What are the rules of behavior for a kept woman?"

We couldn't put them together. A light fixture and a table were rooted to the wall between. Do you think the owner of the bunny rabbits believes his guests would cram lights and side tables into their suitcases along with his hotel towels?

"Ring for room service! Call out the housekeeper!"

No. We had a do-it-yourself fit. It wasn't hard to lift the mattresses off the beds and put them side by side on the floor. I had a practical housewife's fit. "How can anybody make up beds like that?"

You assured me, "Nobody is going to make up this bed."

I thought, "How squalid!" but I kept that to myself. Discretion is the better part of vice. New rules have to be made all the time. I may write that to Ms. V.

I flang myself into the bathtub. You flang yourself right after me. Relaxation was what I craved. You craved fornication, difficult in the bathtub. Too slippery. In bed we fell. You drilled me, your dentistical metaphor, not mine. We are all hung up by the tools of our trade.

"Rum and Coca-Cola."

That's a song my mother used to sing. Now I drink it every afternoon when I come in from school and the oldest child is playing the piano. Yesterday my husband discovered me sitting on the piano bench with drink in hand trying to pick out the tune with one finger. Elusive, that tune. What is the second line? Tomorrow I will give my students ten extra points on a ten-minute quiz if they can tell me the second line. They won't be able to.

Where was I?

What will the Little Flowers of Mercy or the Brothers of St. Poverty do with your skis you left in the men's room of the old Dallas airport at Love Field?

Did love have anything to do with it? I think not. We were two people who had arrived at middle age, that time in life, like adolescence, when we were convinced nothing else was ever going to happen to us. We had to grab fate by the shirt collar. We had to make something happen.

Could you quit floating?

You loved the girls in bikinis with bunny-rabbit tails. It followed that I had to buy the bikini but go tailless into the Caribbean. While you went to ask the manager for a tail for your wife, I went swimming.

Rabbits have no tails atall, tails atall,
Rabbits have no tails atall,
Just a pow-der puff.

Same song, second verse.
Could be better,
But it's gonna be worse.

Rabbits have no tails atall . . .

That's a song my youngest brought home from camp. The youngest sings, the middle one makes papier-mâché dinosaurs, the oldest one plays rock piano. My husband does gravestone rubbings. I have already ordered mine so he can rub while

131

waiting. My epitaph is: Here Lies Melissa Hawkins. She Finally Left Texas. Doing myself in? No, not I. Ennui causes tombstones to be ordered ahead of time. To live in Texas is to live in ennui. I've never liked the landscape here, a great blah, half of it creeping toward the desert to be dried out, half of it oozing toward the Gulf to dirty up the continental shelf. Jamaica was most beautiful, a garden rioting above the sea.

I was in the water floating when you arrived with the bad news.

"The Bunny Mother is very particular about the tails."

She would not sell one, give one, or trade one to a cowboy in tropic white. We consulted. You bought three powder puffs which I cleverly pinned together and sewed onto my black panties. Dear Heloise, I was the one who wrote you asking for directions for rabbit tail construction. Signed: Melissa Makedo. The pins clanked together. For some things there are no substitutes. We had to be content with the ghost of James Bond playing ping-pong with Malcolm X reincarnated in a dashiki. We had to put up with an alloyed steel band. But you cried out when I pinched you. It was real, as real as sun in rum and poinciana blooms in hair.

Oh, what's to do?

Everything would have been all right if you hadn't insisted on the expeditions. A small run-away vacation is simple if you keep it to bed, beach, and bar. Not for you though. You had to see things, to be instructed. We went to Kingston to find Harry Belafonte. He wasn't there. It was hot. There were no ships in the harbor. Port Royal was still mostly under water. The guide kept saying, "Whiskey!" and I kept telling him we didn't have a camera. His disappointment followed us to Bremmer Hall. Did he put a hex on us? You noticed he had beautiful teeth. Nobody else did. Bananas grow up; they point their baby fingers to the sky. That's what I learned at Bremmer Hall. The overseer waited to hear the camera click. Everything was going wrong.

"The other half lives with cameras," I said.

"Never mind," you said.

So, I neverminded awhile.
An interlude, a lull.
"We'll learn to scuba dive."
"OK." But I didn't like the look of the weights they hang around a diver's waist.

Full fathom five thy father lies
With lead weights about his waist.

Literature is instructive.
I took up the snorkel.

I must down to the seas again,
To the lonely sea and the sky.

We went down in an elevator, the only time we used it.
"Is this how the other half lives?"
You said indeed it was.
The elevator opened on the beach. We walked to the pier carrying our flippers, looking quite pro. Out into the blue we rocked in a glass-bottomed boat. You swam under the boat and broke off the piece of coral. I watched. Our instructor went in after you. Wilson was his name. You re-mem-bah Wilson, don't you? He was the one who forgot to warn you sea urchins sting. Yeah, Wilson. Skinny. Wore a red nylon bathing suit. His teeth were filed to sharp points. Wilson. Vampire Man we called him after you came up bloody with sea urchin spines. You were a trifle hysterical then, babbling about sea horses and underwater rodeos. Wilson wanted to hit you. I shook my head. Years of pedagogy were behind that head shake. He held his hand.
The interlude was over. Back to the expeditions, to the last expedition. Dunns River Falls falls hundreds of feet to the sea. The thing to do is to walk up it with a native guide—Tarzan climbing up the boulders through the spray. We approached the sea. Wilson sailed us within the reef all the way.

I said, "Must we?"

"Yes," you said.

Fatal, that yes. Are you floating on your own whim? Where does the truth lie? It lies, and lies, and lies.

On the beach below Dunns River Falls there was a gang of tourists. A black man danced in the midst of them balancing a tray full of rum drinks covered with hibiscus blossoms. Another black man wove green bamboo fronds into hats. Another black man made violins from hollow bamboo canes. He rosined the bow with sea water. Very industrious people, those Jamaicans. What is the Salvation Army going to do with a bamboo hat gone brown and a dried-up bamboo violin? My souvenirs. We danced the limbo with the tourists. Dear Arthur Murray, Do you need a limbo teacher? Inspired by mass frivolity, I played "The Blue Danube Waltz" on my new violin.

That's when we got separated.

A student is standing by my desk. He wants to know why he's failing the course.

I tell him we are all failing the course.

How did we get separated? Some spirit of misadventure lured me. Other people, friendly tourists, took my hands. We formed a human chain. The one who got to hold the guide's hand was the luckiest. I saw you far below holding hands with two strangers. I could not shout. The guides did all the shouting, ha-lo-o-ing over booming water, screeching like mad parrots. We climbed. I watched where I was going. The water was icy; slippery rocks spewed jets of spray. All around the jungle hung. At a turn you saw me and lifted your hand to wave, wrenching yourself loose from the human chain. You were miles below, but I saw you fall. Your body slithered toward the sea. Everyone in your chain stopped while the guide pulled everyone in mine on up. You floated top side down, the deadman's float. I knew it. I passed my Red Cross beginner's test. Our guide was busy imitating the mating call of mynah birds. He saw nothing but the boulders in front of him. The chain of hands pulled me over the boulders. I looked again and saw you floating. Still. People were staring at your back.

I took the coward's choice. Because your life was over, should mine be ruined? Before we had whims. Now decisions were to be made. In my bikini shielded by a see-through shirt, intensely vulnerable and thoroughly shocked, I stepped out of the jungle to the car park and hailed a cab. Back at the rabbit warren I collected my things and dressed myself with lively trembling fingers. Oh, so carefully I printed your name in large, block, childish letters on an envelope. Inside I folded one piece of paper with the following message: Go home to your wife and children. That's all you ever talk about anyway. Signed: Suzy Floozie. Your wife was going to have to pay your double-room hotel bill. It was the most I could do for her. I stomped up to the hotel clerk, simulating our first and only lover's quarrel, pretending great anger which was not hard. Anger is near to fear, neighbor to grief.

"Put this in Dr. Grodall's box." I shoved the envelope over the black marble counter. Funereal. Dear Mr. Rabbit, Down at your hotel in Jamaica sex and death clasp hands and hold on for dear life. Something needs to be done about the ambiance. Love and kisses, Slutina Mae Harlot.

I didn't say please. Tears dribbled down my cheeks. Most undignified.

Slamming out of the hotel was easy. So many doors. Bang! Bang! Bang! July 4th exit. Cab again. Airport again. Only plane there was flying to England. I flew.

"You didn't!" That's what you'd say, your right eyebrow a lofty arch. You used to practice raising your eyebrows in the bathroom mirror.

I did. I must have. There's a ten-pence piece in my coin purse. I bite it now and then to remind myself I went.

London. January. Raining. Cold. Not much money. I couldn't stay inside the bed and breakfast all day. Wallpaper roses swagged and bunched and swagged. Dizzifying. Dear Dorothy

Draper, London needs you. All night I circled the walls with the roses while you floated face down.

Roses are red.
My toes are blue.
I will quit floating
If you will too.

Dear Witch of the West, Could you send me the spell for laying a ghost? Ten pence remuneration enclosed.

I rented a raccoon fur coat (unendangered species) from a costume shop, highly reputed, costumers to H.M. the Queen. MARKS AND SPENCER HAVE GALOSHES CHEAP. An Italian maitre d' at a restaurant in Soho gave me an umbrella left behind by an Englishman emigrating to Australia.

I went to the National Gallery, looked at Venus, Cupid, Folly, and Time and decided it's time I went home.

Art is instructive if you're ready to be instructed.

Three students are standing at my desk. They want to know if they have to take the final examination. I tell them, no. They are going to take it anyway. The course I teach is English 60002.Q. The 19th Century Romantic Novel. The real title is The Will to Fail. Those three will pass, which means they have learned nothing.

Planes again. Airports, Home. Austin Public Library. Newspaper files.

AUSTIN DENTIST DROWNS IN JAMAICA

If we hadn't had two hours between planes a month ago— If you hadn't started talking to me— If I could have gotten to New York without going through Dallas— If we hadn't sat next to each other on the plane from Austin to Dallas, I could still be a not-too-sheltered academic intellectual and you could be back in your office with a sprained ankle complaining about the ski patrol at Sun Valley. Maybe.

Why do you keep on floating?

If I had slipped, I would not haunt you.

Dear Carroll Righter, I was born under the sign of Aries, the Ram, at 3 A.M. on the morning of April 7th. Is tomorrow a good day for sending messages?

I'm putting this in an empty rum bottle, one I emptied while I wrote. Tomorrow the bottle will be dropped into the Colorado River, which flows to the Gulf, which mingles with many seas. The final message is: SINK, PLEASE.

JANET PEERY

What the Thunder Said

It was winter when I first saw Call Lucas, though I'd seen him, sure, before. Ours was more a sudden notice, like a secret thought grown big, then bigger, till you blurt it out and nearly jump inside your skin to hear it said. He was milking Boss, his flat man-rump on a T-bar stool, knees higher, spraddle-legged, shouldered into Boss's flank, arm hoist round her leg to hobble her, neck craned sideways, looking up at nothing, at the pigeons in the rafters, then at me; at me, at Mackie Spoon, eighteen, come in to gather eggs. His wife had a hen that roosted in the barn, and I'd gone out to find the nest.

What we did was wrong, though there can be a way of turning something, seeing how what happens after can add up to make it right. It was milking time, five-thirty, warm inside from cattle, from the little things that live in hay to make it give its own green breathing heat. The sun was tabby orange through the slats, dust and motes around me like I'd walked into a spangled halo, bars of orange slid across me smooth and light as water. I smelled the warm grass smell of hay not cured and dust and cattle, linseed oil and harness leather, swallows' nests of mud and straw and feathers, mice, the foam of milk from Call's pail when he set it down and milk lapped into the dirt as he came toward me, the smell of unwashed work when he got closer, myself in my wool coat with wet snow melting on the shoulders where it fell upon me from the eaves, myself under my dress; and we lay down in all of it, in a way that felt like all the world was gathered into one sweet skin, and though you know it's wrong, down deep, in bone and blood and muscle, you want the one thing your head tells you you're not supposed to want, and in that wanting, in that knowing it's wrong, there is a stillness at the center, calm and full and sly, that comes from knowing you will do it anyway, and you tell your head to cease its thinking, to let the bone and blood and muscle have their way; glad, for what you're doing seems the holiest of human acts. And in that time when everything's afight within you, you are whole as you will ever be, and how I knew the first went gladly out of Eden.

Call was quiet after, gave out one shiver, gathered up his pail and eased back through the stanchion bars to turn Boss out, looked back at me as though he knew me to the center yet had never seen me in his life before, and in his eyes there was a blue-eyed look of staring too long toward the sun, as though they hurt him.

I lived on the place in a little side house. I'd come up in answer to an ad to help Missus in the house. My people lived across the Oklahoma line, but I had had enough of home and of the church I had grown up in. I knew there could be something more. I knew a man could love a woman better than he loved his belt, his Bible, and the way his mouth fit round the word "abomination," that copperheads and bullsnakes were a proof of nothing, that tongues of flame would not consume me if I kissed a boy whose mouth had tasted sweet and clean as broomstraw. I had my own idea of things, and so I left.

Call's was not a rich farm, mostly wheat, alfalfa, flax. He'd been hurt by the dust storms, but not as much as some. The farm was bottomland, sandy loam along the Ninnescah, and willow brakes and cottonwoods and sand plum trees had kept the damage down. Still, you could see it in the scoured look of things.

Missus was a tiny woman, bones frail as a squab's, her hair fine blond, like chick fluff, and she wore dresses in a baby shade of blue. She was sickly, and the Hannah Circle doted on her, bringing covered dishes, cakes and pies to tempt her. They were in the kitchen with her when I got back with the eggs, twelve whites, six brown, two banty.

"Put them on the drainboard, Mackie," Missus told me. "You can wash them later."

"Try some of this peach pie, Lila," one of the ladies offered her.

"Oh, thank you, no," she said. "Maybe after while." I heard her sigh. "Right now I'm not too pert."

The Hannahs clucked around her while I stood at the sink and scalded dishes I'd let sit after supper. I felt my neck go as pink as the spots of rouge on Missus's cheeks. I'd been there four weeks then.

One of the ladies asked after her health. "Poorly," Missus said, "and tired. But I'll bear up."

"Call's so good to hire you help," another said.

"Yes," said Missus. "There's so much work, and we weren't blessed with children."

They started in on female trouble, and I tried to close my ears. I dried the dishes in a hurry, wanting to get out because I knew Call would be bringing in the house milk and I didn't want the warm new smell of it to rise into that kitchen where I stood, my head gone giddy as it ever went at any spirit hoodoo, everybody watching.

Things just went along. I worked in the house and around the yard and with the chickens. I took portions of what I cooked and ate alone at my own place, so the three of us sitting together at the table didn't happen. It was all the bumping into each other. I'd be at the sink and he'd bring in the milk to skim and there we'd be, working, breathing, so close we could smell the things we both remembered, but neither of us would speak. Neither of us acted like the other was alive, but in that ignoring there was more than if we'd tried to talk.

I made up my own world, the one I knew could be, pretending we were married, that I was the wife and he the husband, that I ran the house and saw to things in such a way that didn't need reminding. When we met each other in the barn, I stopped all my pretending and just let be, then afterwards went back to the silent way it was. I came to feel a power over Missus, that I was strong and she was weak and this was only right. I took to slamming things—her teacup at her place, a pair of scissors she had asked for—pretending accident, my slamming, and she would take it with a narrowing of eyes, but say just, "Lightly, Mackie, lightly."

This went on about a year, the three of us moving around, bumping into each other, not talking much, but busy and working, like a boxhive full of bees, until the idea of what was going on became an almost buzzing in my ears.

Then two things happened. Call took Missus to the doctor in Belle Plaine and when they came back she went to bed and didn't get up anymore. To care for her, I moved into the spare room. We put a bell beside her bed so she could call for me. She took this fine, but with her small mouth tightened, and it seemed her belly swelled as though her tumor fed itself on what it knew of me. But until the night in March when Boss had trouble calving and Call yelled out for me to come, I think she just suspected.

Boss bawled and bellowed like the earth was heaving, and we worked by lantern light to turn her calf, me kneading at her hardened belly, Call naked to the waist, his arm full up inside her, wrenching till I felt a give and shifting, slid his arm out red and warm and steaming, and we saw the baby crown. Then, above our breathing, we heard another sound, Missus's bell, but close outside, and when we looked around we saw her in her pale blue nightgown, coming through the doorway toward us in the cold, ringing, calling in a whisper. She cried that she'd forgotten something, cried because she couldn't think of what it was, and then we all three knew she knew, but none of us would say it, and so things went along with Call and me inside the house like man and wife, with Missus as our child.

"I got some broth down her," I'd tell him. "She fussed, but took it."

"She never did eat much," he'd say, and this was how we talked about her, nothing deeper, and we never talked about ourselves and what we were doing or the names we'd have to bear, but my heart sang at the way things worked out, because the second thing that happened was that I was pregnant.

It had happened one winter night the second year when I'd gone to bathe. I'd heated water at the house and carried a ewer out to my place. I lit the lamp and stood at the table washing. I heard him outside, and in my young pride and what I'd learned about desire, I'd figured out that the sight of me could stir him, so I didn't move to cover myself, only turned a bit because we still had never seen each other without clothes. When he came in, I helped him take off his things and washed him until the water went cool.

At first I just ignored the signs that even as Missus lay there I was incubating something of my own. My feet grew sore and swollen waiting on her, and I lost my breakfast soon as I could get it down, but I tried to be kind, and stopped the slamming ways. I didn't tell Call about what I was carrying, but planned to wait for it to grow big enough for him to notice and when she died do the right thing and marry me and just go on. For in that quiet grief-struck house I was happy, and the days could not be long enough. I saw the rightness of the world in everything. When the brood sow farrowed twenty piglets, I knew that number meant my age. If I gathered thirty-seven eggs, it stood for Call's. In April, lightning hit the walnut tree and forked it to the roots, and I knew this meant she would go within a month.

The Hannahs were all over us then, bringing things. More than one looked askance at me, but I kept my eyes down so they couldn't say a word against me for want of charity. "That Mackie Spoon's not missing any meals," one said, but they didn't say more because Call was known to be an upright man.

One asked me, "Where will you go when Lila passes?"

"Don't know," I said. But I knew.

"You might find a place over at the Costin farm," another said. "Bitty Costin's half worn out with all those children."

Another suggested the cafe out on the highway.

"I'll worry about it when the time comes," I said.

"Call looks bad," one said, but I said nothing.

"Feed him, Mackie," they told me. "That's all you can do."

One night in early May I sat beside her bed, sponging her with lemon water. She was wracked, her body meager as an empty grain sack, her skin the color of wet ash, gray-blue and drowned. She asked if I would put the pillow on her face, her nose and mouth, if I would hold it there. "Please, Mackie."

It was the only thing she wanted, the last thing left in her to want. For her, I wanted to, but for everything I'd wanted that I'd taken from her, I couldn't. "I can't," I said.

"A kindness. Please."

I cried into my hands, "I can't," and she cried with me, petting me and saying, "Child, I know."

Call went on about his work all through this time, but I could hear him pounding on the anvil in the toolshed late at night, I saw the blisters on his palms, the axe marks gouged like splintered wounds out on the granary floor. He stayed out of her room all that month, and though I understood it, though I didn't love him any less, I hated him a little.

I was in the kitchen after the service, after all the mourners had gone, wrapping food in dish towels and covering bowls with dinner plates when I heard a sound coming through the open windows from the barn, the way the wind would sound before the dust began to blow. I ran outside with my apron still around my middle, across the yard and toward the sound. I looked inside the barn. He was on his knees beside the hay, and I knew he'd maybe started out to pray but ended up just howling. I saw her pale blue nightgown and I saw that he was stuffing it with hay then tearing at it, stuffing it again and moaning and I watched and listened till I couldn't stand it any longer and I turned and ran with my hands over my ears and the hard weight of the baby like a stone inside me. I ran inside the house and slammed the door and cried, for me, for her, for him, for anyone who ever wanted something that was gone.

In the morning when I got up he was asleep on the floor beside her bed. I went around the kitchen quiet, fixing his breakfast. I went outside. The day was fine and beautiful. Swallows flew in and out of the barn with wisps of straw to build new nests. Off in the timber I heard the bawling of a calf. Cottonwoods were sending off their seedling puffs to gather on the clothesline wires like batting. I went to turn the chickens out, feeling wifely and washed clean as the bedding I had hung upon the line. In the air I felt a message for me that Lila was happier, and I began to feel happy for myself. I knew I could make Call happy, too, and I began to sing the "Do Lord" song—*oh, do remember me*—and I began to feel remembered in all the turning world, and when I came to the part about the home in gloryland that outshines the sun, the sun itself rose over the barn and glinted off the roof until it looked as red as flame. I took this as a sign that the world had turned itself to right again, all wrongs forgiven, and when the rooster crowed it was the trumpet blowing in the Year of Jubilee.

When I went back to the house, the door was locked. I knew better than to try the front because it was sealed shut always, since the dust storms. My suitcase was on the step. On top of it was a square white envelope, no writing on it or inside it, not my name, just five smooth twenty-dollar bills.

I've worked at every cafe from Blackwell to the Waco Wego at least once, some more. I didn't marry. I didn't tell a soul what really happened. I told my son his father was a boy I'd loved who'd moved away before he knew, and only I see Call's straight chin in my son's son. I waited thirty years for Call to speak to me, to say he knew me. I stopped the world with waiting, not to start again until he walked through the door of whatever place I worked and told me, "Mackie Spoon, I'm sorry," for I believed that day would come.

I waited for it, and in the turning of a hundred seasons I saw only Call come begging. Winters moved through springs and summers, and I waited. Sand plums fell, their ripeness gone to bruise, so he could see the shame in waste. Leaves blew from their bare and reaching branches just to show him that the wrong he'd done me was a grievous one. Frost was to remind him of a harsher cold; ice, the sharp, cracked color of his heart. But I, I would forgive him. All he had to do was ask. This moment I could see in rain, and we would then be whole again and new, and he would melt with gladness at the way I had forgiven him.

I saw him many times, caught glimpses of his truck, of him, but only once in thirty years did he look back at me, last summer when Costin's old place caught heat and burned and everybody gathered there. The barn was still burning, but the house had gone. People shone flashlights over the ash pile, but there was nothing left to see but charred wood and one lone teapot on a blackened stove. Across the ashes that had been the house, against the blaze that was the barn, stood Call. I thought I'd gone past fleshly things, but deep inside me something moved at seeing his remembered mouth. He looked at me across the burned-out house, full-face, the fire behind him hot and whipping in the wind, the flames so bright they made his eyes a shadow I could not see into, and I knew the day had come.

There is a way a summer storm will come up from the west, from mountains I have never seen but know are there, a sudden way that, seeing the dark cloud tower, you can almost think the walls of dust have come again until you feel the wind is sharp and clean and you catch the smell of coming-closer rain.

In the storm head rolling high and heavy over us, rising like a warning, there was something of a waiting, of a watching of the goings-on on earth, something in the clouds of wrong that will not be forgotten, and I waited for the lightning to appear, for the flash of reckoning that would scorch Call for what he'd done.

But on the last night I was to see him, I saw instead the message of the fool I was on earth to try to fit the signs of heaven toward the purpose of my will, and when the lightning flashed upon his eyes I saw, instead, my own, by awful trick of light, the hard and high and mighty vision of my own.

I felt my bones grow laden at the sight, with years, and with the sudden want of mercy and the very ground to hold me so I wouldn't fall, and I called out to him, "I'm sorry."

What was in him I can never know, but what was in him made him turn away.

I didn't think. I ran into the rubble and the ashes and I grabbed the teapot. The handle seared my skin but I held on and ran toward him as he walked away. The sound my throat made was a noise like none I'd ever heard—a terrible dark language or another tongue—that wouldn't cease until I threw the teapot at him, hard. It struck him in the back, a clank, a rattle hollow as a far-off clap of thunder. He stopped, stood still, began to turn, then caught himself and kept on walking into rain that came in short, quick gusts and then began to fall like rain, like only rain.

HERMINE PINSON

Kris/Crack/Kyle

Kyle hunches under the con- crete refuge of Highway 59 South on Wheeler Avenue, but it's not really my brother there crouching amidst the scavenged garbage of people who have abandoned all but their bodies. It is not my brother, but a man named Kris. At least that is the name he claims among people he's with. Why did he choose this name? Because it sounds the first syllable of Cristina's name? Cristina, who lives with her mother in New Orleans and does not know him, except as a pic- ture her mother carries in her wallet. Cristina does not know he is an unanswered, unfinished blues. I say "Cristina" and see her face behind my closed eyelids: apple-round, sienna touched skin, almond eyes. Did he choose her name to ritualize his grief for the loss of himself? Or to simply remind himself that he is someone's daddy, that a new birthing in the French Quarter has made up for his deliberate demise. His connection to the world of the living is not smoke-thin after all, not rotting rope, but as real as her voice on the phone when he calls sporadically to see how his "sugarcake is makin' out."

Of all the names he could have chosen—Maceo, his childhood friend from the 'hood; Bubba J., the only boy in high school who could run faster or jump higher than he; or Macky B., his old army buddy, he chose this one. I cannot imagine the mouths of strangers shaping her name on their tongues. Does "Cris" sound right in misery's mouth? Better yet, does my brother need to hear syllables that recall a little girl untouched by Belial's blues in the hell he has stumbled into? What difference can her name make in the crackling silence of smoke rising, its disciples bent over a glass bowl in the unhallowed heat of Houston's meaner parts.

Perhaps in his mind is a locked door to memory's weedy garden where he has stashed his laughter and his dreams, too. And yet, the hastily sealed cracks won't hold, so in spite of himself, he leaves a trail by which we can follow him. Papa, David, Veda, and I know where he hides from himself in broad daylight. We come one by one, like drug seekers, and park our cars under the freeway to ask desperate or dazed loiterers if they've seen Kyle, only to be told they don't know anyone by that name. When David comes he cannot describe Kyle to them, because the robust army veteran with barrel chest and shrewd eyes does not exist for these people. And David does not know how to describe "Kris," a ghost with shriveled body and eyes of running sand—a man who shambles around in a spittle and vomit grimed T-shirt that says, "It's a long way from 3rd World Country to 3rd Ward, Texas," a man whose rough, crispy curls have yielded to salt-and-pepper dreadlocks without the prayers of Zion.

After seeing his last patient for the day, Papa drives his Lincoln Continental from his southeast Houston office to Wheeler Avenue. He parks at the Fiesta Supermarket across the street from this concrete wasteland under the freeway, a place where brothers are not keepers. Papa, sixty-three years old, has spent most of his life holding his family together, sometimes clutching the rope of familial coherence with his bare hands, his wife having let go and let God some fifteen years before. Papa must cross more than the street to reach Kyle. He must cross his own heart's bridge between love and rage, pity and contempt. His heartbeat does not keep time like it used to, each calamity messes with its rhythm. He pulls out his handkerchief to wipe away the sweat that rains down his face. He cannot cry and so his grief pours down his forehead.

Papa must trick himself to get his legs to cross the street. He puts on his doctor's mask of professional kindness to scan the faces of the walking dead for a sign of his son. Treading the city's battlefield of loose stones, broken glass, discarded bits and butts of lives, he catches sight of Kris and approaches the man with the measured concern of one who has spent his life in emergency rooms. The man he approaches is not the boastful boy he saw off to Frankfurt, Germany, twelve years ago. Nor is he the frightened, bloody-headed child whose mother rushed him to the emergency room of Meharry Medical College twenty-five years ago, when he knocked himself out trying to catch a flyball. That day Papa wiped the blood from his son's head and handed the boy to a colleague to stitch up, because he could not bear to sew up his own "blood." He did not want his son to associate him with pain.

When they come face-to-face, Papa cannot see beyond Kris's eyes, which refuse to acknowledge any part of the past. Stone eyes or brash ice? Papa calls out, "Kyle?" his voice a harsh question. Kyle does not answer. "Kyle, you hear me callin' you." "Huh? I don't know nobody by that name," Kris mumbles, wiping his eyes. "You must got me mixed up with somebody else. Ain't nobody here by that name," Kris deliberately spits half blues words at this seeming stranger. ". . . get on further . . . what y'all want here?" he hollers as if Kyle had never attended Mt. Carmel High School or escorted libidinous debutantes to the Jack and Jill Ball at the Shamrock Hilton, as if he'd never been a boy scout, or a little league baseball player, or a father, or a son.

Papa cannot hold his peace. "Son, you might as well put a .45 to your head. You killin' yourself," he shouts. "What about Cris, your baby girl," Papa's voice whispers its most lethal bullet. Kris/Kyle, I cannot say which one, turns his back and sprints toward the refuge of the urban wilderness.

Papa must trudge back to his car alone. He drives aimlessly around 3rd Ward, circling like a homing pigeon without a home. He would go to the Groovy Grill, but it's closed. He would drop by C.J.'s Barbecue, but it has changed hands. The strong black women who sweat in the kitchen to make the meat just right are the same, the name's the same, but Papa does not feel as if he owns any part of the meat he puts in his mouth anymore. Mr. Broussard, the former owner, is now a solemn retiree, relieved that the Vietnamese gentlemen took the restaurant off his hands, when his children did not wish to carry on the family tradition. So Papa drives himself home to a strong shot of Johnnie Walker, his self-prescribed remedy for nightmares and dreams to boot.

I search for my brother, my friend, though I avoid unfamiliar streets. I start at heartways, because it's there that I left him last. February, three years ago and two days before his thirtieth birthday, was unusually cold for Houston. Icy rain and darkness dared the city to stay open and forced the most recalcitrant street-sleepers to seek the flea-ridden refuge of shelters. Kyle rang my doorbell at half past eight. At first, Payday wouldn't let him cross the threshold, as if to do so would be to welcome an evil spirit. "Brother, why are you here?" Payday asked his brother-in-law. "I'm here cuz I ain't all there 'Day. Come on, bronlaw, it's cool. I ain't holdin'," Kyle coughed these last words for emphasis or pity. "Let him in, Payday, just for tonight," I said. "He's not even holdin' himself." I let him in, a stranger who was using my brother's name as a familial password. I fed him, allowed him to bathe, gave him some of my Payday's clothes to wear, and placed his tattered shirt and trousers in the trashcan. I couldn't talk to him, although as children we'd told each other stories before the ten o'clock news to ward off sleep and silence. Black Hansel and Gretel always outwitted Miss Louella, the fat nappy-headed witch who hoarded Three Musketeer bars and candy corn in her purse during church services. Kyle always fell asleep just before Gretel could rescue Hansel from getting lost in Miss Louella's embrace when he reached out to take a piece of her delicious candy. I couldn't tell him if I'd wanted to, couldn't say the words that would have healed us, having reserved my wittiest anecdotes for mentor-colleagues and promising undergraduates, having reserved my compassion for Haitian refugees who would never get past customs to share my house, my life in the suburbs. And when I caught Kris pocketing Mama's gold rings, bracelets, and the photograph they'd taken together at Kyle's high school graduation, the material legacy of the woman who had loved him best, I treated him like the stranger he had become. I ran to the closet where we kept our rifle, cocked it, and aimed it at him. "What you gonna do, sell her stuff for crack? You are Miss Louella's child, aren't you, never stayed awake for the end of the story, didja? Put down my mama's things and get out before I blow you to hell where you belong." I couldn't believe I was saying these things. Couldn't. Kyle blinked, his mouth a cipher; he did not know this woman. "Come on, sister, it ain't that deep. Put the gun down," he coaxed. "Don't call me sister, bastard, I ain't no crack annie off the street," my words carried no tune he could recognize. "Cool . . . I'm gone," he sighed as if talking to himself. I don't know how long I stood there after he left. I put the rifle back in the closet, but my arms trembled for days afterward. And I chainsmoked to keep from singing; smoke is soundless anesthesia that sucks up all the air and leaves the stench of its absence.

I have not seen Kyle since that day. I see Kris sometimes on my way home from work. He is either coming from the crack house, or going, his mouth gaping, eyes running sand. Or I see him in the faces of men who will not look at me as they hold out their hands for a quarter, a dime, a nickel. "Sister-girl, you can spare dat!" I have heard my brother in the aimless curses of the untribed, people who have mutilated the part of themselves they no longer wish to know; like Kris said, they "ain't all there."

Other days I find parts of him in the scalding lyrics of old Isley Brothers songs, ". . . so I can't be concerned with the other side of the road"; or I find him in the tink-tink-tink of an earnest mechanic who performs rough magic on my car; or I find him in the green smell of evening in early Spring when a game of hide-and-seek beckons and from some tree-shaded lawn, someone calls a brother I do not know.

KATHERINE ANNE PORTER

The Jilting of Granny Weatherall

She flicked her wrist neatly out of Doctor Harry's pudgy careful fingers and pulled the sheet up to her chin. The brat ought to be in knee breeches. Doctoring around the country with spectacles on his nose! "Get along now, take your schoolbooks and go. There's nothing wrong with me."

Doctor Harry spread a warm paw like a cushion on her forehead where the forked green vein danced and made her eyelids twitch. "Now, now, be a good girl, and we'll have you up in no time."

"That's no way to speak to a woman nearly eighty years old just because she's down. I'd have you respect your elders, young man."

"Well, Missy, excuse me." Doctor Harry patted her cheek. "But I've got to warn you, haven't I? You're a marvel, but you must be careful or you're going to be good and sorry."

"Don't tell me what I'm going to be. I'm on my feet now, morally speaking. It's Cornelia. I had to go to bed to get rid of her."

Her bones felt loose, and floated around in her skin, and Doctor Harry floated like a balloon around the foot of the bed. He floated and pulled down his waistcoat and swung his glasses on a cord. "Well, stay where you are, it certainly can't hurt you."

"Get along and doctor your sick," said Granny Weatherall. "Leave a well woman alone. I'll call for you when I want you. . . . Where were you forty years ago when I pulled through milk-leg and double pneumonia? You weren't even born. Don't let Cornelia lead you on," she shouted, because Doctor Harry appeared to float up to the ceiling and out. "I pay my own bills, and I don't throw my money away on nonsense!"

She meant to wave good-by, but it was too much trouble. Her eyes closed of themselves, it was like a dark curtain drawn around the bed. The pillow rose and floated under her, pleasant as a hammock in a light wind. She listened to the leaves rustling outside the window. No, somebody was swishing newspapers: no, Cornelia and Doctor Harry were whispering together. She leaped broad awake, thinking they whispered in her ear.

"She was never like this, *never* like this!" "Well, what can we expect?" "Yes, eighty years old. . . ."

Well, and what if she was? She still had ears. It was like Cornelia to whisper around doors. She always kept things secret in such a public way. She was always being tactful and kind. Cornelia was dutiful; that was the trouble with her. Dutiful and good: "So good and dutiful," said Granny, "that I'd like to spank her." She saw herself spanking Cornelia and making a fine job of it.

"What'd you say, Mother?"

Granny felt her face tying up in hard knots.

"Can't a body think, I'd like to know?"

"I thought you might want something."

"I do. I want a lot of things. First off, go away and don't whisper."

She lay and drowsed, hoping in her sleep that the children would keep out and let her rest a minute. It had been a long day. Not that she was tired. It was always pleasant to snatch a minute now and then. There was always so much to be done, let me see: tomorrow.

Tomorrow was far away and there was nothing to trouble about. Things were finished somehow when the time came; thank God there was always a little margin over for peace: then a person could spread out the plan of life and tuck in the edges orderly. It was good to have everything clean and folded away, with the hair brushes and tonic bottles sitting straight on the white embroidered linen: the day started without fuss and the pantry shelves laid out with rows of jelly glasses and brown jugs and white stone-china jars with blue whirligigs and words painted on them: coffee, tea, sugar, ginger, cinnamon, allspice: and the bronze clock with the lion on top nicely dusted off. The dust that lion could collect in twenty-four hours! The box in the attic with all those letters tied up, well, she'd have to go through that tomorrow. All those letters—George's letters and John's letters and her letters to them both—lying around for the children to find afterwards made her uneasy. Yes, that would be tomorrow's business. No use to let them know how silly she had been once.

While she was rummaging around she found death in her mind and it felt clammy and unfamiliar. She had spent so much time preparing for death there was no need for bringing it up again. Let it take care of itself now. When she was sixty she had felt very old, finished, and went around making farewell trips to see her children and grandchildren, with a secret in her mind: This is the very last of your mother, children! Then she made her will and came down with a long fever. That was all just a notion like a lot of other things, but it was lucky too, for she had once for all got over the idea of dying for a long time. Now she couldn't be worried. She hoped she had better sense now. Her father had lived to be one hundred and two years old and had drunk a noggin of strong hot toddy on his last birthday. He told the reporters it was his daily habit, and he owed his long life to that. He had made quite a scandal and was very pleased about it. She believed she'd just plague Cornelia a little.

"Cornelia! Cornelia!" No footsteps, but a sudden hand on her cheek. "Bless you, where have you been?"

"Here, Mother."

"Well, Cornelia, I want a noggin of hot toddy."

"Are you cold, darling?"

"I'm chilly, Cornelia. Lying in bed stops the circulation. I must have told you that a thousand times."

Well, she could just hear Cornelia telling her husband that Mother was getting a little childish and they'd have to humor her. The thing that most annoyed her was that Cornelia thought she was deaf, dumb, and blind. Little hasty glances and tiny gestures tossed around her and over her head saying, "Don't cross her, let her have her way, she's eighty years old," and she sitting there as if she lived in a thin glass cage. Sometimes Granny almost made up her mind to pack up and move back to her own house where nobody could remind her every minute that she was old. Wait, wait, Cornelia, till your own children whisper behind your back!

In her day she had kept a better house and had got more work done. She wasn't too old yet for Lydia to be driving eighty miles for advice when one of the children jumped the track, and Jimmy still dropped in and talked things over: "Now, Mammy, you've a good business head, I want to know what you think of this? . . ." Old. Cornelia couldn't change the furniture around without asking. Little things, little things! They had been so sweet when they were little. Granny wished the old days were back again with the children young and everything to be done over. It had been a hard pull, but not too much for her. When she thought of all the food she had cooked, and all the clothes she had cut and sewed, and all the gardens she had made—well, the children showed it. There they were, made out of her, and they couldn't get away from that. Sometimes she wanted to see John again and point to them and say, Well, I didn't do so badly, did I? But that would have to wait. That was for tomorrow. She used to think of him as a man, but now all the children were older than their father, and he would be a child beside her if she saw him now. It seemed strange and there was something wrong in the idea. Why, he couldn't possibly recognize her. She had fenced in a hundred acres once, digging the post holes herself and clamping the wires with just a negro boy to help. That changed a woman. John would be looking for a young woman with the peaked Spanish comb in her hair and the painted fan. Digging post holes changed a woman. Riding country roads in the winter when women had their babies was another thing: sitting up nights with sick horses and sick negroes and sick children and hardly ever losing one. John, I hardly ever lost one of them! John would see that in a minute, that would be something he could understand, she wouldn't have to explain anything!

It made her feel like rolling up her sleeves and putting the whole place to rights again. No matter if Cornelia was determined to be everywhere at once, there were a great many things left undone on this place. She would start tomorrow and do them. It was good to be strong enough for everything, even if all you made melted and changed and slipped under your hands, so that by the time you finished you almost forgot what you were working for. What was it I set out to do? she asked herself intently, but she could not remember. A fog rose over the valley, she saw it marching across the creek swallowing the trees and moving up the hill like an army of ghosts. Soon it would be at the near edge of the orchard, and then it was time to go in and light the lamps. Come in, children, don't stay out in the night air.

Lighting the lamps had been beautiful. The children huddled up to her and breathed like little calves waiting at the bars in the twilight. Their eyes followed the match and watched the flame rise and settle in a blue curve, then they moved away from her. The lamp was lit, they didn't have to be scared and hang on to mother any more. Never, never, never more. God, for all my life I thank Thee. Without Thee, my God, I could never have done it. Hail, Mary, full of grace.

I want you to pick all the fruit this year and see that nothing is wasted. There's always someone who can use it. Don't let good things rot for want of using. You waste life when you waste good food. Don't let things get lost. It's bitter to lose things. Now, don't let me get to thinking, not when I am tired and taking a little nap before supper. . . .

The pillow rose about her shoulders and pressed against her heart and the memory was being squeezed out of it: oh, push down the pillow, somebody: it would smother her if she tried to hold it. Such a fresh breeze blowing and such a green day with no threats in it. But he had not come, just the same. What does a woman do when she has put on the white veil and set out the white cake for a man and he doesn't come? She tried to remember. No, I swear he never harmed me but in that. He never harmed me but in that . . . and what if he did? There was the day, the day, but a whirl of dark smoke rose and covered it, crept up and over into the bright field where everything was planted so carefully in orderly rows. That was hell, she knew hell when she saw it. For sixty years she had prayed against remembering him and against losing her soul in the deep pit of hell, and now the two things were mingled in one and the thought of him was a smoky cloud from hell that moved and crept in her head when she had just got rid of Doctor Harry and was trying to rest a minute. Wounded vanity, Ellen, said a sharp voice in the top of her mind. Don't let your wounded vanity get the upper hand of you. Plenty of girls get jilted. You were jilted, weren't you? Then stand up to it. Her eyelids wavered and let in streamers of blue-gray light like tissue paper over her eyes. She must get up and pull the shades down or she'd never sleep. She was in bed again and the shades were not down. How could that happen? Better turn over, hide from the light, sleeping in the light gave you nightmares. "Mother, how do you feel now?" and a stinging wetness on her forehead. But I don't like having my face washed in cold water!

Hapsy? George? Lydia? Jimmy? No, Cornelia, and her features were swollen and full of little puddles. "They're coming, darling, they'll all be here soon." Go wash your face, child, you look funny.

Instead of obeying, Cornelia knelt down and put her head on the pillow. She seemed to be talking but there was no sound. "Well, are you tongue-tied? Whose birthday is it? Are you going to give a party?"

Cornelia's mouth moved urgently in strange shapes. "Don't do that, you bother me, daughter."

"Oh, no, Mother. Oh, no. . . ."

Nonsense. It was strange about children. They disputed your every word. "No what, Cornelia?"

"Here's Doctor Harry."

"I won't see that boy again. He just left five minutes ago."

"That was this morning, Mother. It's night now. Here's the nurse."

"This is Doctor Harry, Mrs. Weatherall. I never saw you look so young and happy!"

"Ah, I'll never be young again—but I'd be happy if they'd let me lie in peace and get rested."

She thought she spoke up loudly, but no one answered. A warm weight on her forehead, a warm bracelet on her wrist, and a breeze went on whispering, trying to tell her something. A shuffle of leaves in the everlasting hand of God, He blew on them and they danced and rattled. "Mother, don't mind, we're going to give you a little hypodermic." "Look here, daughter, how do ants get in this bed? I saw sugar ants yesterday." Did you send for Hapsy too?

It was Hapsy she really wanted. She had to go a long way back through a great many rooms to find Hapsy standing with a baby on her arm. She seemed to herself to be Hapsy also, and the baby on Hapsy's arm was Hapsy and himself and herself, all at once, and there was no surprise in the meeting. Then Hapsy melted from within and turned flimsy as gray gauze and the baby was a gauzy shadow, and Hapsy came up close and said, "I thought you'd never come," and looked at her very searchingly and said, "You haven't changed a bit!" They leaned forward to kiss, when Cornelia began whispering from a long way off, "Oh, is there anything you want to tell me? Is there anything I can do for you?"

Yes, she had changed her mind after sixty years and she would like to see George. I want you to find George. Find him and be sure to tell him I forgot him. I want him to know I had my husband just the same and my children and my house like any other woman. A good house too and a good husband that I loved and fine children out of him. Better than I hoped for even. Tell him I was given back everything he took away and more. Oh, no, oh, God, no, there was something else besides the house and the man and the children. Oh, surely they were not all? What was it? Something not given back. . . . Her breath crowded down under her ribs and grew into a monstrous frightening shape with cutting edges; it bored up into her head, and the agony was unbelievable: Yes, John, get the Doctor now, no more talk, my time has come.

When this one was born it should be the last. The last. It should have been born first, for it was the one she had truly wanted. Everything came in good time. Nothing left out, left over. She was strong, in three days she would be as well as ever. Better. A woman needed milk in her to have her full health.

"Mother, do you hear me?"

"I've been telling you—"

"Mother, Father Connolly's here."

"I went to Holy Communion only last week. Tell him I'm not so sinful as all that."

"Father just wants to speak to you."

He could speak as much as he pleased. It was like him to drop in and inquire about her soul as if it were a teething baby, and then stay on for a cup of tea and a round of cards and gossip. He always had a funny story of some sort, usually about an Irishman who made his little mistakes and confessed them, and the point lay in some absurd thing he would blurt out in the confessional showing his struggles between native piety and original sin. Granny felt easy about her soul. Cornelia, where are your manners? Give Father Connolly a chair. She had her secret comfortable understanding with a few favorite saints who cleared a straight road to God for her. All as surely signed and sealed as the papers for the new Forty Acres. Forever . . . heirs and assigns forever. Since the day the wedding cake was not cut, but thrown out and wasted. The whole bottom dropped out of the world, and there she was blind and sweating with nothing under her feet and the walls falling away. His hand had caught her under the breast, she had not fallen, there was the freshly polished floor with the green rug on it, just as before. He had cursed like a sailor's parrot and said, "I'll kill him for you." Don't lay a hand on him, for my sake leave something to God. "Now, Ellen, you must believe what I tell you. . . ."

So there was nothing, nothing to worry about any more, except sometimes in the night one of the children screamed in a nightmare, and they both hustled out shaking and hunting for the matches and calling, "There, wait a minute, here we are!" John, get the doctor now, Hapsy's time has come. But there was Hapsy standing by the bed in a white cap. "Cornelia, tell Hapsy to take off her cap. I can't see her plain."

Her eyes opened very wide and the room stood out like a picture she had seen somewhere. Dark colors with the shadows rising towards the ceiling in long angles. The tall black dresser gleamed with nothing on it but John's picture, enlarged from a little one, with John's eyes very black when they should have been blue. You never saw him, so how do you know how he looked? But the man insisted the copy was perfect, it was very rich and handsome. For a picture, yes, but it's not my husband. The table by the bed had a linen cover and a candle and a crucifix. The light was blue from Cornelia's silk lampshades. No sort of light at all, just frippery. You had to live forty years with kerosene lamps to appreciate honest electricity. She felt very strong and she saw Doctor Harry with a rosy nimbus around him.

"You look like a saint, Doctor Harry, and I vow that's as near as you'll ever come to it."

"She's saying something."

"I heard you, Cornelia. What's all this carrying-on?"

"Father Connolly's saying—"

Cornelia's voice staggered and bumped like a cart in a bad road. It rounded corners and turned back again and arrived nowhere. Granny stepped up in the cart very lightly and reached for the reins, but a man sat beside her and she knew him by his hands, driving the cart. She did not look in his face, for she knew without seeing, but looked instead down the road where the trees leaned over and bowed to each other and a thousand birds were singing a Mass. She felt like singing too, but she put her hand in the bosom of her dress and pulled out a rosary, and Father Connolly murmured Latin in a very solemn voice and tickled her feet. My God, will you stop that nonsense? I'm a married woman. What if he did run away and leave me to face the priest by myself? I found another a whole world better. I wouldn't have exchanged my husband for anybody except St. Michael himself, and you may tell him that for me with a thank you in the bargain.

Light flashed on her closed eyelids, and a deep roaring shook her. Cornelia, is that lightning? I hear thunder. There's going to be a storm. Close all the windows. Call the children in. . . . "Mother, here we are, all of us." "Is that you, Hapsy?" "Oh, no, I'm Lydia. We drove as fast as we could." Their faces drifted above her, drifted away. The rosary fell out of her hands and Lydia put it back. Jimmy tried to help, their hands fumbled together, and Granny closed two fingers around Jimmy's thumb. Beads wouldn't do, it must be something alive. She was so amazed her thoughts ran round and round. So, my dear Lord, this is my death and I wasn't even thinking about it. My children have come to see me die. But I can't, it's not time. Oh, I always hated surprises. I wanted to give Cornelia the amethyst set—Cornelia, you're to have the amethyst set, but Hapsy's to wear it when she wants, and, Doctor Harry, do shut up. Nobody sent for you. Oh, my dear Lord, do wait a minute. I meant to do something about the Forty Acres, Jimmy doesn't need it and Lydia will later on, with that worthless husband of hers. I meant to finish the altar cloth and send six bottles of wine to Sister Borgia for her dyspepsia. I want to send six bottles of wine to Sister Borgia, Father Connolly, now don't let me forget.

Cornelia's voice made short turns and tilted over and crashed. "Oh, Mother, oh, Mother, oh, Mother. . . ."

"I'm not going, Cornelia. I'm taken by surprise. I can't go."

You'll see Hapsy again. What about her? "I thought you'd never come." Granny made a long journey outward, looking for Hapsy. What if I don't find her? What then? Her heart sank down and down, there was no bottom to death, she couldn't come to the end of it. The blue light from Cornelia's lampshade drew into a tiny point in the center of her brain, it flickered and winked like an eye, quietly it fluttered and dwindled. Granny lay curled down within herself, amazed and watchful, staring at the point of light that was herself; her body was not only a deeper mass of shadow in an endless darkness and this darkness would curl around the light and swallow it up. God, give a sign!

For the second time there was no sign. Again no bridegroom and the priest in the house. She could not remember any other sorrow because this grief wiped them all away. Oh, no, there's nothing more cruel than this—I'll never forgive it. She stretched herself with a deep breath and blew out the light.

★

LISA SANDLIN

The Old Folks Wish Them Well

Mama has finally given me permission to car date, but the first Saturday I can go out is the Saturday of Andy Meaux's wedding, so that's where we go. They're holding the reception at a roadhouse right across the state line in Vinton, La., the bride's hometown. The decorations are beautiful. They've pinned white and pink crepe paper to the skirts of the buffet tables, looped it on the walls, double-twisted it around the six-decker cake— they've even got streamers spinning from the ceiling fans. I feel like I've stepped on a great big merry-go-round just waiting to start up.

The musicians are already tuning. They blast into pieces of songs, then stop dead to concentrate. The oldest one tests his bow on a fiddle he is nestling like a pillow. When they're ready, they lead with a thumping waltz, and oh! the whole room goes crazy cheering Andy and the bride.

The singer's eyes are smooth shut. He pulls out one note until he's stretched it fine like taffy. No jumping, no strutting; Cajuns when they sing they might be asleep standing up. It is a mystery how they feel the music. But they do, they do. And the dancers: they bounce and they trot, they ride every beat, they are wild. *C'mon cher*, they take you by the elbow, *c'mon and dance now, have a good time.*

Mama does. She sits over at the Arceneaux's table drinking Pearl and smoking menthols. Her eyes are shiny wet when she looks at me and she says, "Fifteen and a half already." She says I'll be next, before she can turn around, I'll be out the door in a shower of rice. She has the pattern picked for my wedding dress. She describes it for Trudie Arceneaux, who is almost blind from diabetes and insists on every detail. Just because she can't see, don't mean she don't get the picture, Mrs. Arceneaux wants us to know. Well, Mama hums, inset sleeves that V right down to the index fingers, baby seed pearls, a peplum. Peplum! My God, Mama, I tell her, that's from the '40s, that pattern's twenty years old. And who says I'm getting married tomorrow? She just smiles. She's made the voile minidress I'm wearing, and but for one dumb touch it is pretty. When I wasn't looking, Mama stitched my name KAYLA on the shoulder and embroidered it with vines. Vines.

Jerry Hooks and Wayne Barnett won't leave me alone for a minute. They are cousins; I've known them all my life. When I shut my eyes with the singer up there, something simmers in me I swear I don't know what it is, though I think . . . I just think, it has nothing to do with Jerry Hooks or Wayne Barnett. Still, I don't mind them hanging around. I raise up my arms and stretch my white pumps under the table, ready to get up and start this party.

Jerry and Wayne both want to dance, but they have to wait for Mr. Arceneaux to get done saying what he is fixing to say. Jack Arceneaux sets his beer down and points at me with his lit cigarette. He lowers an eyebrow until it crowds his eye. His mouth is seriously open; he looks like he's about to give the boys job advice. Mr. Arceneaux says, "You can tell how a girl will go by looking at her mother, boys. It is a proof." He says this to flatter my mama, who is a widow with a 26-inch waist. Her chin is lolling on her hand. "Shoot, Jack," she says.

Mrs. Arceneaux's fingers spider out to find her husband's cup. When she gets hold of it, she guards it to her chest. She smiles and tips sideways toward Mama's shoulder without turning her face. Mama has seen her sign checks, bless her heart, Mama says, she scrawls right across the numbers the clerk has filled in for her. "Irene," Mrs. Arceneaux asks her, "why you don't get married again?"

The band rolls straight into "Johnny Can't Dance." Kids in little suits and dresses with dragging sashes race in between the tables, knocking into the folding chairs. I jump up, but Mama's fingernails have got my wrist. Now she has advice. Mama gives advice to everybody. They come to our house and lurk outside the screen door till I let them in, so she can read the cards for them. She has told me, though, that the cards are only an aid, something for the people to fix their minds on. Mama has a power. She says that power is a strange thing because it is so ordinary. Sometimes, she says, she stiffs up and pretends to let a message hit her when all the time the answer has floated into her mind just as common as any other thought, like if it's going to storm or not. Sometimes she guesses the puzzle behind the Concentration game before Hugh Downs has ever turned a square. She just knows what it is.

Mama stares deep into my eyes. "What Jack says, that goes for boys, too," she whispers, inclining her head toward Jerry and Wayne. Mama likes Wayne Barnett because she says he will grow to be a man a girl can count on, like his daddy. Not like Jerry's father, mean Gaston Hooks. "Those two are night and day." She rolls her eyes. "Devil and angel." Mama says Wayne's daddy is a sweetheart man.

But Jerry Hooks gets my hand. He is tall, slump-shouldered, and grave as a judge; he has slitty Hooks eyes that fear to look at me. Up on the bandstand a white man with a vacant stare squeezes accordion. A negro man sings, *Oh Johnny can't dance.* Older couples jounce by us. They hug and pinch, their plaited hands go up and down. The negro man sings, *He's got the ants in his pants.* My dress sticks at the waist where Jerry's hand is. He steers me like a car.

In between dances, I light for a minute at the family tables; that is the polite thing to do. Mama has advised me to listen to every word the fathers say. Mr. Gaston Hooks wears his white hair short on the sides and tall on top, poofed like Porter Wagoner. He has three cups of beer in front of him and his elbows have made holes in the white paper tablecloth. When he empties one cup, he sets a full cup inside it. He is loud. He says, " 'Member that no-count who had the gall to take Darlene out to the rice fields and when she wanted to go home, he slapped her? Slapped my baby? My oldest son Loy, he hemmed that sucker in his car and throwed in two fair-sized cottonmouths and a gunny sack of garter snakes. He let him perch up on the top of the seat, wiggling and carrying on, for two solid hours. Fellow was relieved to get beat up when Loy finally let him out. It was a favor!"

Wayne stands there next to his uncle, waiting and grinning. His smile is something to see. Now, Mama has called the Barnetts the angel side of that family and Mama is always right, and Wayne Barnett for sure does not look like the devil. But he looks like he might know him. He has Barnett eyes rather than squinty Hooks ones, blue with eyelashes like a girl's. He has black, black hair, and he wants to dance. When we lace hands, he rubs his fingers in mine. He slings me out and reels me in and twirls me like a daisy. *Ohhhhhhhhhh,* the white singer with the accordion on his stomach reels back, back, back as his voice goes up. When he has pulled the note to its natural end, he snaps forward over the accordion like a rubber band. *Jol-ie Blonde!*

When that dance is over, I sit down at the Barnett's table and listen to Wayne's father. Everybody pushes cups of beer at me; it is a wedding. Mr. Tollie Barnett is telling the story of how he came to marry Vangie Hooks. He has one foot perched up in the folding chair. He talks with a toothpick in his mouth, which slurs his soft voice. He says, "Vangie wore blue taffeta and I couldn't get me one whole dance with her. I about developed a hump, holding up my shoulder to ward off the tapping hands. Finally one poor soul spilled his beer on me. I allowed as how it might of been a accident and kept on dancing. But then he came right up and put his hand on her you know what. Well—"

Jerry whirls me away, but we have to wait it out because the groom's older brother Weldon is about to dance with the broom. Weldon's barefoot and his pants are rolled up. He's a knobby little guy, at least twenty-seven years old and still not married, so he has to go along with the fun. Now I've seen older brothers, and sisters too, cut loose in high style and jitterbug with the broom flying. But Weldon is shy and hangdog. The broom is the perfect height for him. Everybody laughs a lot at poor Weldon, so stiff and mannerly, waltzing on the empty floor.

Then the kids get onto him like mosquitoes. Little Judy Leger circles him in her mother's spike heels. She's wedged her feet in the toes; the empty heels flop. She is giggling and not discouraged for a minute. Her brother is helping her wart him, making running stomps at Weldon's bare feet.

Jerry and I plop down at the Hooks' table, which sports a marching line of cups, full of beer. We get two of them. Mama's chin rides by on Clovis Guidry's shoulder. Gliding down, she flicks her finger in time to the music, and teases Mr. Hooks, "Gaston, around my daughter, you watch your smart mouth." She winks at me. Mr. Hooks cocks his jaw at her. The pearl buttons on his shirt swell out. He murmurs, "Irene, Irene." When she has danced away, his narrow eyes beat a path to mine. He says, "I asked Loy, I said, why'd you throw in them garter snakes, they's not poisonous. Loy he said, 'Atmosphere, Daddy.' " Next to me, another Hooks relative spurts out his cake, laughing.

Wayne grabs me away; I have to swallow my beer in one fast gulp. He says, "C'mon to the Fair with me, Kayla, after the party. It don't shut down till midnight." Wayne has a soft voice like his father Tollie Barnett, who is repeating his courtship story for Myrtle Melancon's benefit. Mrs. Melancon's purple lace dress is fancier than the bride's; you can see her chest dividing until the purple lining covers it up. Mr. Barnett says, "Lord knows I ain't no fighter! But I must have been getting ready all that time, because I didn't take off my coat and that was the only coat I had, I just jumped right over Vangie and took him backward on the floor. I swung at his face with my eyes closed, then waited for him to hit me back, but one of Vangie's slit-eyed old brothers pulled me off him, laughing. 'Man's gone to sleep, Tollie,' he said, 'you can quit now.' Gol-lee, I felt bad about it later. That fellow went down on the Arizona."

As soon as we're back out on the floor, Jerry Hooks steps on my foot smack in the middle of a waltz. He's tongue-tied, but he mentions the Fair, too. He leaves a 1-2-3 step for me to say something back. Then he leads left and I follow right and he rushes on to tell me they have a booth where you can get your picture taken and they'll blow it up into a poster and mail it to you in ten days. He says this because his hobby is cameras—and because he doesn't think I'd go with him if he has only himself to offer.

But Wayne snatches me before I can answer. Back and forth—if I wasn't so soothed by the beer, I'd get aggravated about acting the crownpiece in this checker game. Wayne has me a plate of dirty rice and a pile of saucy shrimp he's bothered to pick out of the gumbo. He's got me another foamy beer. I've heard enough by now to know that Mama is right about these fathers, mean and nice, sour and sweet. Mama makes Judge Simon Hightower wait on her while she listens to Mr. Barnett. Sitting out the dance is probably a relief for Judge Hightower. He is old as the hills, and so is his stripey suit. Twirling the toothpick between his thumb and finger, Mr. Barnett says, "Didn't want old man Hooks to see me scuffed up, so I took

Vangie to my room while I changed. Left her standing by the door. I took the only chair, feeling foolish, and I gave her a out. I told her she deserved a better man. 'Vangie,' I said, 'this here's the most fearful man you'll ever see.' I was just waiting for that taffeta to swish out the door. But then I heard it rustle—"

Mama cuts him off with an "Ooh la la!" She got that from the Everly Brothers.

While Wayne is brushing sauce from his good jacket, Jerry leads me off. It is a drawn-out slow dance, all in French. The negro man is singing, not playing his rub-board; his hands with the silver rings dangle loose at his sides. The floor is solid old people, draped all over each other. The little kids sit at the tables and kick their feet, eat more cake and wait to chase around again. Mrs. Leger ties up Judy's sash and tries to buckle her shoes back on. Judy is wailing for the spike heels. "Kayla." Jerry Hooks surprises me to death. He stammers, "The turns of your face m-m-make a valentine."

When we sit at his table, Jerry keeps my limp hand pressed between his two hot ones. I think, Now that was a sweet, sweet thing he said. But then Mr. Hooks starts up. His white poof has expanded; it looks like a tube balloon sitting on his head. He glances at Jerry and says, "Nowadays young people are down-right sissies. Got my youngest a twenty-two for his grad-u-ation, said no thank you Daddy, what I want me is a Kodak camera. Can you beat it? Sissieeeees!" His voice skids, drawing out the end of the word like a Cajun yell.

Poor Jerry, he drops my hand. Wayne Barnett says get my purse. I'd like to sit still a minute. My head is buzzy-thick from the beer and the dancing. The room is twisting like a crepe-paper streamer. My best vision is a round spot right in front of me, where all the cupbottoms have left overlapping rings—the paper tablecloth looks like a tub of bubbles. But I am hauled across the floor again. Mama fingers the carnation in Wayne's buttonhole. She is all charm. She sighs, "Well, I promised her. Fifteen, my God. Eleven o'clock, young man."

She pulls me aside so Wayne can't hear and she holds both my shoulders. Sloughing off the charm, she says, "Kayla, I got not a doubt under heaven about you." She says it in the quiet voice she uses when her card-reading customers have left, when any need for sugar-coating is gone. Then she stands back, winking—she is so full of winks; it's like she knows everything that's ever happened in the world. Jerry dogs us to the door. Andy Meaux's bride is bouncing across the dance floor and I could swear that underneath the long white dress she has brass springs on her feet. The last thing I see before getting into Wayne's truck is Jerry, slouched against his Chevy, kicking a storm of oyster shell in the parking lot.

This is truly my first car date; Wayne scooches me next to him. He hangs his nice suit jacket with the boutonniere on a coat hanger, and hooks it on the empty part of the seat by my window. Then he stows a beer bottle between his legs. "First thing we go on is the ferris wheel," I tell him. My daddy used to call the ferris wheel the king of rides. He liked the soft breezes up there above the lights. He used to say nobody could reach us up there, that we'd never fall out because he had ahold of us both. Before I know it, twenty miles of woods and fairyland refineries have whizzed by and we're back on the outskirts of Beaumont, Texas, out by the rice fields.

Wayne lets the truck idle at a stop sign. A ways over, where the blacktop runs into dirt, farm roads curve out like fingers into the rice. It's nothing but dark out there. The rice fields are flooded. If we were to turn that way, we'd end up on a raised strip of muddy road, surrounded by low black water.

All of a sudden it's like a sparkler tip has lit in my stomach, sizzling, but not burst yet. I've heard the police cruise these farm roads to catch kids parking. Just to scare them, maybe get an eyeful. Because everybody knows what kids come out to the rice fields for. Wayne puts the neck of the beer bottle in his mouth and takes a swallow. Pulling it from his lips makes a soft sucking noise. "You want some?"

I'm still squinting toward the rice fields. Wayne gets flustered. He leans over to say something, and when he does, his beer bottle tips and spews warm foam over my dress. My whole lap is soaked.

"My God, Wayne!" I yell.

Wayne heaves the bottle about fifty yards out the window. He runs his fingers through his black hair and pulls on it. "Dammit, I messed it all up now. I just wanted ten minutes alone with you, before we got around another crowd. I swear that's all."

He takes hold of my shoulders then and pulls us face to face. Farther away his nice jawline had a blur to it. So close up I can see him fine, except for his eyes are not blue; they're swimmy gray. "Let's just stay a minute, Kayla," Wayne says. And he gives me the longest kiss I've ever had. It is in fact the third kiss I've ever had, and now I see the others were only practice. This one starts a soft roaring in my ears, like something is coming from far away. As he pulls back, Wayne lets out a breath and says, "I won't turn down that road without it's all right with you. Kayla, I . . . I . . . if anybody was to say a wrong word about you, it'd be their last, you understand what I'm saying?"

Pride puts an arch in my back. "All right, but then we've got to go, hear?"

"We'll go, Kayla," Wayne promises. He shifts out of idle, turns right toward the farm road. When we reach it, he guns the truck around and jams it into reverse. He sticks his head out to see. We roll backward into the curve, back, back, back on down the road, right in between the spreading rice fields.

Wayne cuts the motor and kisses me again. He puts his hand on my ribs right beneath my breast. And he keeps it there. He keeps it there till it moves up and we slide down on the plastic seat and go on kissing. He's promised and I believe him, so I let that sparkler catch, to find what it tells me. It's this: I like being alone out here on this big, black road. I like Wayne's hand on me. It makes him new, like he's got a mystery side to him that maybe not even he knows about yet. And me—I'm not me, not Kayla, not a solid girl or a person in the world, I am this pure *feeling*. When I shut my eyes, I can be all around Wayne like water.

Pretty soon, Wayne's white shirt is stuck to his chest. He takes it off because it's so wet and he says I should take off my dress, too, so it can dry off. I get a shivery twinge, but the moon and stars are shining through the truck window, and Wayne's voice is every bit as soft as his sweetheart father's. He says, "A slip is just exactly like a dress, now isn't it?" He has to take his mouth off my neck to say it.

My voile dress is mashed with creases, and sure enough soaked with the beer and sweat. "Are we about to go to the Fair, Wayne?"

His index finger flips twice across his heart. "You bet we are, Kayla," he says. "I want your mama to stay liking me." My backbone tickles. Air hits my wet skin. My zipper's undone. Wayne puts the dress on his hanger, hooks it on the mirror and we lie back down. My slip hikes up on the sweaty seat. The crickets are singing by rubbing their legs together. Wayne starts kind of moving on me.

Then there's a crash so sharp it's like a gunshot in the window. We both jump bolt upright. Wayne whacks his back on the steering wheel. But all it is, is down in the floorboards, my decoupaged box purse has tumped over. We laugh a little bit, each of us sitting at our own window. We sneak one good look at each other. I'm surprised by how fast everything has changed. I'm not a *feeling* anymore. That's Wayne Barnett over there. I'm going to put my dress back on.

But Wayne touches my arm. "Kayla," he says, "You like me more than Jerry?"

I'm relieved to be talking. I set my elbow out the window, lifting my hair up from the back of my neck so it will catch the air. "I like you, Wayne."

Wayne grips the steering wheel like he's going to drive off, but he hasn't started the truck. "Jerry's real smart," he says. "Jerry's going to go to college, Kayla."

"So?"

"So I'm probably going to wind up in the army."

"So?" I am not catching on to this conversation. Why won't he look at me? Wayne is holding to the steering wheel for dear life, and his voice is very quiet. It is low and soft, and it has a tinge of sadness, like the smooth black water out there, with the moonlight floating through it.

"So maybe you should of gone to the Fair with him, Kayla." Wayne's voice is husky soft. "Maybe you'd of done better to go with him."

Now I get it, and his saying that makes me want to be so good to him. All my feelings gather at one place in my chest and I get up kneeling on the truck seat with my stocking feet under me, and lay my hand on his shoulder. His shoulder muscle flinches, like my hand has burnt it. "Wayne," I say, "I came with you, didn't I?"

His hands drop off the steering wheel, and he breaks into a smile, a huge bright-eyed smile, like he's won something. His fingers start running over my back. He says, "I know we should go. But let's just stay one more minute, Kayla." Then he accidentally brushes the straps off my shoulder. Now I am awfully mixed up. It *is* sweet what he said. But . . . am I imagining this, or does Wayne seem to know just exactly how sweet he was? Did a sweep of light just cut down the road and then wink out? I start to take my dress off the hanger so I can see out the windshield.

But Wayne settles both his hands on my waist and pulls me to him. We are sinking back down. He wedges his knee between mine. "Hey, Wayne," I protest. I figure he'll laugh and get off now. My head is mashed against the door. For a second, Wayne trembles above me—then his breath breaks on my face and his weight rushes down. He's grinding on me. "Wayne." I nudge him. But he's not listening. It's like he can't hear. His body is bearing down on me, all hard muscle and bone. It takes a while for my feelings to catch up, but they do. He's scaring me. I'm blinking, but my eyes burn and burn until they fill up. I struggle one hand in between us.

Wayne opens his eyes and looks at me. He must can see I'm crying because he gets off me and sits up. He just sits in front of the steering wheel. Then he yells, "Jesus!"

177

I crowd back against my door, startled and resentful. Why is *he* mad? I'm the one should be mad. But he starts saying he's sorry. He says it over and over until he's whispering like the crickets out there in the rice fields.

It's when he stops apologizing that we more feel than hear a creeping motion, a throbbing purr in the dark. Something is out there on this muddy road, coming to get us. Something big and stalking is headed for this truck. My God, my head is stark clear and the very first thing I know is that a slip is not a dress. There's a bump! and the truck shudders. Wayne yells Jesus! again and jerks his shirt off the floorboard. I grab for my dress, but there's a white flick, on-off like a light switch. Wayne and I look out our windows. *Flick.*

Jerry Hooks has nosed his Chevrolet right into Wayne's front bumper. He is long-gone drunk. He sits cross-legged on the hood of his car, taking pictures. Of my dress hanging in the windshield. KAYLA stitched on the shoulder. With vines.

Jerry's rocking back and forth, crushing and booming the hood. He says, "Yearbook." He says, "Blown-up. Poster." It is the meanest trick I've ever heard of. Jerry sets the Kodak on his lap and wipes his eyes. He calls, "Kay-laaaa."

I slide out in my white slip, all stitched up so it would be shorter than my dress. Wayne jumps out right behind me, his shirt flying open. Mud squishes, oozing on my stocking feet. My voice is shaky, but I really do want to know. I ask him, "Jerry, how can you say my face is like a valentine and still do this?"

Wayne strides past me. Mama has said a girl can count on the Barnetts. She has said they are sweetheart men. My faith in Mama is taking a beating. Night and day, she said, devil and angel, but as far as I can see it's plenty of both. Wayne leans toward Jerry; he's got his arm out. Is he going to grab that camera?

Wayne swipes at it like he might be swatting a mosquito. "Hey, c'mon, Jerry," he says, and he kicks the Chevy's fender, but not hard enough to do more than knock some mud off it.

Jerry hugs the camera to his chest. He is a big grinning hump on the car hood. He gives a snort, almost a snicker . . .

. . . *or was that Wayne?*

Jerry aims the camera at his cousin. He's about to squeeze the button. I keep my eyes on Wayne, I could stand here forever. Because now I know what that flash will show me. When I catch his face, it will not be ashamed like it was a minute ago. Wayne's face will wear no consternation at all. I will see buck pride and a pucker of slyness around his mouth.

Flick.

The moon cuts the watery fields in a knife-straight stripe. A step beyond me there, it cuts right through the road. Plain ordinary moonlight that you might see on any night. But as I step forward, its white blade lights me and shines me. Fills me to bursting, like a kind of love. Mama didn't tell me, she expected me to learn: You've got to step into the power before it's yours. It will miss you if you don't. Just like Mama knows which cloud holds the next spire of lightning, I know what I can do.

Gritty mud sticks to my nylons as I go over to Jerry. He sputters, choking on the last word: "K-Kayla, you are my hear-rrrrt." Wayne slides his hand beneath my elbow; he thinks he is with me. I aim for the tender scallop of his ribcage. I poke him so hard he doubles over, coughing.

My slip is blinding white, it can be seen for miles. The crickets are playing their little tiny legs like fiddles. I know what to say and when I say it my voice is mean. It is mean and it is joyful. "Jerry Hooks, you give me that camera," I say.

"Jerry Hooks, you give me that camera," I say, and that is just what Jerry Hooks does.

After climbing back into the truck, I plunk his prisoner polaroid down then scoot to the very edge of the seat so my feet can reach the pedals. Wayne hollers as I start her up. Reverse is pull toward my chest and shove up, first straight down from there. The rest will come to me.

ANNETTE SANFORD

Six White Horses

In the summer of 1947, Lila Bickell took an interest in a salesman named Terrence V. Dennis.

Her brother Hector said, "*Terrence,* for God's sake!"

Hector was thirty-eight, a teller at the Farmers Union Bank and nice enough looking except for a certain hardness of heart that showed up as a scowl on his nice-looking face.

"If I were named Hector," Lila said, "I wouldn't throw stones."

Lila, at forty, was pretty in a careless sort of way that kept people from noticing how small and fine-boned she was, and how generally appealing. She wore any old thing and when she got up in the morning, if her hair misbehaved, she pulled a tam over it and went off to her job at the Quality Shoe Mart about as content as she would have been otherwise.

Lila and Hector shared a home, a yellow stone cottage that had belonged to their parents until their parents died. Hector grew vegetables in the rambling old garden, and Lila raised flowers she put around in the dark rooms to lighten the furniture.

They each had their chores. Lila cooked and shopped, and Hector did the laundry and cleaned the house. At night they read in two chairs by the fireplace.

They might have gone on that way for a long time except for Terrence, who came one day and knocked on the door when Lila was at home nursing a summer cold.

She thought at first she might ignore the knock. "If I were at work," she told herself, "whoever is there would give up and go away." Then she got out of bed and put on a dilapidated bathrobe and went to see who it was.

Terrence V. Dennis was an honorably discharged veteran selling reconditioned vacuum cleaners. He wasn't as tall as Lila would have liked, and he had a mole on his chin that she intended to suggest he have burned off as soon as they were married.

"Married!" Hector said. "You aren't thinking of that, are you?"

Lila replied, "If Terrence proposes, I'll accept."

That was later, of course, after she found out more about him and kissed him in the grape arbor a number of times.

"A great many men my age have died, Hector." In the war, she meant, but she steered clear of the war because of Hector's embarrassment at not having gone due to a punctured eardrum.

"I think Terrence and I can be happy," she went on. "And that's all anyone wants, isn't it? Just to be happy?"

"I thought we were."

"How can we be, Hector? We aren't fulfilled."

Through the rest of June, Terrence showed up once a week at least to take Lila to the movies. On the Fourth of July he asked her to marry him and after that he came regularly to dinner on Saturday night.

On these occasions he wore a nice jacket of houndstooth tweed and slicked back his hair with some kind of tonic that smelled like chrysanthemums. Hector inhibited him, sitting like a bulldog at the end of the table, but after dessert he usually said something noteworthy.

One evening he said, "Four out of five women open their doors wearing pink kimonos."

Lila said in surprise, "Mine is tan."

"Four out of five," Terrence reminded.

After he was gone Hector said, "Have you thought about eating with him day after day?"

"He'll be easy to cook for," Lila said. "He eats whatever I put on the table." She was doing what she always did, which was to hum something catchy while she put away the leftovers.

"Does he read at all?"

"Of course he reads."

"I'd like to know what."

"Then ask him, why don't you?"

By then, Hector had let up a little about the vacuum cleaner Lila had bought without consulting him.

The first afternoon he took on terribly. "*I* clean the house. Why should you choose the vacuum?"

"As a little surprise." Lila brought him his gardening boots. "Do you know who you remind me of? Silas Marner, when he smashed his waterpot."

"Why didn't you call me? You knew where I was."

"He was about to break down," Lila continued, "and then he found Eppie under the furze bush."

"Under what kind of bush have you hidden my Hoover?"

"This is a good machine, Hector, with quality parts. Terrence sprinkled wet sand on the carpet and it sucked up the whole mess with only one passover."

Lila went on humming and storing what was left from the Saturday night dinner. Hector swept around the table, particularly around Terrence's chair where crumbs of biscuits were strewn like dandruff.

He called out to the kitchen. "Terrence V. Dennis thinks all he has to do to support a wife is knock on doors."

"Well," Lila called back, "that's how he found one."

She hung up her apron and went upstairs to look over the trousseau she was assembling in their parents' bedroom.

The trousseau consisted so far of one white nightgown with flowing peignoir, two ivory-colored slips, shoes both black and brown, a serviceable coat that wouldn't show spots, and a print blouse with roses on it.

While she was trying the blouse on, Hector appeared with a new pronouncement. "You'll be at the Quality Shoe Mart for the rest of your life."

"I might have been anyway," Lila said. "But if that's the way it works out, I won't mind too much. We aren't planning on babies."

"Babies!" said Hector. "You're too old for that."

"Oh, do you think so?" She slipped on the coat. "Well, anyway, I don't want any. I wouldn't make a good parent and neither would Terrence."

"I can't think of anything Terrence would be good at."

"You aren't fair, Hector. You're rude to him, in fact."

"He asks for rude treatment. He's oily, Lila."

"Oily? What does that mean?"

"Slick," Hector said. "He can't be trusted."

"How do you know?"

"It sticks out all over him."

Lila folded the nightgown and the peignoir and laid them again with the ivory-colored slips in a drawer smelling of lavender leaves she had picked from the garden. "You'd better get used to him. We may live nearby." She hung up the coat. "We could live here if you like."

"Here!" said Hector.

"There's plenty of room. He could help with the vegetables."

Lila went off to take her bath. When she came out after awhile wearing her worn-out robe, Hector was downstairs reading in their father's chair.

Lila hunted up the book she was halfway through and sat down across from him in their mother's chair.

184

"I think you hold it against Terrence that he grew up in a carnival."

Hector breathed through pinched nostrils. One of their rules was that neither of them talked while the other was reading. "I thought it was a circus."

"Oh, maybe it was." Lila leaned forward to do a little house-keeping on one of the ferns banking the fireplace.

"No," she reconsidered, "I think it was a carnival. I remember being surprised that a carnival had a band."

"What does a band have to do with it?"

"Terrence's father directed it."

"Terrence's father sold tickets. You told me that yourself."

Lila explained patiently. "He sold tickets first, while the crowd was coming in. Then he put on his uniform and directed the band." Lila moved around in the chair until her spare frame fit it. "It was interesting really. They played from a collapsible platform set up in the midway to keep things lively. When a crowd feels lively, they spend more money."

Hector said sullenly, "What did Terrence do while the band was playing?"

Lila shrugged. "Lessons, I guess. What other children do." She nibbled her lip. "His mother was the circus seamstress."

"Which was it, for God's sake? A circus or a carnival?"

"There's not much difference, is there? Except for the animals. And the trapeze artists. Terrence sang now and then. Have I told you that?"

"No," Hector said, as if more on the subject was too much to bear.

"One of his songs we used to sing ourselves. You remember it, don't you? It went like this." Lila looked toward the rug where Terrence had thrown out the wet said. " 'She'll be coming a-round the moun-tain when she comes—' " She labored with the melody like a train having trouble going up and down hills. " 'She'll be dri-ving six white hor-ses when she comes—' "

She went through all the verses, the one about killing the red rooster and all the rest, and then she was quiet.

Hector revived slowly. "Terrence sang that? To a crowd who paid money to get on a Ferris wheel?"

Lila shifted her glance to Niagara Falls, confined in a black frame since 1920. "He did very well, I think, standing up singing in front of people who were eating and talking and not paying attention."

She looked again at Hector. "What do you think of when you hear those words?"

"I don't think of anything. They bore me senseless."

"I think of us when we were children. We never had celebrations."

"We were too poor for celebrations," Hector replied. "The whole world was poor."

"The woman in the song wasn't. Or if she was, it didn't matter." Lila's gaze glazed over with dreamy absorption. "She was just jouncing along in that empty wagon, rushing into town, rushing toward excitement."

Hector scowled. "What empty wagon?"

"The one the horses are pulling. Can't you hear it rattling?" She looked brightly at Hector slumped in his chair. "Everything to fill it is waiting ahead. Like in marriage," she said.

He burst out suddenly, "I hate this damned business with Terrence V. Dennis!"

"Yes. Why is that?" She peered at him closely. "Is it because I'm your sister and you feel you ought to protect me? Or because when I'm married you'll be discommoded?"

She blew out her breath in a despairing little puff. "It's both, I suspect—though I've never been sure just how much you care for me."

"What do you mean by that?" Hector asked tensely.

"Oh, it's not your fault. No one in this house was ever demonstrative."

She flung out something else as carelessly as a dropped handkerchief. "Our parents never kissed. Have you thought about that?"

Hector got to his feet. "I'm going to bed."

"Oh, do sit down. You ought not to run off when we're finally getting to something."

186

"Getting to what?"

"To sex," Lila said. "That's why I'm marrying, you know. To experience sex." She watched him sink down again. "Well, haven't you ever wanted to?"

"This is not a topic I care to discuss."

Lila said peevishly, "You didn't shy away from it when you showed me those horses—the ones across the creek that we watched through the fence."

"That was thirty years ago!" Hector said in astonishment.

"I know when it was. I remember everything about it—and it's not a happy prospect, realizing I could go to the grave knowing only about horses."

Hector closed his eyes. "Do I owe all this to a summer cold?"

"Terrence would have come along anyway," Lila said. "He was just slow turning up because of the war." She saw Hector flinch and went on more strongly. "That's something else, Hector. We've tiptoed too long around the war."

"For pity's sake, Lila!"

"You were classified 4-F for a legitimate reason. You aren't a coward who has to slink around ashamed for the rest of your life."

"This is worse than the Johnstown Flood!"

"You're making it worse," Lila told him crossly." But why not, I suppose? Look how we've lived—like two dill pickles shut up in a jar."

Lila brooded with her chin in her hand. "If it hadn't been for Terrence prying the lid off, we might have had a blow-up instead of this civilized conversation."

"Our *life* is civilized because we don't have conversations."

"We're opening locked closets, Hector." Lila gazed dispiritedly at the pale line of his lips. "The trouble is, most of them are empty."

"You can't possibly judge the extent of my experience!"

"When would you have managed any?" Lila asked. "In all your life you've spent three nights away from this house. Two for your tonsils and that one other time when you camped on the river and the bears chased you home."

"It was coyotes, dammit!" Hector leaped from his chair.

187

"You think you know so much. You don't even know that a man and a woman don't necessarily require darkness."

Lila sighed. "If you know it, I know it. We've read the same books."

The following Saturday while Lila was stuffing cabbage for Terrence's dinner, Hector went out in the back garden and ripped up a pear tree. He left a hole the size of an icebox where the roots had been, and green ruined fruit all over the lawn.

"Our tree!" cried Lila when she stepped out at five to pick mint for the tea. "What's the matter with you, Hector? Are you having a breakdown?"

Hector lay on his back, panting like a lizard. "Can't a man hate pears?"

"You never hated them before. What about in pear marmalade?"

"The worst thing in the world is pear marmalade."

The week after that, he took to wearing red socks and calling up girls.

On Saturday evening he sailed through the kitchen at five minutes to five. "Tell Terrence I'm bowling," he said to Lila.

"I will," said Lila, watching him go. "If he happens to ask, that's just what I'll say."

Hector continued his Saturday night absences. Summer wore down and fall came on before he perceived that the situation with Terrence had altered somehow.

The first thing he noticed was Lila going to work in her serviceable coat. Next he was dripped on by an ivory-colored slip drying in the bathroom. Then he spotted the print blouse with the roses on it laid out for pressing.

He said to Lila, "What's happened to Terrence?"

"Nothing that I know of." Lila hummed. She was putting away meat loaf and *au gratin* potatoes with nice little beans out of Hector's garden.

"You're wearing your trousseau."

"Yes," she said. She didn't explain. She went off upstairs and ran enough water to drown a crocodile. When she came down again, she had on her lace nightgown and matching peignoir.

She smiled at Hector, owlish by the fire, and then at the pear logs, smoking and popping. "Have you seen my book?"

"Your book!" said Hector. "I want to hear about Terrence."

"Oh," said Lila. She took her time sitting down in her mother's chair. "He's off in Oklahoma selling Watkins vanilla."

"Since when?" Hector asked.

"Since the last week in August."

"Well, you might have mentioned it!" Hector recalled wrenchingly the Saturday nights wasted eating restaurant stew and hanging around pool halls until the coast was clear. "Is he gone for good?"

"Yes," said Lila.

He could scarcely believe it. Terrence was gone! In deference to Lila in her celebration raiment with nothing to celebrate, he summoned his scowl. "It's too bad," he said. "The dolt threw you over. But of course he would, anybody fool enough to wear tweed in the summer."

Lila cleared her throat lightly. "He didn't read either—only the funnies."

Hector observed her. She was lovely in white—like a slice of angel food cake—and not at all dampened by her sad experience.

"What was the *V* for?" he brought out of nowhere.

"Victor," said Lila. She consulted the ceiling. "Or perhaps it was Vincent. Or Vernon or Virgil."

Hector stared at her, pop-eyed. "You never asked?"

"I intended to once. But he wasn't around."

"Well," said Hector. "It was plain from the start he had nothing to offer."

"Plain to you maybe. You have a man's eye for things." A piece of bright hair tumbled over her shoulder. "To me he seemed interesting. He grew up in a circus."

"In a carnival, Lila."

"Whatever it was, he had a very good childhood. He was out in the world, having adventures."

189

"Now he's selling vanilla. In Oklahoma."

The hall floor creaked. Geese gabbled in the sky.

"I should tell you, Hector." Lila looked toward Niagara in its tame black frame. "Terrence is gone because I asked him to go."

"You ran him off, Lila?" Hector's neck bowed forward. "When you were so bent on marrying him?"

"I was bent on fulfillment."

"It's the same thing, isn't it?"

"It's not the same thing at all."

Hector sat still. Once in a fall on the stairs he was knocked unconscious. The way he felt now, he was just coming to.

"Lila," he said after a suitable pause. "If you've sent Terrence off, you realize, don't you, that you'll have to forget—whatever you hoped for."

"Maybe," said Lila. She twiddled with her hair. "Or maybe I'll find it somewhere else."

The room heaved gently, like the sealed-down crust of a steam-filled pie. "Where?" he said.

"Wherever it is."

She rearranged her white skirts, revealing to Hector's numbed gaze a number of pink toes and pink painted toenails.

"Terrence," he said. "Terrence upset things."

"He did," Lila said as softly and smoothly as if she were slipping on slippers at the Quality Shoe Mart. "But he cleared the air too. We can be grateful for that."

Hector shuddered. "Grateful to Terrence." He had breathed ether once. It was nothing to this.

Finally he said, "It's too late, I suppose, to back up and start over."

Lila smiled on him kindly. "It was too late for that when you hacked down the pear tree."

The Gift Horse's Mouth

"Are those hawks or buzzards?"

"I think, honey," Estelle said, "those are buzzards. Hawks fly alone."

I'm like a hawk, she thought, coming out here on my own. If Ed wants to come down later, fine, we can fly in. But I've had it with Houston, and I'm tired of him talking about nothing but that new building of his. That and that stupid fishing trip he's on in Mexico. So if I feel like getting some peace and quiet in the country with just Barbie, and I feel like driving, why then, that's just what I'll do.

"Rio Ancho thirty-two miles, Jackson's Creek seven," Barbie read.

Estelle thought Barbie had lost her case of the squirms after they had stopped for a hamburger in New Braunfels, but now she was back to reading every sign along the road. She liked best the long, wordy signs for film development, political candidates, and gala country music weekends, which she would try to read completely before the car was past.

Estelle thought again that it was strange to name a town "Rio Ancho" when it was the Sangre River that cut over the limestone along the west side of town before flowing into a broad pool below the plateau on which the town set.

"Welcome to Rio Ancho, Guest Ranch Capital of the World, Enjoy Yourself in the Beautiful Texas Hill Country," Barbie read. As they turned onto the main street, Barbie began reeling off "Circle R Trading Post, Horseshoe Bar, James Kelcy, Attorney at Law, NAPA Auto Parts" until the signs came so quickly she gave up and lapsed into silence.

A pickup truck coming toward them suddenly made a U turn without signaling.

Estelle hit the brakes. Barbie pitched forward but awkwardly braced herself on the dash with her hands. Recovering, Barbie reached across the seat for the horn. Estelle pushed her hand away.

"Stupid old man," Barbie said. "Why don't you honk at him?"

"He may be right," Estelle said. "We're just too used to the big city. We need to calm down a little, get in tune with a slower pace. It's different out here. Besides, I'm kind of used to that. He drives the way my grandfather used to drive."

Estelle had read a condensed version of *Talking to Your Child* in one of her ladies' magazines. She didn't remember the fine points of the article, but she did recall that you don't argue with your child when the child is experiencing emotional difficulties.

"I know you feel frustrated at not being able to honk the horn," Estelle tried, "but we do things differently in the country than we do in town."

The truck turned left, again without signaling.

"He's still a stupid old man."

"I wish you had known my grandfather," Estelle went on.

"Maybe you wouldn't feel that way. Some of the best times of my life were when I'd go visit him and Grandma in the summer. He'd take me with him when he went trading for cattle and horses, and he kept a horse for me to ride." Estelle became a little weepy. "In fact, he was killed driving his cattle truck."

"Ninety-seven," Barbie said, reading the time-temperature sign in front of the bank.

They stopped at the grocery store for supplies. Estelle thought it was silly of the cashier to ask for identification when she had been buying things there for years. Besides that, she was wearing her emerald ring, the big one, which should have been proof to anybody that she wasn't going to write a bad check for a few piddling groceries.

After a stop at Jed's Drive-In where Barbie had her Big Red soda, they went past the Watering Hole, now advertising cocktails, the Cedarcrest Nursing Home, and into the hilly country beyond. The Eldorado swooped across the low-water bridges where families, most of them Mexican, sat on bright-webbed aluminum chairs and splashed in the shallows.

Just as she rounded the bend before their turnoff, she noticed something in the road ahead. She braked and honked. Three buzzards took flight with laborious indignity and glided off to wait in the weeds.

"Gross," Barbie said, looking at the armadillo crushed on the pavement.

Topping a small hill on their road, Estelle saw a truck approaching and pulled over as far as she could. The truck stopped, and both waited for the dust to settle a little before lowering their windows.

"Hello, Mr. Wilson," she began.

"Hello, Mrs. Grady," the rancher returned. He lived on the ranch beyond theirs, and, for the privilege of running some of his cattle on their land, he kept an eye on their place and looked after their horses when they were gone. "Hot enough for you?" he asked.

"Certainly is warm, isn't it?" she replied. "Are the horses down?"

Wilson nodded.

"How are you getting along?" she asked.

"Can't complain," he said.

After a pause, Estelle said, "I guess we'd better be getting along. We'll see you later."

The electric window sealed out the heat and dust, and they eased down the hill. Off to the left, a deer stand stood like a sentinel tower.

The house was hot and stuffy. Estelle opened the windows and started the air conditioner to drive the heat out. She put the groceries away, turned on the water, made the beds, and then closed the windows, resealing the house.

"Well, what do you want to do?" she asked Barbie as she mixed a big pitcher of iced tea.

"I don't know," Barbie said.

"How about going riding?"

The summer before she had been so enthusiastic about riding they had bought her a horse plus a second one so somebody could ride with her.

"It's too hot."

"How about a walk then?"

"It's too hot for that, too."

Having driven the entire morning and then some so they could enjoy the ranch, Estelle was irritated at the nebulous refusal to utilize the opportunities.

"How about a swim? That'll cool you off."

"There're snakes down there."

"I know it's different from swimming in a pool like at home," Estelle said, "but it's very safe. Let's go get our suits on."

"All right," Barbie said and heaved herself off the couch.

They drove the half-mile to the river, the Eldorado bumping over the road, which was little more than two tracks through the grass. One reason Estelle had argued for buying the place was that the river made a big curve as it cut around a bank and provided an ideal swimming hole. Swimming in the clear water, Estelle thought for a moment of shucking her bathing suit. As long as she was out to enjoy nature, why not be totally natural? But then she would have to explain to Barbie why she was running around naked. In the end, she undid the straps on her top when she lay down to soak up the afternoon sun.

As they drove up to the house, she noticed that the horses had come up to the fence. She stopped and they got out to pet them. The bay was the one she usually rode, while Barbie or guests not used to horses rode the old sorrel mare. Both leaned against the fence and stretched out their heads.

Estelle scratched them behind the ears while Barbie climbed onto the top rung of the fence. As Barbie talked "nice horse" language to the animals, Estelle watched a solitary hawk rising above the hilltops in wide circles. She felt cleansed by the river. The warmth of the day radiating from the rocks and earth enveloped her.

She knew how to really enjoy the land, just like that hawk she was watching. Relax and get in tune with what was around you. Don't worry what you look like. Let the days float along. In the house behind her there was no schedule, no calendar crammed with appointments. It was rejuvenating to live without demands, and she always felt more alive and fresh when she returned to Houston.

Barbie's cry jerked her out of her reverie. Barbie looked on the verge of crying and was holding the upper part of her left arm. "She bit me," she said as if a trusted friend had suddenly hit her.

The mare shook her head slowly from side to side as if denying the accusation but, prying Barbie's hand away, Estelle saw the large red area and the imprint of the incisors. It looked as if the mare had twisted her head as she nipped so that the skin was pulled and broken in several spots.

Estelle weighed the seriousness of the wound and decided, "We'd better have the doctor look at it."

Barbie began to cry in earnest. "He'll give me a shot. I know he will."

"He may not. First, let's clean it up."

She drove the fifty yards to the house where she washed the arm and bandaged it to keep Barbie from massaging dirt into it. Estelle kept her bathing suit on but threw a bright patterned shift over it and ran a comb quickly through her hair. Thank goodness for blow-dry haircuts, she thought; otherwise I'd be a fright.

Estelle drove quickly, but as they passed the city limits, the digital clock in the dash indicated that it was well past closing time for offices. The doctor's office was a small brick building off the main street. Thank goodness, she was observant and noticed on an earlier trip or they'd have to drive all over town and really be late. As they arrived, a man in boots and checked, jean-cut slacks was coming down the steps. Estelle rushed up while Barbie climbed out of the car.

"Is the doctor still in?" she asked.

"He just left," the man said. He looked in his mid-fifties, but she really couldn't tell with the brim of his western straw pulled low on his forehead. "What's your problem?"

"A horse bit my little girl."

By this time, Barbie had come up, and the man could see her holding her arm. "Let me see," he said and peeled back the three band-aids Estelle had laid over the bite.

"Better go inside," he said, straightening up.

"But you said the doctor wasn't in," Estelle said.

"He's not," the man said, "but as soon as I unlock the door, he will be."

"Oh," Estelle said, but didn't go any further.

The man looked at her tolerantly. "My medical license is on the wall if you'd like to check it against my driver's license," he said.

Estelle smiled her best smile. "Let's just get Barbie fixed up," she said.

The doctor clumped across the waiting room and down the hall, turning on lights as he went. The floor was linoleum tile throughout with nondescript vinyl couches in the waiting room, above one couch a picture of a huge Santa Gertrudis bull. Estelle thought the office looked more like a veterinarian's than an M.D.'s. Still, if anybody was accustomed to treating horsebites a country doctor would be.

"Next time a horse does that," he said as he let them out, "you bite it right back."

Barbie grinned. She was feeling like a survived martyr with the gleaming bandage on her arm and the doctor's judgment that she didn't need a shot. She had had a tetanus booster a month before as part of her precamp physical. To perk her up further, Estelle took her to the Corral Restaurant to eat chalupas. Barbie ordered a hamburger instead.

After Barbie was asleep, Estelle took a walk. The afternoon had upset her, but the night calmed her once more. She walked toward the road until she was well beyond the circle of light cast by the mercury vapor lamp next to the garage. She could not see another light anywhere. She stood for a while, surveying the isolation, looking at the stars bright in the cloudless, moonless night. A gentle breeze came over the land, scattering the heat of the day. As she returned, skirting the fence, she could hear the horses moving quietly and see their dark shapes outlined against the paler earth.

When she woke the next morning, the sky was cloudless still, the sun harsh and bright. Squinting against the brightness, she stopped beating the eggs for omelets and tried to see what was moving in the pasture with the horses. Something or several somethings were on the ground, but she couldn't see clearly because the fence blocked her view.

She put the bowl down and went outside. Before she reached the fence, she had an idea of what she would see, but she forced herself on anyway. The bay was grazing calmly off to one side while straight ahead three or four black buzzards were walking around the mare stretched on the ground as if they were appraising merchandise.

She stood at the fence debating what to do. She climbed the fence and picked up a rock as she approached the group. The buzzards noted her approach and took to the air in an awkward flapping and fluttering before she was close enough to throw the rock. Once aloft, they glided to landings at a safe distance and turned back to watch.

The mare's eyes were open, her head stretched at the end of her neck as if she were reaching for something. Several flies buzzed around her loose, grizzled lips. Estelle looked at the mare's flanks. They remained sunken. Estelle started to nudge the horse with her foot, but drew back. The animal was clearly and indisputably dead.

Barbie had been watching her from the den. "What's the matter with Bootsie?" she asked as soon as Estelle was inside.

Let's be honest, Estelle thought. "She's dead," she said.

"Serves her right for biting me," Barbie said. "Are those buzzards out there?"

Estelle nodded.

"Gross," Barbie said.

"Let's have some breakfast," Estelle suggested. Whatever the problem, she knew, you do better to face it with a full stomach.

"I don't want any breakfast," Barbie said. "A dead horse and buzzards, super gross!"

Estelle managed to coax Barbie into eating a bowl of Count Chocula cereal. As they got into the car and headed back toward town, Barbie said, "One of them's sitting on top of her. And three others are looking."

Estelle didn't look.

"Office Hours 1:00–5:00," the sign on the doctor's door said. She could have sworn the sign said something else when they were in the day before. Whoever heard of a doctor who didn't have morning office hours? She opted for staying in town rather than driving out to the ranch and back.

A Tab, a Diet Dr. Pepper, a Diet Pepsi, and a pair of shoes she really didn't want later, they returned to the doctor's office. He came in ten minutes late and began working his way through the pile of folders waiting for him.

"My horse died," Estelle told him as soon as he swept into the examining room.

He looked around the room for a brief moment as if he expected to find something lying on the floor.

"I'm sorry to hear that, ma'am," he said, "but I'm not a vet."

"I mean the horse that bit my daughter died."

"I doubt we have anything to worry about," he said. "You told me it was an old mare. Probably just old age. But we still ought to check to make sure nothing's really wrong."

"How do we do that?"

"Pretty simple," the doctor said. "Just cut off its head and take it or send it to the public health labs."

Estelle pictured the decapitated horse lying in the pasture.

"When could you do that?" she asked.

He looked at her as if she had failed to understand what he just said.

"I mean," she said, "you don't do anything in the mornings, do you? Doctors are used to cutting on things." Even thinking about it, she could feel her stomach muscles contract, her throat tighten.

"In the mornings I make rounds of the nursing home and invalids. In the afternoons I have office hours, and in the evenings I drive thirty-five miles to see my patients in the hospital. I don't have time to tend to the people in this town, much less take care of that dead horse. Tell you what, go talk to Clyde Morris. He's the vet. You'll have to see him anyway to get the shipping box and forms. Or hire somebody to do it for you."

At the Rio Ancho Veterinary Clinic Estelle was met by a German Shorthaired Pointer and a twentyish young woman with a child.

"Clyde's out in the field," the woman said after Estelle asked to see the doctor.

Estelle looked around but didn't see anything but live oaks and cedars around the house. Maybe he farmed a little somewhere. "Could you go out in the field and call him?" she asked.

"I mean," the woman said, "he's out making calls. I can try to raise him on the radio."

Estelle and Barbie followed the woman through a back entryway stacked high with cartons of medicine.

"This is Pig Cutter One calling Pig Cutter Two," the woman intoned into the microphone. "Can you read me?"

How quaint, Estelle thought.

After several tries, a man's voice came over the speaker. "I read you. What do you need?"

"Lady here has an emergency."

"Put her on."

Estelle took the microphone gingerly from the woman. Estelle never used the CB her husband gave her for Christmas because she couldn't stand the static.

"Hello," she said.

"This is Morris," the voice came back. "What do you need?"

She wasn't going to make the same mistake with him that she had made with the doctor. "Our horse bit my little girl," she began.

No reply.

"And then the horse died," she added.

"What's the emergency then?" the voice asked.

"The horse might have had something wrong with it."

"If it died, I'd say that was a pretty sure bet."

Estelle thought she heard the wife snicker behind her, but she didn't turn to look.

"But I mean something bad." She could not bring herself to say "rabies."

"If you're worried about it being rabid," the vet said, "fill out the forms and ship the head off to Public Health in San Antonio."

"That's my emergency," Estelle said.

"My wife'll give you the forms and the address."

"But I can't cut off the animal's head."

"Neither can I," the voice said.

"But you're a vet."

"That's right, but I'm a vet with a sow that's ready for a caesarian and a call twenty miles away from a rancher with a sick stud bull. No way I'll be home until after dark. Tomorrow's the same thing. It's no big deal. Just get a sharp knife and have at it."

"But I can't," she protested.

"Try Phil Murphy. He might be willing to do it for you. I have to get back to this pig. I've taken almost too long already."

"Thank you," Estelle said automatically as she handed the microphone back to the wife.

She spent an hour trying to track down Phil Murphy but couldn't find him.

She filled up the car at the filling station she usually patronized, led up to the topic as easily as she could, and asked the owner if he knew anybody who might help her out.

"You do have a problem," he said and called over the boy who worked in the station. In between servicing cars, they conferred for ten minutes, one proposing a name, the other judging the nominee. "I'm sorry," the owner finally reported, "but I can't think of anybody right off who might do that kind of thing."

She stopped at the Watering Hole. She ordered a Coke for Barbie and a light beer for herself. Halfway through the beer she sauntered over to the group of men at a corner table.

They must have been occupying the table for a long time, judging from the piled-up ash trays and how loudly they guffawed at her story of the dead horse.

"Lady," one of them said, "I'd be happy to go out to your place."

"You would?" she said.

"But not for no dead horse."

She stopped short of throwing her beer in his face, whirled, and walked away, feeling their laughter hit her square between the shoulder blades.

On the way home she remembered her neighbor, Mr. Wilson, dependable Mr. Wilson who looked after everything for them.

"He's gone cattle buying," Mrs. Wilson told her. "Making the rounds of the auctions. Won't be back until Thursday."

Dinner was burritoes and canned chili microwaved back to life. Barbie took her plate to the TV and watched a rerun of "Gilligan's Island" while she ate. When she brought her plate back, she asked, "Am I going to die?"

"Of course not," Estelle said. "We just want to check and make sure Bootsie wasn't sick when she died."

"Will I have to get lots of shots?"

Where did she pick up all this business about shots, Estelle wondered. "I don't think so," she said.

Barbie showed instant relief. "What happens to the head when they're through with it?"

"I suppose they dispose of it some way or the other."

Barbie clouded up again.

"It's kind of bad," Estelle comforted, still following the article she had read, "thinking about an old friend like Bootsie dying and being worked on in a laboratory."

"It's not that," Barbie said.

"What is it then?" Estelle asked.

"I wanted to take it to school," Barbie said. "It'd be a lot neater than the bird's nest Billy brought in last week."

Estelle let Barbie stay up late and watch the movie on television to make up for the problems of the day. In bed, Estelle tried reading. The book's cover pictured a young woman in a pale dress fleeing from a decrepit mansion set on the cliff behind her, but the story didn't hold Estelle's attention. She thought of taking a walk to calm herself, but somehow she didn't want to go outside. She went to the bar and mixed a pitcher of martinis.

Halfway through the pitcher, she hit upon a solution. She would think of it just like packing a suitcase. They would get up, eat, pack to go home, she would pack the horse's head, and they would close up the house and leave.

She drifted off to sleep in the recliner chair. She dreamed she was having an affair with a friend of her husband. He took her to a discreetly located hotel with a luxurious decor. At the door to their room he kissed her passionately, then pushed open the door, and swept her inside. In the middle of the king-sized bed was a horse watching Johnny Carson and working a crossword puzzle. "Enjoy your stay," her lover said and left.

She woke up, staggered into the king-sized bed in the master bedroom, and fell asleep.

When she pulled the pillow off her head in the morning, she thought for a moment of ringing for room service instead of going down to breakfast. As the familiar items in the room focused, she remembered where she was. She felt nauseous.

She thought of just leaving, period.

But if anything happened to Barbie, she'd never forgive herself. Her husband would never forgive her. Barbie would never forgive her. Why did that stupid horse have to die?

She showered, dried her hair, and examined her wardrobe, trying to decide what she should wear for cutting off a horse's head. She finally put on a pair of jeans and a bandana blouse.

She did everything neatly and overly precisely. They had breakfast. They packed. She put things in the car.

Opening the knife drawer, she felt like a character in one of her novels presented with a case of dueling pistols and told to choose. Except none of the knives looked very efficient. You would think with all the deer that bunch of boozers slaughtered, they would keep a decent knife in the place, but then they all took their kill to the processing plant in town. The cost made a handy tax write-off since they donated the meat to the children's home outside town. She couldn't find a cord long enough to use the electric carving knife. Even though it didn't feel very sharp, she took the biggest one she could find, a butcher knife. She wanted to sharpen it, but the electric can opener with the sharpening attachment was in town. She put on her sunglasses, picked up the packing box in the garage, and started for the pasture.

It was hot already. Around her she could feel the land reflecting the heat it didn't absorb. The sky was cloudless. In the distance, she could see a hawk riding the air currents between two hills. The buzzards were riding the dead mare. One was perched on her flank while the others hopped off and on her. As Estelle approached, they turned, one by one, to watch her. Only when she was close enough to see their featherless heads in detail did they begin to move sullenly away from the horse. She beat on the box with the knife and shouted to hurry them away. They sailed off a short distance to watch her as if she were auditioning for a part.

The birds had begun working on the mare on the softest part of her body, her anus. They had torn the opening larger and were working down her stomach. Except for her ravished flesh, the mare looked as she had the day before but stiffer, duller. Her lips were pulled back from the yellow teeth, dried as stone. Her eyes were open and staring but covered with dust. Ants marched in and out of her nose.

Estelle thought she was going to pass out. She shut her eyes and gripped her stomach until the feeling passed. On second glance, the mare didn't look quite as bad as she had originally. The details seemed to have more distance to them. Estelle looked at the head where she was supposed to cut.

She couldn't do it.

She opened and shut her eyes several times more. The dead body by itself was not so revolting as the thought of touching it. She bent down and touched the neck and drew back immediately, shivering.

204

She poked the horse's neck again. She shut both eyes and lowered the knife until she felt it touch the horse. She squinted one eye to see where the blade lay.

Keeping her head turned away, she placed the knife behind the curve of the large cheekbone and pulled the knife toward her. Slowly she looked to see the rend in the flesh.

All she could see was a little disturbance in the dust on the horse's neck.

With both eyes open, the pushed the knife back and forth more, bearing down a little. The hair bristled up about the edge of the knife and went flat at one spot. The skin was parting.

She stopped, leaving the knife resting on the horse's neck, and covered her face with her hands.

Where were *they?*

She was not supposed to be out in a rocky pasture, getting her pants filthy dirty, sweating through her blouse, getting sick at her stomach, cutting off the head of a horse that did something as stupid as bite her daughter and then die. She cursed her husband floating around in the Gulf, harassing harmless fish, cursed the kickers in town, cursed the horse, cursed Barbie for being bitten, cursed the buzzards, cursed the pasture, cursed the heat, and cursed the stupid idea of having a place outside town.

She thought about just leaving and just seeing what would happen. But what kind of a mother would she be if she did that?

Holding her stomach with one hand, she started sawing the knife back and forth again.

If she didn't look at the head and the rest of the body, it was kind of like cutting up a big roast. She put both hands on the knife and bore down.

Except that roasts weren't hairy. And roast didn't make the sickening popping sounds that the cartilage in the throat did.

She waited for her stomach to calm down again and attacked furiously. She tired quickly and stopped to catch her breath.

She was almost halfway through, she thought, but she couldn't tell for sure. She stood up to check and noticed that the buzzards had eased closer, like spoiled pets who stop for a moment after a reprimand and then begin again. She shouted at them, threw rocks at them, and drove them back a little farther.

She touched the horse's head with her foot and shoved. It didn't move very far. She felt her leg muscles pull when she shoved it a second time, but the nose moved out, turning the cut from a slit to an open wedge. The ground underneath was stained with blood and fluids. She retched and found her mouth dry. She was afraid if she ever went back into the house, she wouldn't finish the job. She stepped over the neck and resumed cutting.

She worked steadily, brushing the sweat off her forehead with her wrist. It was like stuffing envelopes for the Heart Fund or Muscular Dystrophy or whatever it was she volunteered to work on that year. You were supposed to feel good for helping, for doing your duty, and all it was was boring. Her clothes were already ruined, so she knelt and put her full weight into each downstroke and pulled on the upstrokes.

The knife grated against the neckbones and she stopped. It was like trying to cut a rock. How did she do chicken joints? She either wedged the knife in and twisted or she whammed down with the biggest knife she could find. She tried slipping the knife between two vertebrae but she couldn't force it.

She beat on the vertebrae, both hands on the knife. Meat scraps flew around her. One landed on her forehead, and she wiped it away, almost poking herself in the eye in her haste.

She found that she was crying, kneeling on all fours and crying. Then she was hiccuping and retching, and then she was vomiting coffee, eggs, and English muffins, her throat raw and burning.

She spat out the dregs of breakfast and started back toward the house. She washed her mouth out with the hose at the side of the house and marched into the garage. It took her a moment to find the ax, but when she did she yanked it off the floor and started back outside.

Holding the ax across her chest, she put each foot down as if she were stamping on some vile insect. At the horse's head she didn't think about taking a deep breath but did and brought the ax down with all her strength on the neck. She jerked the ax back up, clumsily, both hands on the end of the handle. She swung it in a wide arc, aimed for the same spot, and stepped sideways to brace herself for the blow. Her foot hit her own vomit, slipped, and she fell headlong across the horse's neck, the ax flying out of her hands.

She jumped up, repulsed. Breathing heavily, she spat the dust out of her mouth. She half-walked, half-ran to the ax, picked it up, and slammed it into the horse's neck as soon as she had her footing. Again and again she put all her force into the blow. Some hit the splintering vertebrae, some hit the flesh, splattering it in chunks. Even after the last white cord in the spine had severed, she continued slamming the axhead into the dirt between the severed head and the neck.

She leaned on the ax, panting, wiping the perspiration from her forehead. She let the ax fall and pulled the box over to the disembodied head still staring at the cloudless sky. She considered the problem for a while, then grabbed an ear in each hand. They were fuzzy and stiff. She heaved. The head was much heavier than she thought it would be. She heaved again, feeling her stomach muscles strain, and lifted the head off the ground. But it wasn't high enough, and she only hit the side of the box, knocking it away.

She heaved a third time, pulling the head up her leg, trying to lift it with her knee. She poised it over the open box and let it drop. She closed the lid and stood up.

She dusted herself off, erasing the line the horse's head had made up her leg. The buzzards had eased closer and stood in an ugly and studious circle around her.

She flung rocks at the birds. She grabbed the ax and ran at them ready to chop off their heads. She raced from one side of the circle to the other, screaming at them. Clumsy and slow as they were, they moved out of range. She threw the ax at one with all her might, but it fell short by a wide margin. She did not bother to retrieve it.

Her back muscles popped as she lifted up the box and started toward the house, staggering from time to time as she stepped on a rock. She put one last effort into the task and worked the box high enough to drop it into the car trunk.

She slammed the lid and sat panting on the bumper. She wiped her brow and flung her hand out, spattering the concrete floor with sweat. When her breathing became more regular, she went inside. She grabbed a can of Pearl Light out of the refrigerator and took a long drink. She shivered with the cold beer and the air-conditioned temperature and told herself she would be better outside until she cooled down.

Sipping the beer, she stood in the shade of the garage, her eyes squinted against the glare, and watched another buzzard glide to a landing in the pasture. She shivered again but not with the cold.

It wasn't pretty, she told herself. The land wasn't the least bit pretty. It was hot and hard and life died on it and was eaten by other life. The land would burn your skin, wrinkle your face, and turn your hands into tools. People out here didn't care any more than they did anywhere else. She could break her leg and nobody would know. The house could burn down and no help could save it.

The only things that made you civilized were flush toilets and electricity. That was all. She followed the power line from the corner of the house until it disappeared in the cedars along the road. That one thin wire was the only thing that made the country livable, cooling the drinks, cooking the food, running the air conditioner, pumping the water.

She saw the wire running on through the cedars to join the other wires along the highway which ran into the co-op electric company. Wires were all along all the highways; they traced and followed all her journeys. They crossed and crowded each other, and she could follow them all the way to Houston, but Houston was nothing more than a bigger tangle of wires.

All along, she had been thinking of going the moment she finished her task. Now she found she wanted to stay. One place was like another. Besides, she had met the country as it was. She had done what needed to be done. Nobody had helped her. Nobody. Not her husband, not her child, not her neighbors, not the people you expected to help you. She was the one who had done the sickening work. Now she wished she had been braver as she did it. Surely she could have kept her stomach if she had tried a little harder.

It would be better to go, though. In another day the corpse would begin to rot and stink. When they returned there would be nothing in the pasture but a heap of bones. She would leave a message for Wilson to take the bay back to his place. Maybe he could drag the body to the far end of the pasture.

She finished the beer but didn't go back in immediately. She heard nothing but the wind in the cedars and liked the sound.

"What did you do with Bootsie's head?" Barbie asked as Estelle passed her on the way to clean up.

"It's in a box in the trunk," she said.

"Gross," Barbie said.

Estelle spun and pointed a finger straight into the child's face. "I am sick and tired of hearing that word! You say it one more time and I'm going to slap your face!"

Barbie didn't say anything else until they were on the other side of Rio Ancho, headed for San Antonio.

"Are we going home?" she asked.

Estelle had thought that after she left the head at the Public Health Offices she would reward herself with a shopping trip. Somehow, that no longer seemed attractive. Spending money was something anybody could do.

"Yes," she said. "We're going back to Houston."

She wasn't sure what she would find once she returned to Houston, but whatever it was, she felt ready for it.

Angels Prostate Fall

All spring and summer Stanley Morris has gone around with odd old tunes in his head that no one else would think of or remember.

Now, in dog day August, it's "Twilight Time" that keeps threading through his mind.

"Heaven-ly da of da da da, it's—twi-light time . . ."

Doodle-de da da da . . . The Platters? The Coasters? The Drifters? Ink Spots? Sun Spots? The Plates? Saucers? The Forks? The Spoons?

Stanley gets in his big old car and drives over to the complex of professional buildings by the hospital off the freeway. With the crazy traffic and drivers in the "metroplex" he would drive a semi cab if he could get away with it. He parks and goes into Building A to get his records from Dr. Fishbein so he can take them over to Dr. Miller in Building C.

Stanley's university is forcing them to choose to give up their old doctors to go on a new medical plan with higher benefits and better coverage. Stanley's old friend and internist Dr. Witherspoon is threatening to retire anyway so he has referred him to young Dr. Whittle. His eye doctor, whom Stanley has seen since the strange incident suffered in the mountains, is off the list anyway, so that leaves just the urological base not covered, so to speak. His old buddy Fishbein is off network too so Witherspoon has recommended Miller.

He has had a long, rich relationship with Fishbein, Stanley thinks as he goes into his office. It's a shame to have to change. Like twenty years. Stanley has called Fishbein jokingly "the Man with the Golden Finger." Actually the jolly little man has a finger of steel. Once, in the midst of a digital rectal exam Fishbein is moved to tell Stanley about his only son, Albert, who has flunked out of med school and is now in the submarine service. Stanley has been to see him just two months ago, so he has no worries on that score. "Smooth as a walnut!" Fishbein has yelled at him in glee. "You sure don't have cancer!"

Da da da—da da da dah—la da de da . . .

"I called for my records in order that I can transfer them to Dr. Miller," he says to the young woman at the desk. She's different from two months ago. Fishbein always seems to have different people out front, as opposed to dear old Witherspoon, whose wife and nurse, who look so much alike they may be sisters, are always sitting in matched chairs smiling placidly at you.

"Mr. Stanley?" she says.

"Mr. Morris," Stanley says.

"Oh. Yeah. That's right. Morris."

"I believe it is."

So much for twenty years.

Humming the Platters or Coasters or Drifters ditty, he walks through the maze of halls and byways between Building A and Building C. He passes nurses and men in white smocks and in green caps and smocks and a lot of people moving slowly along the halls shaking, shambling, being helped, or rolled, shuffling with canes, on crutches, or like himself a month ago with patches or bandages on their eyes.

Dr. Miller's office or the office he seems to share with Drs. Martz and Dong, is not bright and jolly like Fishbein's. It is stark, with just a print or two of hunting dogs and a somber tapestry on the walls. He hands the folder to the woman at the desk. She has very large eyes, like fish that swim in a bowl, behind her thick, magnified glasses. She looks startled to receive such an object as this folder.

"What can we do for you?" she says.

"Oh—Nothing. Right now, I mean. I called. You said—someone did—that you, actually that Dr. Miller, would accept me as a patient. I'm changing medical plans. I am newly on the Uni-Pro Coalition Network. Okay?"

"Mr. Morris?"

"Right," he says. They seem to be able to read the name on a folder.

"Have a seat," she says. "Dr. Miller will want to see you."

"Thanks, but there's no need. I am just delivering the records."

"Have a seat," she says. "I'll tell him. He'll want to see you."

This sounds like an order. He sits.

In a little while she takes him in to an examination room and asks for a urine sample.

"Really," he says. He did not come here today to be examined. It's just been a couple of months. Smooth as a walnut. But he kind of has to go anyway, so he yields on the urine front. A nurse comes and nods at him and collects the cocktail. Then the door opens and a massive, not to say apelike, figure appears. It has a black beard and a thick neck and head and terribly penetrating black eyes and a white coat with *Dr. Miller* written on the pocket. He shifts his feet and seems about to leap up or sideways and holds out his hand.

Stanley takes it. This Miller has a small, strong hand.

"What can we do for you?" he says.

213

Stanley shrugs. He feels small and out of place, as if he is engaged in a bad joke. He knows he is fine. The last thing he desires or needs is an examination. "Nothing," he almost says. "Not a thing. I was just passing by and thought I'd drop the folder off and behold you, and I must say you have surpassed my expectations."

"Really," he says. "Not much. I am just checking in, as a new patient. Thought I'd say howdy."

"Take off your pants and shorts," the doctor orders. "We'll see what's what."

"I just had the old exam," Stanley says. "Not long ago. Dr. Fishbein—"

"You want to be my patient, I'll say what's what. Take 'em down," Miller says, black eyes glinting with a strange obsidian light, cutting to the chase. Stanley sees that he is not the tapestry. That is Martz or Dong. This one is the hunter.

"You bet," he says.

Dutifully he resigns and aligns himself to what the comedians used to call "the fickle finger of fate."

This guy is gentler than Fishbein, anyway.

As Stanley turns around, assembling himself, Miller pulls off the white prophylactic glove with a "pop." His dark doctor eyes hold Stanley.

"I think I felt something," he says.

Stanley stares at him.

This mountebank. Charlatan. Pretending to be a doctor! Jesus! This massive black-eyed demon or fool staring back at him. This incredible trickster. Jokesmith—

"Right on the left edge. Just a—tiny—rough spot."

"That is impossible," Stanley says, but only to himself. "You are wrong. Perhaps demented. You are a demented person, thank you very much, and I am putting on my trousers and buckling up my belt and leaving here in search of a sane doctor. Kidding around is okay, but—Jesus—"

"Miss Hish will make you an appointment for a biopsy," Dr. Miller says. "Then we'll take a look and see what's what."

He extends again his remarkable small, strong hand.

"Pleasure to meet you, sir," he says.

"Oh my," Stanley says.

Back home, air conditioning thrumming in the old house, Stanley tells Olive he may have a little problem.

Her green eyes take on a shade of blue in concern.

"There are all kinds of reasons for a rough spot," he says. "The odds are heavily against it being malignant, or anything like that."

"Did he say so or are you saying so?" she says.

"I'm saying so," says Stanley. "It's ridiculous. The semester is about to begin. I have a full teaching load. I have committee duties. I'm supposed to make a talk to the new students. Housman one more time? I don't have time for foolishness. Art Baker had a biopsy, he said it hurts like hell. They shoot a needle into you. *Ka-ping!*"

"Would you like to be sinful and have a steak tonight?" she says. "A little wine?"

He nods. "And a little Scotch beforehand," he says.

" 'Afore ye go,' " she says.

He shrugs. That's a little more levity than he wishes.

Dr. Miller does the biopsy in his office, with the help of a bland man called Johnny who runs the machine. He laughs that he should be called "Dick" instead of Johnny. "Moby Dick the harpoon guy," he says. Ha ha.

"Moby Dick was the whale, not the harpoon guy," Stanley says. "That was Queequeg."

"Oh no, I wouldn't want to be called that," says Johnny, hands caressing the dials and screens on his smooth machine. Dr. Miller swings in and without a word hurls six consecutive harpoons through Stanley into his target chestnut. Each arrives with a delicious little blossom of pain.

"I'll call you in four days," the doctor says.

"That wasn't bad, was it?" Johnny says.

"How does it work exactly?" says Stanley.

"The needle goes in, makes the hit, and takes a core that comes back out through the needle for the lab. Pretty slick, eh? Couldn't do it this easy just a couple of years ago."

"Hurray for technology," Stanley says, though he feels ambivalent.

All week long, as the campus gears up to begin the term, Stanley goes around consciously humming upbeat old tunes like "Yankee Doodle Dandy" and "Pack Up Your Troubles In Your Old Kit Bag" while "Twilight Time" keeps oozing up from his subconscious.

The earnest, beaming chaplain encounters him on campus and takes Stanley's lapel and leans to confide to him. "You remember," he says, "Jack Bompers? He went on to Virginia?"

"Do I remember him?" Stanley says. "He just left last year, he was our dean, for Christ's sake."

"Has prostate cancer," Chaplain says. "Just found out. Going to have a prostatectomy. I talked with him by phone last night. He is sore afraid but he is coming to terms with his mortality."

"I am very glad," says Stanley.

There are a dozen reasons you can have a rough spot, just a tiny spot, on your chestnut, he thinks. (He has come to think of it as his chestnut since he saw the big color picture of the male and his parts on the wall in Dr. Miller's examination room: the prostate there being characterized as the size of a chestnut. Seeing the picture worried Stanley. The chestnut was up there right in the middle of things, it looked pretty inaccessible, and wired up to all the rest. Oh well.)

Why in the hell didn't Fishbein find it, feel the little lump? No wonder he had gotten to be so jolly, he was getting senile. But Stanley had liked old Fishbein. Every time he'd taken him a book or an article, for Fishbein was a reader and a thinker of sorts, the jolly fellow would stick his head out into the hallway and yell up to the desk, "This one's on the house for Stanley!" You had to love old Fishbein.

In five days the doctor's office calls, Stanley wondering if they had forgotten or lost the cores or what, to say the pathologists in their city can't tell, they disagree over one of the cores, the one right at the left edge that Miller had felt. Can't tell if it's malignant or not. They are sending it on to Mayo's, it will be a few days more.

"They're sending it to Dr. Pfimmelphlammel, or whatever his name is, the nation's most respected and famous and expert pathologist."

"Hey, don't you feel special?" Olive says. "But, really, doesn't that make you feel like it probably isn't?" Her eyes are kind, but there's a lot of blue in them.

Stanley rolls his own brown eyes, one good, one bad. He would like for it to sound encouraging but somehow it really doesn't. It just sounds even more ridiculous, that in this city full of pathologists and labs and medical expertise they have to send his prostate sample to the Mayo Clinic.

Another three days go by and he is still bleeding a little from the Moby Dicking.

When the call comes the nurse says Dr. Miller himself will speak to him.

"It's a malignancy," he says. "Just that one spot. The good news is that it appears to be contained, though we can't be sure it hasn't spread outside the prostate. The bad news, of course, is that you have cancer. It's a Gleasons Five."

Involuntarily Stanley laughs, seeing Jackie Gleason in his mind. Have they named prostate cancers after Jackie Gleason?

"What? Is something funny?" Miller asks.

"Gleason's what?"

"Five. Meaning a mid-level malignancy. Not way up there but requires attention. Yes?"

Yes. Oh yes.

Dr. Miller suggests he come in and talk about it, the alternatives, which seem to be leave it alone, take it out or radiate it. He'll send some information. Stanley says he'll be there, with Mrs. Morris.

* * *

Dr. Miller's private office, as opposed to his stark reception area and sterile examination rooms, is pleasant. Homey. He seems a different man in here. A person.

Retrieving dogs are on the wall. Hunting and fishing magazines are on the coffee table. Stanley's wingback chair is slipcovered in a pattern of muted colors. Olive sits on a smaller chair beside him. Dr. Lester Miller sits behind a small desk wearing small round glasses intensifying the penetrating blackness of his eyes. He rolls a Mont Blanc pen in his small hands.

They talk about it.

It's really pretty simple. If you're fifty or sixty and in good shape, go for the fence, he says, go for the cure. If you're seventy, radiate. Some younger men choose to radiate anyway. It can be as effective. If you're eighty, smile and be glad you just got it, right? It's probably not going to kill you sooner than anything else. Every man gets cancer of the prostate sooner or later.

There are hazards to the surgery or to radiation. The doctor explains them. It's a tricky little operation. Slit you from the belly to the groin. First, you get the lymph nodes in the stomach. If they're okay, go on. Delicado. Take a lot of stuff apart and put it back together. Bleeding is a possibility, so you give two units of your own blood before. God! Suddenly Stanley thinks of Jim Anderson, the anthropologist. Then, if it hasn't spread outside the prostate you can save the veins, maybe avoid impotence. Later, after a successful removal, there can be bad, degrading urinary problems.

"I suppose you have a good success rate with this operation?" Olive says.

The doctor nods, up and down but crossways too. He's honest, not willing to claim perfection. He does it almost every morning, this operation. He always operates with his partner, Dr. Martz. No urological surgeon would ever operate alone.

Reassuring, eh?

So?

"I think I want to go ahead and have it out," says Stanley.

"Think about it," Miller says. But he smiles and nods. This is a good man, he smiles. His smile is warm and wonderful, really reassuring. Go for it, Stanley, babe, it says. How could Stanley have thought he looked apelike? Actually, he resembles Moses.

And now, through the absurdity of it, the feeling that you are witnessing something happening to someone else, Stanley is vaguely glad he wandered in here with his file from old Fishbein.

"I don't think he's all that stern, or forbidding," Olive says, impressed with Dr. Miller. "I think he's very human and answers straight. Professional. Careful to let you know what's what. He spent a lot of time with us."

Da da dah, da da da dah, Stanley hums.

He goes to see his old buddy Doc Witherspoon, the retiring internist. The old doc has toy soldiers on his shelves and desk. Dragoons and lancers and marching Scots in kilts. He is a homeopath by nature, though pretty regular by prescription, basically against surgery.

"You're in good shape. You can stand it. But it's a damn traumatic operation, Stanley. You know—I've got some literature here."

He threshes around and comes up with an article in a medical journal.

"There's good opinion that says just leave it alone. Keep checking it. There are odds it may just stay the way it is."

That might make you a little nervous, Stanley thinks. He has made up his mind.

He gets his affairs in order. He tells his chairman, a few others. He makes a day to day schedule of his teaching and other obligations. He speaks to the incoming students, transfers but mostly freshpersons, on A. E. Housman's *Introductory Lecture.* The only pleasure that does not diminish with fulfillment is learning. "Other desires perish in their gratification, but the desire of knowledge never." He believes this. It goes by them, or over them. In the midst of leaving home and beginning college, in their vitality and gleaming youth, they do not in this moment seem to comprehend this message, or care. In time to come, he thinks, they will.

He talks to Dr. Miller again. Ten years ago, this friend of his, Jim Anderson, died during this same operation, bled to death on the operating table. Miller looks at him darkly. We have improved our techniques greatly in the last decade, he rejoins. But do not ever think I said it is not serious and has no risk.

The operation is set for September 16. Stanley sees in his pocket diary that this is the date of Rosh Hashanah. He thinks of his brother in the East, who has just had his foot removed because of diabetes. Old Barry will think he's trying to upstage him. He asks his grad student Joe Green to take over his writing section while he's out. Joe says he will, though he is just hanging in there, he may leave school and go back to playing music in New Orleans or L.A. This worries Stanley. Surely Joe is meant to be a teacher. He pays all his bills and pre-notifies the medical plan of the operation. He goes to the bank with a signature card so that Olive can get into the strong box should he expire. He knows in his heart that he will live forever but he prepares.

In the blood donor substation in the shopping center he has an eleven o'clock appointment to give blood for himself. He will need to give twice. It's crowded. The woman volunteer at the desk says it'll be a wait of an hour or more. He sits to wait.

An old man starts yelling at a nurse. "I think you are too old to give," she says.

"I'm only eighty-one," he yells.

They take him back to where you give, and in a while they wheel him back out. He has collapsed.

"I told him!" says his wife.

"Mr. Stanley," the woman at the desk calls out.

"Mr. Morris," he says. "Stanley Morris. Just like it says on the form."

A short fellow in a white smock that says *Claude, Blood Specialist* on the front comes shuffling up to the desk. He takes the form with a palsied hand, so the form shakes. He looks at Stanley with an askew, bloodshot eye.

"Mor-ris?" he says. "Morris? That your name? Morris?"

"Yes," Stanley says.

The man, Claude, starts spasming in his side, his arm and shoulder jerk. He slams the form down on the desk.

"Ain't you got no middle initial?" he demands.

"What?" Stanley thinks he must be demented. Must have had a stroke. Doing the best he can. "Oh, yes," he says. "I do. *N.*"

"*N*?"

"Yes, sir. *N.*"

"*N*? *N*?" The man twitches and shakes convulsively. He hands Stanley a ballpoint from his pocket in a quivering hand. "All right! Slide that *N* right in there—"

Stanley bends and slides the *N* in between the *Stanley* and the *Morris* on the form.

"All right," the man says as a convulsion turns him around and he shuffles, or half-topples, into the doorway of the room beyond.

Stanley hears him fall in there. The nurse runs in. They get him on a stretcher. Stanley stands against the wall. The ambulance comes. They take the man away.

"We're closing now. No more blood today," the woman says. They close and lock the door.

"God," he says to Olive. "I thought he'd had a stroke. Dear God, he was having a stroke! And I just stood there. I thought he was demented. While all the time he was doing his duty to the end . . ."

"Don't feel guilty. What could you have done? That's terrible."

But he feels guilty.

"Oh yes—Claude. We buried Claude on Wednesday," says a new woman at the desk when he goes back a few days later to give again. "We'll miss Claude. He'd been here a long time, they tell me."

He goes to have a CAT scan to see if it has spread.

Never having been scanned before—never having been in a hospital since the old appendix at fourteen—Stanley is taken unawares. The portly woman in greens tells him to jump into the machine and lie down. It is a rectangular machine. He takes his shoes off and hops in. Immediately she starts it up and tells him it will take half an hour. Don't move at all or it will have to be done all over again.

He is lying on his back. The machine comes down an inch or so from his nose. He panics, almost screams. Let me out of here! He can't breathe. He has not known what would happen. He has not composed or arranged himself. He needs to crack his arthritic wrist. His head is not on his neck right. He itches. His foot itches, his face itches, his ear itches. His balls itch. He is in a coffin that grinds and moves above and around him. He really is going to scream for them to stop it. He can't lie still in here. He is suffocating. He gasps—

He tries to say the Lord's Prayer but can't remember it. It comes to him disjoint, the pleas seem to have no coherence. The twilight ditty comes floating in, but he can't breathe. He tries to think of poetry. His grandfather could recite Gray's *Elegy in a Country Churchyard* through. "Buffalo Bill's defunct—" No, that won't do. "Let us not to the marriage of true minds admit impediment—" Yes. All right. "Apeneck Sweeney—" Yes. "Mrs. Porter and her daughter wash their feet in soda water—" "Stately, plump Buck Mulligan—" Ah. Ah, hell. An old horror movie, as the mechanism rolls so slowly from the head, so slowly, to the feet, and turns and comes grinding back at you again. Poe. Buried alive. Living death . . .

Finally it stops. He staggers up.

All weekend he is numb, waiting for the result.

It's okay. It hasn't spread to the bones. It's in the chestnut, and we are going to get it.

His daughter and her husband call from New York. Martin's parents are both doctors. All his uncles are doctors. The advice of these experts is don't do the knife, go with cryosurgery. Freeze it. It's the best and coolest method. Freeze that chestnut.

"Freeze it?" Stanley says. "Freeze it? What happens when it thaws?"

On the evening before the operation, drinking the gallon of Golitely, on and off the toilet, Stanley stops himself from going in his study and writing on his desk pad, "It's been wonderful."

He goes out into the big back yard where every spring he plants a garden of tomatoes, squash, cucumbers, beans, and seven kinds of peppers. There used to be, years ago, a colony of bees in the wall of his old house by the chimney. They had to take off the side of the house to get more than a hundred pounds of blackened honey out after an old man came and led the bees away. And still bees love this house, this yard, this place. Every spring, for a day or two, hundreds come down the chimney and lie on the rugs in the living room and den and just quietly lie there and die, and Stanley gently sweeps them up. Now a new hive has come and settled in the honeysuckle on the back of the old garage by where he plants his garden. They fly around his head in slow circles as he digs and waters, picks and prunes. Olive worries about their returning like this. She has visions of their cousins the African killer bees slowly making their way up here from Mexico.

What should he do? Try to get rid of them? Poison the bees? When it gets cold, he'll take the honeysuckle off the back of the garage, and see if—

See if.

In the black early morning, cleaned out and clear as a bell, he goes with Olive and is admitted to the hospital.

He chats with the anesthesiologist, to whom he has lied, saying he has no history of breathing difficulty whereas all through childhood he had asthma. Let's just do it, right? She gives him a little something and says she'll be right here by him.

Drs. Miller and Martz greet him. The old tune now in his mind is a hymn, an oddly humorous hymn. "All hail the power of Jesus' name—Let angels—" Nice play on words, eh? Prostrate/prostate. Ha. Martz is smaller than Miller. He has kind eyes. They wear masks.

"What faith do you have?" Stanley thinks he says.

"Jewish," they say.

Yes. On Rosh Hashanah. What a good conjunction. Stanley smiles up at them, their strong, quick, white-sheathed hands. A new beginning. In a book by a former student on Jewish holy days he has found the prayer they pray this day. He has it in his mind. It is a prayer for healing and for mercy. Drifting really off, Stanley, forcing his eyes to open, looks up and thinks he says the prayer to them, to the doctors.

He does not know if they hear the prayer.

DONNA TRUSSELL

Fishbone

The other girls from Grand Saline's senior class were off at college or working at jobs. Not me. I stayed alone in my room and played The Game of Life. Mama didn't like it.

"Wanda, are you on drugs?" she asked.

I shook my head. I spun the plastic wheel—it made a ratchet sound—and moved the blue car two spaces, up on a hill. The great thing about The Game of Life is all the plastic hills and valleys. No other game has such realism.

"You need a change," Mama said. "You're going to Meemaw's."

My bus was leaving early the next morning, so I had to pack in a hurry. But I took the time to put a matchbook in my purse. I don't smoke, but I thought it might come in handy if I needed to send a message to the bus driver: Hijacker, ninth row, submachine gun under his coat.

The sky was overcast, and it was a slow, pale trip. The only rest stop was in Centerville, where I got a sandwich at the Eat It and Beat It.

Meemaw was waiting for me at the bus station. She smelled like cold cream and lilacs.

Ed was there. He grabbed my suitcase. "Yo," he said.

"Yo," I said back.

On the floor of Ed's pickup was a stack of *Soldier of Fortune*s. I rested my feet on a picture of a tank. Meemaw's life sure had changed since she married Ed.

"My little girl," she said. She patted my knee the way a kid flattens Play-Doh.

"She's not your girl," Ed said. "She's your granddaughter."

"She *is* my little girl."

A chain link fence surrounded Meemaw's garden. "Keeps dogs out," she said. The fence made her farm look even less farmish than it used to, with its green shack for a barn and refrigerator toppled on its side out back and Meemaw's giant new house modeled on the governor's mansion.

She fussed over me at supper: Wanda, can I get you more roast, would you like another helping of butter beans, how about some corn bread?

Ed had three cups of coffee. He poured the coffee into his saucer and blew on it. I asked him why he drank his coffee that way. He didn't answer. Finally Meemaw said, "To cool it down."

Ed's cup and saucer were monogrammed in gold. My plate too.

"Meemaw, where's your dishes?" I asked. "The ones with purple ribbons and grapes?"

"Well, we have Ed's china now."

He slurped his coffee, staring straight ahead. He might as well have been talking to the curtains when he said, "I'm glad you're here, Wanda, because I've been wanting to ask you something. I've been wondering—who paid the hospital when you had that baby? The taxpayers?"

I smashed a butter bean with my fork. "Excuse me," I said and went outside.

I looked out across the pine trees, dark green. In my book *Myths and Enchanted Tales* trees had people inside them. I wished some God would change me into a tree. That wouldn't be a bad life—sun, rain, birds. Kids looking for pine cones. Me shaking my branches.

The peat moss in the garden was warm. I lay down and pulled a watermelon close.

Meemaw came out and sat down near my head, in the snapdragons and cucumbers. Meemaw planted vegetables and flowers together. Except for the gladiolus, off by itself. Pink, peach, yellow, white—a thousand baby shoes shifting in the wind.

She smoothed my hair.

"Meemaw, what happened to your strawberries?"

"Birds," she said. "But that's all right. Plenty for the birds too."

Every morning we went to the garden. We pulled weeds while Meemaw told me how important exercise was. Or she told me uplifting stories about people she knew. Struggles they'd had. A young man wanted to commit suicide because law school was so hard. Once a week his mother wrote him letters full of encouraging words.

"What encouraging words?"

"Oh, 'don't give up.' That sort of thing."

When the man finally graduated he found out his mother had been dead for a month. She'd known she was dying, and had written the last letters ahead of time.

Meemaw had lots of stories about people who "took the path of least resistance" and ended up sick or poor. I got back at her by asking personal questions.

"Meemaw, have you ever had an orgasm?"

Yes, she said. Once. "I was glad to know what it is that motivates so much of human behavior." She smiled and handed me a bunch of glads.

Afternoons I stayed in my room. Mama wouldn't let me bring The Game of Life. I stretched out on the bed a lot. The light fixture on the ceiling had leaves and berries molded in the glass. One time I wrapped my arms around the chest of drawers and put my head down on the cool marble top.

Meemaw would call me to supper. There wasn't much discussion at the table. If anyone said anything, it was Ed talking to Meemaw or Meemaw talking to me. Except for once, when I went to the stove to get some salt. Ed told me I'd done it all wrong. "You don't bring the *plate* to the salt. You bring the *salt* to the plate."

After supper Meemaw and I walked to the barn. She milked Sissy and I fed the chickens. I'd throw a handful of feed and they'd move in at eighty miles an hour.

Ed never came with us. He hates Sissy, Meemaw said. "He's jealous."

"Jealous of a cow?"

"Why of course. I spend so much of my time with her."

Evenings Ed watched *Walking Tall* on his VCR. Or he went inside his toolshed. He never worked on anything. He looked at catalogs and ordered tools, and when they came he hung them on the walls. He read books about the end of the world. The whole state of Colorado will turn into Jell-O, and people will drown. "You've got five years to live, young lady," he said. "*Five years.*"

He kept his guns in his study. A whole caseful. He polished them all the time.

"What are you looking at?" he asked me.

I walked away. He shut the door.

One day when I was watching Meemaw through a little diamond made of my thumbs and two fingers, Ed asked, "You planning on sitting on your butt all summer?"

"I haven't thought about it."

"Well, start thinking."

Meemaw knew a man in town who was looking for help. She knew everybody in town.

"It's a photography studio," Meemaw said.

"I don't know anything about photography."

"He's willing to train. It's a nice place. There's another studio in town, but people say it's Lamont's that puts on the finishing touch."

She made the phone call. Ed was smiling behind his newspaper. I *knew* he was.

Ed showed me all the things I had to do to Meemaw's Ford Falcon if I was going to drive it, because "service stations don't do a goddam thing anymore." He told me to check the oil about ten times a day, and never, never, *never* drive the car without washing the tires first. "Ozone," he said. "Ozone layer."

I washed the tires and drove to Lamont's Studio.

Mr. Lamont wore horn-rimmed glasses and a pair of green polyester pants that were stretched about as far as they could go.

"Wanda, you put here that your last job was back in December. What you been doing since then?"

"Nothing."

"Nothing?"

"Nothing you'd wanna know about."

"But I *do* want to know."

"OK. I was in love with this guy. We were going to get married, but then we didn't. Then I had a baby boy."

"Oh."

"He's been adopted."

Mr. Lamont tried to act natural. He looked down at his desk and poked his index finger with a clear plastic letter opener. Inside was a four-leaf clover, frozen forever. Millions of years from now aliens might dig up that letter opener. Some alien might write a term paper on what the clover means. Luck, I thought, as hard as I could, in case aliens can read the minds of people who used to be alive. *It means good luck.*

"I can't pay minimum wage," Mr. Lamont said.

"Whatever." Might as well be here, I decided, as out on the farm with Ed.

After supper Ed gave me a lecture about jobs and responsibility and attitude. People don't think, they just don't *think*. World War III is coming, and no one's prepared. All the goddam niggers will try to steal their chickens.

"But I'm ready for them," he said. "I've been stocking up on hollow points. They blow a hole as big as a barrel."

He punched his fist in the air. Meemaw jumped, but didn't say anything. She clanked the dishes and hummed "Rock of Ages" a little louder.

I went to bed with the pamphlet Mr. Lamont gave me, *The Fine Art of Printing Black and White*. The paper is very sensitive, it said.

The next day Mr. Lamont showed me the safelight switch. "See that gouge? I did that so I could feel for it in the dark."

"Why not just feel for the switch?"

He shook his head and laughed. "You're trouble," he said. "Now I have to patch that hole."

Mr. Lamont made a test strip. "Agitate every few seconds," he said, rocking the developer tray.

He let me print a picture of a kid holding a trophy. "Next time, make it light and flat," he said. "The newspaper adds contrast. See how this one came out?" He pointed to a clipping of a bunch of Shriners. They looked like they had some kind of skin disease.

After a week I got the hang of it, and Mr. Lamont left me in charge of black and white. I liked the darkroom. No phones. No people, except for the faces that slowly developed before me. Women and their fiances. Sometimes the man stood behind the woman and put his arms around her waist.

Jimmy used to do that.

Jimmy and I went to the senior picnic together. It was windy. Big rocks pinned down the corners of each tablecloth. Blue gingham. The white tablecloths had to be returned because the principal thought they'd remind students of bedsheets. Jimmy and I laughed. We'd been making love for weeks. We got careless in the tall grasses by Lake Tawakoni. Night birds called across the water.

When I was two weeks late, I told Jimmy. He looked away. There's a clinic, he said, in Dallas. I covered his lips with my fingers.

At the auto parts store they said they'd take him on, weekends and nights. At the Sonic too, for the lunch shift. Jimmy and I looked at an apartment north of town on Burning Tree Drive. A one-bedroom. He stared at the ceiling. Jimmy? I said.

Goodbye, goodbye, I told the mirror, long before I really said it.

I read every book I could find about babies and their tadpole bodies. I gave up Pepsi and barbecue potato chips. I felt great. Hormones, the doctor said.

At first my baby was just a rose petal, sleeping, floating. At eight months I played him music, Mama's *South Pacific* and Daddy's bagpipe music. I stood right next to the speakers, and my baby talked to me with thumps of his feet.

You want to feel him kick? I asked. Mama shook her head and kept on ironing. Daddy left the room.

I didn't get a baby shower. Mama told everyone I was putting it up for adoption. "It," she called him. I made up different names for him. Fishbone, one week. Logarithm, the next.

Mama bought me a thin gold wedding band to wear to the hospital. Girls don't do that anymore, I told her. Some girls even keep their babies.

Not here in Grand Saline, she said. Not girls from good families.

My little Fishbone got so big that two nurses had to put their hands on my stomach to help push him out. Breathe, they said, pant. Now push.

Please let me hold him, I said. *Please.*

Now, Wanda, Mama said. You know what's best.

He cried. Then he slipped away, down the hall. The room caved in on me, with its green walls and white light. Mama held me down, saying, we've been through this. We decided.

At the nurse's station Jimmy left me a get-well card. Good luck, he wrote. That's all.

Mama took me home to a chocolate cake, and we never talked about Fishbone again. She never mentioned Jimmy's name.

Now, before driving home to Meemaw's house, I always stopped for a minute at the trailer court on the edge of town. I watched people. A woman would frown and I'd think, that's me, heating up a bottle for Fishbone and the formula got too hot. A man would take off his cowboy boots and prop his feet on the coffee table. A woman would tuck herself next to him. He'd kiss her hair, her neck.

I remembered love.

Now I felt thick and dull, something to be tossed away in the garage.

"How's the passport picture coming?" Mr. Lamont said, knocking on my door.

"Don't come in. Paper exposed."

"The man going to Morocco is back."

The man was worried about his eyes. I've got what they call raccoon eyes, he'd said. Can you can lighten it up around the eyes?

He was disappointed when I gave him the picture. "I know you did the best you could," he said. He smiled. He didn't look so much like a criminal when he smiled.

At home I found Meemaw cutting up chicken wire and putting it over holes in the chicken coop. Making it "snake proof," she said. I took over the cutting. I'd never used wire cutters before. Everything is just paper in their path.

"It looks so bare in the chicken coop," I said. "Why don't you put down an old blanket or something?"

"You know, I did that very thing when I had a batch of baby chicks. I put down a carpet scrap, so they'd be warm. And they died. Every single one! I was heartbroken. You know what I found out? They'd eaten the carpet."

"How'd you find that out?"

"I did an autopsy."

"Ooooooo Meemaw! I can't believe you did that. That's awful."

She shrugged. "I wanted to know."

"I could never be a doctor," I said.

I read somewhere that these psychologists asked some surgeons why they became doctors, and they all said they wanted to help people. Then the psychologists tested the surgeons and found out they were sadists. They like knives.

"How about photography?" Meemaw said. "I hear they teach it in college now. I would pay for you to go."

I rolled up the leftover chicken wire and put it away. "Almost time to milk Sissy," I said. I went to get the milk pail.

"Wanda, wait. Tell me what you want to do with your life."

"You promised not to ask me that anymore."

She laughed and patted me on the back. "Yes, I did." She set the pail under Sissy, and then turned to face me again. "But what *are* you going to do?"

"I don't know, Meemaw."

Lately I'd been thinking about the homeless on TV. I live in the gutter, I could say. It has a nice ring to it.

"Wanda, I once read a book that began with a quote from the Bible. It's the most beautiful of any Bible verse I've ever read. It says, 'The Lord will restore unto you the years the locusts have eaten.'"

She waved her arms. "Isn't that *beautiful?*"

"Uh huh."

The barn door swung open. Ed.

"How many times do I have to tell you not to leave the wheelbarrow out? It's been sitting in the garden since this morning."

"I told her it was OK," Meemaw said. "It doesn't hurt anything."

"The hell it doesn't. If you leave it out, it rusts. If it rusts, you have to buy a new one."

"I don't think it'll rust for ten years at least," Meemaw said.

"Either you use tools or they use you. That's all I have to say about it." He stomped off.

Meemaw rubbed my arm. "Don't worry about it. Ed's upset because yesterday you left his mail in the car instead of bringing it in to him. He's afraid somebody could have stolen his pension check."

"Who'd steal it out here in the middle of nowhere? Who'd even know it was there?"

Meemaw shook her head and went back to milking Sissy. I always thought milking a cow would be fun, till I tried it. The milk comes out in streams the size of dental floss. It takes forever.

"You know how Ed is," Meemaw said.

"Yeah, I know. Why did you marry him, anyway?"

"He needed me."

"But why not marry someone you needed?"

"I don't need anybody. I just need to be needed. They say money is the root of all evil, but I say selfishness is. Selfishness and lack of exercise."

That got her started.

"Sweetie," she said, "I once read about a mental hospital for rich movie stars. It costs a powerful lot of money to go there. And you know what the doctors make those rich ladies do? Run in circles. That's right! Why, one movie star had to cut wood for two hours."

I thought about that, but I just couldn't see how cutting wood could make a difference.

That night I wrote Jimmy a letter: "I hope you like it at college. Do you ever think about our baby? Whenever I take a shower, I think I hear him crying. Do you have this problem too?" I signed it, your friend, Wanda. I sent the letter in care of his parents.

"Let sleeping dogs lie," Mama wrote me. "Think of the future. Pastor Dobbins will be needing a new receptionist soon, and he's willing to interview you. It's very big of him, considering."

I dropped the letter in the pigpen. The next day I could only see one corner, and after that it was gone.

I did pictures of Dwayne Zook, his sister Tracy Zook, and then I was done with the high school annual. Mr. Lamont asked me to sit at the front desk to answer the phone and give people their proofs.

"Lovely," they'd say. Or, "Your boss surely does a fine job." No matter what they said, I was supposed to reply: He had a lot to work with. There was this one girl, though, who looked like Ted Koppel. I didn't know what to say to her.

We had a lot of brides. I patted their faces dry and gave them crushed ice to eat. I spread their dresses in perfect circles around their feet.

One day Mr. Lamont asked if I'd like to go into the other darkroom to see how he did color.

"It looks like pink," he said, "but we call it magenta."

He held up another filter. "What would you call that?"

"Turquoise?"

"Cyan," he said.

"Sigh-ann."

He let me do one, a boy sitting with his mother on the grass. The picture turned out too yellow, so I did another.

"Perfect," he said. "You learn quick."

We goofed off the rest of the day. He showed me some wedding pictures that were never picked up. "A shame," he said. "That's the best shot of the getaway car I've ever done."

He'd go to Food Heaven to get lunch for both of us. We ate Crescent City Melts and talked. He asked if it was true that Ed got kicked in the head by a mule when he was a kid.

"Does he really have two Cadillacs?"

"Three. They just sit out back, rusting. He drives his pickup everywhere."

Sometimes Mr. Lamont came into my darkroom. He'd check on my supply of stop bath or paper. Then he'd lean in the corner and watch me work. He never touched me. We'd just stand there in the cool darkness.

He told me about his mother and why he couldn't leave her. "Cataracts," he said. "I read to her."

I told him about the book I got at the library, *The Songwriter's Book of Rhymes.* Also-ran rhymes with Peter Pan, Marianne, caravan, Yucatan, lumberman and about two hundred other words.

In Meemaw's attic I found an old textbook. Nebraska had tiny bundles of wheat in one corner. New Mexico was full of Indian headdresses. One night I dreamed I was high above Texas, watching the whole pink state come alive. Fish flopped high in the air. Oil wells gushed. Little men in hard hats danced around.

"I don't want to go to college," I told Meemaw the next morning. "I want to buy a car and drive to west Texas. Or maybe California."

"You can't do that," Meemaw said. "A young girl, alone."

"Why not?"

"It's just not done."

"Then why can't I be the first to do it?"

"Oh Wanda."

Meemaw believes in Good and Evil. She doesn't understand how lonely people are. Anyone who tried to hurt me, I'd talk to him. I'd listen to his tales of old hotels and wide-hipped women who left him.

On my 77th day at Meemaw's I came home and found Ed filling up the lawn mower.

"It's time you earned your keep," he said.

"What about supper?"

"Forget supper. You're going to mow the lawn."

"Is that so?"

"Yes ma'am, you betcha that's so." He sat down on a lawn chair. "Get started."

A vat of green Jell-O swallowed him up, chair and all.

I thought of another death for him—a giant cheese grater with arms and legs. Ed ran and ran, and then stumbled. The cheese grater stood over him and laughed as Ed tried to crawl away.

I didn't get to the big finale because the lawn mower made a crunching sound and stopped. Ed came running over, asking how come I didn't comb the yard first, how come I can't do anything right? "You're as lazy as a Mexican cat."

His red, puffy face pushed into mine. In the folds of his skin I could see the luxury Meemaw had given him—her flowers and food and love. He just lapped it up.

He followed me into the house. Young people! Welfare! Good-for-nothings!

"You're a fine one to talk," I said, turning to face him. "I've never seen you lift a finger around here."

He moved towards me, and then stopped. His eyelids quivered. I could hear the hands on the clock move.

"You ungrateful bitch," he said. "Your grandmother thinks you're different, but I told her. I told her what you are."

It got dark while he told me what I was. He must have been rehearsing. He used words I'm sure he got out of the dictionary.

Meemaw twirled yarn and cried.

Ed walked down the hall. He came back with my suitcases and threw them at my feet.

"Get out! Now." He turned to Meemaw. "If she's here when I get back, I'll send for my things."

He slammed the door. His truck roared out, spitting gravel into the night.

"He's a child," Meemaw said. "A grown-up child, and I can't do a thing about it." She held my face in her hands. "My little girl. My sweetie. What are we going to do?"

She put my head on her shoulder. We stood there, rocking.

"I named my baby Fishbone," I said. "Did I tell you that?" She shushed me and patted my back.

He'd be seven months old now. In twenty years he'll come looking for me. We'll have iced tea and wonder how to act. I wanted you, I'll tell him, but I was young. I didn't know I was strong.

"There's a bus to Grand Saline in the morning," Meemaw said. "I'll call your mother."

We rode a taxi into town. Meemaw got me a room at the motel. She brushed my hair and put me in bed.

"You can go home now, Meemaw."

"Yes, I suppose I can."

She wouldn't leave until I pretended I was asleep. But I couldn't sleep one bit. I found a *Weekly World News* under the bed and read every story in it. Then I read the ads, about releasing the secret power within you and true ranches for sale and the Laffs Ahoy Klown Kollege in Daytona Beach.

At five in the morning I went for a walk. The air was cool and clear as October.

Waffle Emporium was open. Something about dawn at a coffee shop gets to me. Pink tabletops and people too sleepy to talk. New things around the corner. Carlsbad Caverns. White Sands.

I thought about what to do next. I had six hundred dollars in my shoes. I could go anywhere. San Francisco, to work at the Believe It or Not Museum. Or Miami—I could take care of dolphins. I thought about Indian reservations. Gas stations in the desert. Snake farms. The owner would be named Chuck, probably, or Buzz.

I walked to the bus station and read the destination board. I said each city twice, to see how it felt on my tongue.

MILES WILSON

On Tour with Max

We're heading west, somewhere near the Texas/New Mexico line, driving from Canyon to Socorro. Max is in the back seat drinking Shiner Beer and hiccuping. He has been complaining about his rough handling in the question-and-answer session after last night's reading. The girl didn't look like the sort who would mix it up in public, although you really can't tell anymore, but she knew Max's early poetry a lot better than he did and was grimly partisan about its bald misogyny. When Max tried to jolly her out of a scrap, she creamed him, and the local faculty host had to step in flapping it all away and inviting everybody to the reception. Max drank and sulked his way through the party, but I got him back to the motel before any serious damage was done.

We're on our way to New Mexico Tech because Max's last live-in was a grant writer and twenty-five years ago Maximilian Pfluger was a big item in American poetry. John Ciardi called him a "pivotal countermotion in American letters." Max's friend parlayed this history into a National Endowment grant for a reading tour. Why I'm here is that the grant has a gimmick designed to give a younger poet some exposure while the colleges take an old gray reputation to the bank. Happily for Max, most faculty members apparently don't read once they leave graduate school, so reputations on the circuit lag a generation or so.

Unofficially, I'm expected to keep Max mostly in line: colorful, but on time for the next reading. Before I signed on, an NEA staffer sized me up over lunch, pointing out that NEA didn't need any bad press in this political climate and that the organization would certainly want to review my own grant needs following a successful tour.

As it turns out, keeping Max in line hasn't really been much of a chore. He is generally no worse than cranky, and when he drinks too much he tends to get sullen or sleepy instead of outrageously memorable. Still, I've had to behave more responsibly than suits me.

So instead of a one-trick pony, we give the schools a dog and pony show. Most nights, though, Max is the dog. Max fancies himself a good reader, but he is mainly loud. His gestures are all choreographed and his inter-poem patter was scripted in about 1958 and hasn't changed since as far as I can tell. He still makes jokes about the Beats. There are probably literary antecedents for our act, but I don't really think I want to inquire too closely.

Although I'm the warm-up act, I usually draw a better reception. Max doesn't mind. He's getting some attention for a change, the booze is mostly free, and he's even finagled a couple of coeds into the sack. He also wets a line at every school for a visiting writer job. Some of these places are odd enough that he just might land one.

The tour is supposed to last four months and take in Texas, Oklahoma, New Mexico, Utah, Colorado, Wyoming, and Nevada. There must be two hundred schools in Texas alone, counting junior colleges, and it feels like we've hit most of them.

The National Endowment deal doesn't require matching funds, so even places who've never seen a live poet order us up like examination copies of a textbook they have no intention of ever using.

Max also bootlegs a few extra readings on the side to supplement the NEA money. Mostly, though, he doesn't have the stamina to be much of a hustler so he settles for what's at hand, which is me. NEA wires us each a check every two weeks and Max is already into me for $800 I'll never see again. This is more or less OK because Max claims to have assurances that he is next in line to judge the Walt Whitman competition, although he has the decency not to remind me of this as he consummates another loan. He may be lying, but I can't take the chance that he isn't. A WW would jump-start my career which keeps refusing to turn over, starter grinding away while my battery goes on losing juice.

Max is done with the Shiner and on into a bottle of Wild Turkey that he lifted from the reception. I've tried to broaden his range of chemicals but he is unreconstructible: "Whatever killed Berryman and Thomas is good enough for me."

It's only April, but already the road feels like a strip of bacon under the sun and I know how much I wouldn't want to be here when summer really gets down to business. And I think about all those schools. Make no mistake: this is the satellite circuit, not the main tour. We do not stop at Southern Methodist or Boulder or the universities of Texas or Oklahoma. We read at colleges where the faculty mournfully says, "This isn't the end of the world, but you can see it from here." Places nobody but William Stafford goes.

At most of these schools, there's an MFA from somewhere sunk up to his axles in freshman essays. They press sheaves of poems on me, asking if I'll intercede with Max on their behalf. Nobody seems to get an MFA in fiction writing anymore.

I don't tell them that Max pretends to read only the work of attractive women and that he has trouble getting his own stuff published these days. All the old editors are dropping off; the only automatic Max has left is *The Norton Anthology* which is not a bad gimme at that. He stays in year after year because he's got something on one of the editors from graduate school days—some irregularity with sources in his dissertation, as far as I can gather.

Mostly, though, Max is out of touch in the poetry biz: he thinks Galway Kinnell is still a comer. So I read their poems. They're usually pretty competent and they all sound alike, as though they were written by sleepwalkers with elaborate sensibilities. They remind me of my own poems; we're all slicing up the same pie. Which is why each first book must be hailed as the appearance of a distinctive new voice. These are the manuscripts that Yale and Wesleyan and Pittsburgh will not be publishing. After a while, the poets will give up or publish at some dinky press with the half-life of a subatomic particle and be tenured or not be tenured. Some of them already divine this and are a little brittle with visiting writers and their preferments.

Everywhere, though, you see them being buffed by thousands of freshman papers, worn smooth by the handling of chairmen and deans until there are no rough spots for a poem to stick to. At a party, a drunk and funny MFA from Cal Irvine—a lopsided man who had just switched from the raw, Third World witness poem to the somnambular lyric in hopes of publishing in *College English,* the benchmark of contemporary verse for his chairman—told me that he often thought of his senior colleagues as occupying the rocking chairs of literature while he and his like held the folding chairs of literature. There are a lot of decent, desperate people dying out there in the polar reaches of academe.

This is too depressing to dwell on, so I try as I can to make little notches in the academic conveyor belt. I tell one chairman that the best journals are now publishing so much haiku that the Academy of American Poets has lobbied for Congress to put import quotas on Japanese verse just as it did on Toyotas. At another school, I lament to the student paper our shocking neglect of muscularity in American poetry and reveal my plans for a publishing venture to redress that disregard: The Bench Press. At a college in eastern Colorado, I whittle a bit on a dean who read three Edna St. Vincent Millay poems by way of introducing me on a night when Max's aesthetic digestion gave out and I had to solo. The next morning before we left, I bought mauve ink and rose paper at the college bookstore and in my best imitation of a woman's hand wrote "Flee, all is discovered." I tucked the flap into the envelope without sealing it and put it in campus mail for the dean. And so on. Nothing really outrageous, just little nicks here and there, a gesture.

The Wild Turkey has made Max nostalgic. He remembers fondly his role in making American poetry safe from Eliot. He has chronicled these campaigns before, but it comes out different every time he repeats himself.

"We were just routing the last of the footnoters at Princeton when Bill Empson turned up on a panel and had me hanging on at the bell. But Doc Williams was working my corner that night as cut man; he patched me up and I got back after it in the next round. Even *Partisan Review* gave me the decision."

From the poetry wars of the fifties, Max moves on to literary slugfests in other venues. Though he now sags considerably, Max once fancied himself a brawler. Edmund Wilson wrote in his memoirs that Max had the sneakiest left hook in American letters. Max's history in the ring is checkered, to be sure, but he's enjoyed some notable successes. He KO'd Alan Dugan twice and Delmore Schwartz once, and it took Mailer a combination followed by a shove to put Max down. He threw James Dickey into a briar patch in Tuscaloosa and once decked Dylan Thomas unfairly when Max was young and Thomas was drunk. Later, though, he loaned Thomas money. Now Max laments that nobody cares enough about poetry to get into fights about it anymore.

Max rouses himself from the legendary past to ask where we're heading. He is apprehensive to learn that we have entered

New Mexico. One of his former wives may be living in Santa Fe and there's apparently a matter of some delinquent alimony. He worries that she might somehow conspire to seize his earnings the way the IRS used to grab Sonny Liston's purse after every bout.

But mostly he's sorry to be leaving Texas and its petrodollars behind. Don't believe those twangy howls about the price of oil. The colleges are still awash in it like academic sheikdoms. The faculty looks as scruffy as anywhere else, but the schools are outfitting themselves handsomely. They move up a notch in NCAA football classification, they endow a chair in petroleum engineering or laissez-faire, and they amass a phalanx of new vice-presidents. They also throw elaborate receptions for itinerant poets. Max has fattened on Texas.

I figure it's going to be early evening before we make Socorro. Max's bladder is not what it used to be and we have to stop every fifty miles or so. Max has a quaint sort of modesty and always squeezes through the fence to find some kind of scrub cover. I'm not entirely sure how I feel about Max, but when I see him there hunched forward pissing into the wind and distance of New Mexico, I feel a tenderness towards him that takes me by surprise.

But sentimentality is a quick ride and we're not down the road too far before I'm filling time by erecting headlines for the tour: "Pfluger Flops in Fort Collins: Max No Factor on Poetry Scene"; "Poet Pukes at Podium: Grody to the Max." Headlines don't have much staying power either so I start doodling with dialogue. I've been thinking about trying my hand at fiction after the tour. A guy I knew in grad school is a junior editor at Simon and Schuster which ought to give me a leg up. Anyway, it's fun to fool around with stuff I'll never get into my poetry. Usually, it goes something like this.

"When Meryl Streep takes off her clothes it's art. When I take off mine, it's $300 or thirty days."

"Your tits are prurient. Hers look like two big bowls of Wheaties or something. Besides, you didn't go to Yale."

"How do you know where she went to school?"

"I saw it in *Parade Magazine.*"

"You said you didn't read anymore."

I try to make up lines that have some ginger to them; if you can write snappy dialogue, there's no telling how far you can go.

Pretty soon it's late afternoon and the sun is going down like a slug of hot lead. We're still a hundred miles or so from Socorro and I'm getting hungry, so when we top out a long rise I'm glad to see a sign inviting us to stop at Ryan's Crossing.

Ryan's Crossing turns out to have all the comforts of home. Besides a cafe, there's a bar, general store, post office, and TV satellite receiver franchise all in roughly two and a half buildings. I gas up the Hertz while Max goes on inside. When I'm done, I park the car around the side where the pickups are. As I walk out front, I can see another truck maybe five miles out, busting its springs down a dirt road heading in, a long shroud of dust in its wake.

Max is sitting expansively at the one table that's right in the middle of things. I figure it's OK since the place is mostly empty and we'll be long gone before the Friday night crowd arrives. Max's bar etiquette is not all it should be, and he's not quite enough of a relic to get away with some of the stunts he pulls. But his luck is generally good, he's got a quick tongue in a pinch, and so far I've managed to bundle him out the door the two times when luck and wit were clearly not going to forestall mayhem.

Although the sign over the bar reads "This Property Insured by Smith & Wesson," Ryan's Crossing is pretty genial. The chili is great and the bar whiskey is cheap. There's not a video game in sight and the jukebox has some old tunes that Max plays over and over. Before I know it we're both looped and the place is full of cowboys, maybe twenty or so, all in hats they don't take off and two or three of them with women. My automatic warning light goes on, but the whiskey keeps shorting it out and I finally switch to manual override. On the one hand, no one's talked to us which is not a good sign, but Max has no contention in him tonight and the bartender, clearly a veteran and therefore a finely tuned barometer of trouble, seems not the least uneasy.

So I'm not ready for it at all when I come out of the john and see three guys around Max at our table. The rest of the bar is quiet so I can tell right away that this is not a friendly get-together. I check the bartender, but he's going to let it happen. Max has just finished saying something, but his back is to me and I can't make it out. The cowboy across the table from him lets out a sort of laugh that seems to narrow his face.

"A poet? Well, tell you what. I never heard a real poet say a poem out loud."

"Careful, Tommy, them poets is all queers. He might take a shine to you."

"Queers and Jews."

A snappy line might still pull it out, but Max is saying nothing and the only thing I can come up with is trying to pass us off as good old goys which is not true and which I don't think anyone here would get anyway.

"So what you're going to do is climb up top that pool table and start saying poems till I tell you to quit."

"I never seed a naked poet neither. Let's strip him down, Tommy."

And I'm thinking that I should have taken up industrial hygiene in college instead of poetry. Or that with just a little luck I could have been on the road with someone a lot sweeter who stayed out of bars. Or maybe a real brawler—Jim Harrison or Philip Levine, say—people who get left alone. Instead, I've got Max who is sour and paunchy and couldn't go two rounds with a sonnet anymore. I'm still hoping that maybe we can ride it out with nothing worse than humiliation when Max swings his elbow off the table into the groin of one of the cowboys and gets knocked sideways off his chair. I figure I'm next, so I start to move and get a pool cue flat across the kidneys and then the lights go out.

246

When I come around, they've propped me up in a chair and Max is on the pool table. They've left Max's clothes on—a break for Max, a break for them—and he is reciting poetry. One eye is swollen and he keeps pawing at his nose which is bleeding. He's a little unsteady, tilting above the felt, but his voice is OK and gets stronger as he goes:

> The land was ours before we were the land's
> She was our land more than a hundred years
> Before we were her people . . .

"Hey, that ain't poetry; it's got to rhyme. You trying to mess with us?"

Max stalls and it hangs in the balance. I don't think Max knows any poems that rhyme. The man nursing his groin looks like he's getting ready to climb up on the table.

"Louise, you been to college. Is it poetry if it don't have rhymes?"

Tommy is still running things and he's going to do this right. I try to shape a prayer that whoever taught Louise her obligatory literature course did not give her a "D" and a loathing for anyone who reads poetry or writes it. I pray rather than bet, because the odds are not good.

"It used to have to rhyme. But I don't think it has to anymore."

Max coughs a couple of times and starts up again when Tommy breaks in and tells him to do it from the beginning.

When Max is through, nobody says anything until Tommy tells him to keep going. He recites two more Frosts, a Robert Penn Warren, and something I don't recognize. It turns out that once he gets rolling Max can rhyme like a bell. The next time he stops, somebody hands him a beer.

Tommy turns out to be a tough-minded but fair critic: "It ain't Willie, but it ain't bad at that. You know some more?"

Max is warmed up now and begins to use the table like a stage, working the audience that horseshoes around him. He does Roethke and Dylan Thomas and Housman. The beer is replaced by whiskey bought by Curley who says no hard feelings about the elbow in his balls. Max has his foot to the floor now, redlining it, ad-libbing between the poems. He's sweating up there in the smoky light with a little blood caked around his nose, his eye squeezed shut and already going purple. They're clapping and cheering after each poem and I can see a few boots tapping along when Max leans into a rich iambic. He does two encores and then finishes with Yeats:

> Heart-mysteries there and yet when all is said
> It was the dream itself enchanted me:

Max is almost singing it now and I can see that it's not just the words, maybe hardly the words at all, but the current they generate that carries us along.

> . . . that raving slut
> Who keeps the till. Now that my ladder's gone,
> I must lie down where all the ladders start,
> In the foul rag-and-bone shop of the heart.

The bar is bedlam: hooting and piercing whistles and stomping. Louise is up on the table wrapping Max up and leaning into a long, looping kiss. Curley pounds me on the back and someone is passing the hat. It comes back full of wrinkled bills, and Max, down from his perch, sets the hat on the bar and says we'll drink it dry. Tommy shakes his hand and apologizes and someone gives him some ice wrapped in a bar towel for his eye. When Louise asks Max who wrote the poems, Max tells her he did.

"All the ones you liked anyway, honey. Why would I go around remembering what somebody else wrote?"

I can see that Louise is not too sure about this, so I ask her to dance. She wants to know what kind of guy Max really is and

I tell her that I wouldn't even try to guess. After someone cuts in, I go back to the bar. Max's flush has faded and the jaundice he gets from drinking is starting to rise. I go to work on him, but it still takes me most of an hour to pry him loose. By then he's said a couple of things that could have been taken wrong except for all the sloshy goodwill.

Finally, there are good-byes all around. Curley asks Max his name and Max says it's Wallace Stevens. Then we're out in the dark which nips me like a tonic. We walk around to where our car is, but instead of getting in Max opens the door of a pickup and hoists himself up so he's standing hunched in the door frame, holding himself there with one hand hooked around the back of the cab. I can't see what he's fooling around with in his other hand, and then he starts to recite "The Windhover." So I ask and he says whenever he can't get a stream started he recites Hopkins.

"If I want to puke, I do some late Auden."

What he's doing is pissing on the driver's seat. He gets three more trucks before I give up on talking him out of it and back the car out into the rutty lot. Max comes shambling then, stuffing himself back in, and even though a dog has started to bark I can see that we're going to get away without getting shot.

Max picks the back seat again. I've about run out of patience with myself because I can't begin to sort out how I feel about all this.

"They'll think twice about screwing with the next poet that comes along," says Max. He unlimbers a long, foggy belch and settles in. "And kid, let that be a lesson. If you want to grow up to be an artist, you can't ever let them get too familiar." Then he rumbles off to sleep.

And we're ninety miles out of Socorro, steady at 80 with all the windows down, taking our luck and chances down the road.

Biographical Notes

Donald Barthelme published twelve books, including two novels and a prize-winning children's book, before he died in 1989. He was a regular contributor to the *New Yorker* and taught creative writing at the University of Houston. He won a Guggenheim Fellowship and a National Book Award, among other honors.

John Bennet was born in Athens, Texas, in 1945. He was raised in and around Dallas, and attended the University of North Texas and the University of Texas at Austin. Bennet moved to New York City in 1966 and later studied writing at Columbia University. In 1975 he joined the *New Yorker* magazine, and has been a full editor there since 1980.

James Lee Burke, a native of Houston, is the author of sixteen novels, many starring the Cajun detective Dave Robicheaux, and *The Convict*, a collection of short stories. He has been the recipient of a Breadloaf Fellowship, a John Simon Guggenheim Fellowship, and the 1989 Edgar Award for best crime novel for *Black Cherry Blues*.

Robert Olen Butler, a self-proclaimed Texaholic, has written seven novels and two volumes of short fiction, *Tabloid Dreams* and *A Good Scent from a Strange Mountain*, which won the 1993 Pulitzer Prize for Fiction. His stories have appeared in many publications including the *New Yorker*, and have been anthologized in *New Stories from the South* and *The Best American Short Stories*. He teaches creative writing at McNeese State University.

Sandra Cisneros has been awarded a MacArthur Fellowship, three National Endowment for the Arts Fellowships, and the 1991 Lannan Foundation Literary Award. Her published works include *Bad Boys*, *The House on Mango Street*, *My Wicked Wicked Ways*, *Woman Hollering Creek*, and *Loose Women*. She lives in San Antonio, Texas.

Matt Clark grew up in Decatur, Texas, and currently teaches writing and literature at Louisiana State University. A finalist for the 1994 Faulkner Prize, he won the 1994 Robert Olen Butler Short Story Award and the 1994 Lillian Hellman Playwriting Prize. His work has appeared in *Alaska Quarterly Review* and *Gulf Coast*.

Tom Doyal, a fifth-generation Texan, was born in Lubbock and grew up in Medina County. He now writes and practices law in Austin. Nine of his stories aired on KAZU-FM in Pacific Grove, California, and four have been read at "Texas Bound." His story "Mambo Panties" appeared in the premiere edition of *@austin* magazine in 1997.

Dagoberto Gilb has been awarded fellowships from the National Endowment for the Arts, the Guggenheim Foundation, and the Whiting Foundation. He is the author of the novel *The Last Known Residence of Mickey Acuña* and a collection of stories, *The Magic of*

Blood, which won the PEN Hemingway Foundation Award and the Texas Institute of Letters Best Book of Fiction Award in 1993, and was a PEN/Faulkner finalist. He lives in El Paso.

Dave Hickey, born in Fort Worth, teaches theory and criticism in the Department of Art at the University of Nevada at Las Vegas. His books include *The Invisible Dragon: Four Essays on Beauty*, *Air Guitar: Essays on Art and Democracy*, and *Prior Convictions*, a collection of short stories. He received the Frank Jewett Mather Award for Distinction in Art Criticism in 1994.

Barbara Hudson was born in El Paso and currently lives in Cullowhee, North Carolina. She received her MFA from the University of Pittsburgh. Her stories have been published in *Writers' Forum*, *Apalachee Quarterly*, *Quarterly West*, and *Story*, and anthologized in *New Stories from the South: The Year's Best*, in both 1991 and 1993. She is at work on a collection of short stories.

Arturo Islas (1938–1991) was born in El Paso. In 1971 he received his Ph.D. from Stanford University, where he became a professor of American and Chicano literature. His novels include *The Rain God*, which won the best fiction prize from the Border Regional Library Association in 1985, *Migrant Souls*, and the posthumous *La Mollie and the King of Tears*.

Carolyn Osborn, born in Nashville, Tennessee, has lived in Texas since 1946. A former newspaper reporter, radio writer, and English teacher at the University of Texas, she is now a rancher and writer living in Austin. Her stories are published in many journals such as *The Antioch Review*, *Paris Review*, and *Georgia Review*. "The Accidental Trip to Jamaica" won a Texas Institute of Letters Award for best short story.

Janet Peery's stories are anthologized in *Best American Short Stories* and *Pushcart Prize Anthologies, XVI* and *XVII*. Her collection *Alligator Dance* won the Rosenthal Award from the American

Academy of Arts and Letters, and a Whiting Writers Award. Her first novel, *The River Beyond the World*, was a finalist for the 1996 National Book Award.

Hermine Pinson, a native of Beaumont, Texas, received her Ph.D. from Rice University and is assistant professor of American and African American literature at the College of William and Mary. Primarily a poet, she is the author of a collection of poems entitled *Ashe*. Her poetry and fiction have been published in *Common Bonds: Stories by and about Modern Texas Women*, *African American Review*, and other literary journals.

Katherine Anne Porter (1890–1980) was born in Indian Creek, Texas, and attended convent and private schools. Most of her working life was spent in New York, Mexico, and Europe. Her *Collected Stories* received both the National Book Award and the Pulitzer Prize in 1966. She published one novel, *Ship of Fools*.

Lisa Sandlin was raised in East Texas and graduated from Rice University. She received the 1995 Dobie Paisano Fellowship, awarded jointly by the Texas Institute of Letters and the University of Texas at Austin. Her stories are collected in *The Famous Thing About Death* and *Message to the Nurse of Dreams*. She teaches fiction writing at Wayne State in Nebraska.

Annette Sanford, who was born in Cuero, Texas, was a high school English teacher for twenty-five years before resigning in the mid-1970s to become a full-time writer. She has received two Creative Writing Fellowships from the National Endowment for the Arts, and her stories have been widely published and anthologized. Her collection *Lasting Attachments* was published in 1989.

R. E. Smith's stories have appeared in a number of literary magazines including the *Texas Review*, and "The Gift Horse's Mouth" was anthologized in *Best American Short Stories, 1982* and *South by*

Southwest: Twenty-Four Stories from Modern Texas. Currently a professor at Purdue University, Smith returns to Texas several times a year to visit his family, whose roots in the state go back to 1848.

Marshall Terry founded the Creative Writing Program at Southern Methodist University and presently serves as Associate Provost for Undergraduate Education. He has written five novels, including *Land of Hope and Glory,* and a short fiction collection, *Dallas Stories.* In 1992 he received the Lon Tinkle Award from the Texas Institute of Letters for "a career of excellence in letters."

Donna Trussell is a fifth-generation Texan. She now lives in Kansas City, where she writes a film column, teaches creative writing to children, and collects bad art. Her poems and stories have appeared in *Poetry, Chicago Review,* and other magazines. Her widely reprinted story "Fishbone" was performed as a theater piece in Seattle and has been translated for a Polish anthology.

Miles Wilson was born in Belle Fourche, South Dakota, and educated at Pomona College and the University of Oregon. His fiction and poetry have appeared widely in journals. A collection of short stories, *Line of Fall,* published by the University of Iowa Press, won the John Simmons Short Fiction Award. He teaches at Southwest Texas State University in San Marcos.

Kay Cattarulla was born in Ithaca, New York, and was educated at Cornell and Columbia Universities. She helped start New York's Symphony Space theater in 1978 and, in 1985, initiated "Selected Shorts," its nationally known series of short fiction readings by actors. The Texas offshoot, "Texas Bound," began in 1992 as part of "Arts & Letters Live," the literary series she founded at the Dallas Museum of Art.

John Graves, dean of Texas letters, is the author of the classic *Goodbye to a River* and other works, including *Hardscrabble,*

From a Limestone Ledge, and *Still Life with Birds.* He was born and grew up in Fort Worth and now lives in Glen Rose, Texas, on some four hundred acres of rough Texas Hill Country.

TEXAS BOUND® ON TAPE

Three taped editions of Texas short stories read
by Texas actors. Each three hours in Dolby stereo,
recorded live at the Dallas Museum of Art.

Texas Bound
8 by 8: Stories by Texas Writers,
Read by Texas Actors

"One of the year's best in fiction."
Publishers Weekly, 1994

Larry McMurtry's "There Will Be Peace in Korea,"
   read by Tommy Lee Jones
William Goyen's "The Texas Principessa,"
   read by Doris Roberts
Robert Flynn's "The Midnight Clear," read by Tess Harper
Reginald McKnight's "The Kind of Light That Shines on Texas,"
   read by Tyress Allen
Lynna Williams's "Personal Testimony," read by Judith Ivey
Tomás Rivera's "Picture of His Father's Face," read by Roger Alvarez
Annette Sanford's "Trip in a Summer Dress," read by Norma Moore
Lawrence Wright's "Escape," read by Randy Moore

Host: Tess Harper. Produced by Kay Cattarulla. Directed by Randy Moore.
ISBN 0-87074-369-4, $15.95

Texas Bound II
8 by 8: More Stories by Texas Writers,
Read by Texas Actors

Audie Award finalist, 1997

Matt Clark's "The West Texas Sprouting of Loman
      Happenstance," read by Brent Spiner
Mary K. Flatten's "Old Enough," read by Julie White
Arturo Islas's "The King of Tears," read by Octavio Solis
Tom Doyal's "Uncle Norvel Remembers Gandhi," read by Randy Moore
Janet Peery's "What the Thunder Said," read by Kathy Bates
Miles Wilson's "On Tour with Max," read by John Benjamin Hickey
Hermine Pinson's "Kris/Crack/Kyle," read by the author
Larry L. King's "Something Went with Daddy," read by G. W. Bailey

Host: G. W. Bailey. Produced by Kay Cattarulla. Directed by Randy Moore
   and Norma Moore.
ISBN 0-87074-394-5, $16.95

Texas Bound III
7 by 7: More Stories by Texas Writers,
Read by Texas Actors

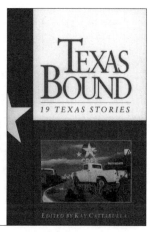

"Barry Corbin brought the house
down, Texas style."
The New York Times

Tom Doyal's "Sick Day," read by Barry Corbin
Marshall Terry's "Angels Prostate Fall," read by
   Randy Moore
R. E. Smith's "The Gift Horse's Mouth," read by Peri Gilpin
James Lee Burke's "The Convict," read by James Black
Robert Olen Butler's "Jealous Husband Returns in Form of Parrot,"
   read by Octavio Solis
Barbara Hudson's "The Arabesque," read by Marcia Gay Harden
Donald Barthelme's "The School," read by Raphael Parry

Host: Barry Corbin. Produced by Kay Cattarulla. Directed by Raphael Parry.
ISBN 0-87074-425-9, $16.95

TEXAS BOUND®
IN PRINT

Texas Bound: 19 Texas Stories
(Book I)

The first anthology contains many of the stories
featured in audiocassette Volume I and Volume
II, with additional stories by Rick Bass, Shelby
Hearon, A. C. Greene, Tomás Rivera, and others.

ISBN 0-87074-368-6, paper, $10.95
ISBN 0-87074-367-8, cloth, $22.50

Available at bookstores, or from:
Southern Methodist University Press
Drawer C
College Station, Texas 77843
Toll-free order number: 800-826-8911
Toll-free FAX number: 888-617-2421
Or visit our website at http://www.smu.edu/~press/TexasBound